Streets of Golfito

by Jim LaBate

Cover Illustration and Inside Illustration by Wendy Nooney

Mohawk River Press

Published by
Mohawk River Press
P.O. Box 4095
Clifton Park, New York 12065-0850
518-383-2254
www.MohawkRiverPress.com

This story is fiction. Characters, places, and incidents are either creations of the author or used in a fictional manner. Any similarities to real people, locations, or events are coincidental.

Photograph on the back cover by Anthony Salamone.

First Printing 2021
Printed in the United States of America
Library of Congress Control Number 2020914306
ISBN 9780966210088
10 9 8 7 6 5 4 3 2 1

While this book is a work of fiction, I did have the opportunity to live and work in Costa Rica, and this book is dedicated to all the wonderful people I met during my time there.

Other Works by Jim LaBate

Let's Go, Gaels – A Novella

Mickey Mantle Day in Amsterdam – Another Novella

Things I Threw in the River: The Story of One Man's Life

My Teacher's Password – A Contemporary Novel

Popeye Cantfield – A Full-Length Play

Writing Is Hard: A Collection of Over 100 Essays

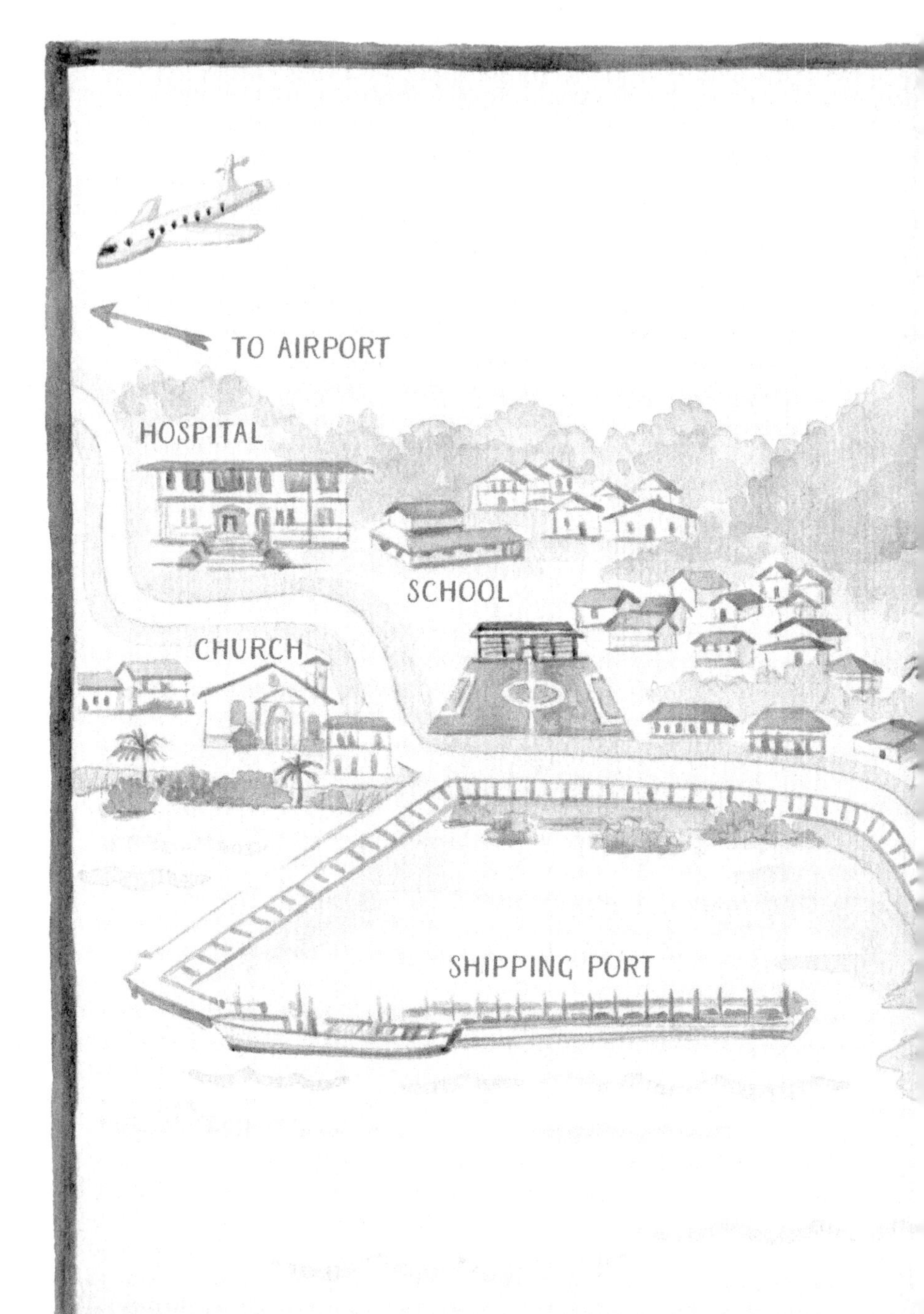
TO AIRPORT
HOSPITAL
SCHOOL
CHURCH
SHIPPING PORT

N
E
W
S
CLUB GOLFITO
14
TO BANANA
PLANTATION
SAWMILL

Chapter 1

The sign sits at the southern end of town near the bus stop on the eastern side of the road, so that first-time visitors to Golfito can read it. The sign itself is beginning to rust, the paint is chipping near the edges, and the post on which it hangs leans a bit to the starboard side. And unlike historical markers in the United States, which often have an illustration or a detailed history of the highlighted person or event, this sign is stark in its simplicity. It reads as follows:

Don Diego
Un Voluntario del Cuerpo de Paz
1974-1975

Chapter 2

Golfito is a somewhat unusual town. Tucked away on the Pacific side of Costa Rica near the country's southern border with Panama, this "little gulf" really has only one street. Sure, many short *calles* and neighborhoods extend away from the main drag, but they don't extend very far, and their residents have to return to this primary artery to visit other parts of town.

The town is like a long belt stretched between the calm waters of the gulf and the steep mountains that frame this five-mile stretch of land. By themselves, those physical characteristics alone would make Golfito unusual, but the human development of this port city makes it truly unique. For when the American Fruit Company decided to install its main banana operation in this quiet and isolated corner of the world, this small community really sprang to life.

For long before planned communities became common in the United States, the American Fruit Company divided Golfito into five distinct sections and began constructing them at the northern end of town.

First, the Company cut a path through the trees and constructed one solitary runway for the Golfito Airport with an accompanying building that was only slightly bigger than a two-car garage. This airport allowed the American executives to fly in and out rather than have to fly into San Jose and take an eight-hour car trip on the Pan American Highway. And since these same executives might also like to play a round of golf while they were in town, the Company built a nine-hole, par-three course alongside the runway: four holes on the eastern side and five on the western side with a clubhouse between the first tee and the putting green for the ninth hole.

The second section, and the first residential section, is called the "*Zona Americana*" because it was initially inhabited primarily by these American executives and their families. The president, the vice-president, the treasurer, and all the other key people who would oversee this new operation lived here, and the more important the position, the bigger the house and the closer it was to the airport and the clubhouse.

Besides the homes, this American section also included the Company office building, the Company grocery store, the Company hospital, the Company school for grades kindergarten through eighth, and the Company recreational facility which included not only an outdoor swimming pool but also an indoor facility with a room big enough, and high enough, for a game of volleyball. The swimming pool was open daily, and they showed movies in the big room three nights a week: Sunday, Wednesday, and Friday. The families who lived in this zone never had to leave the zone if they didn't want to, and they rarely did so.

The third section was the first for the Costa Rican residents who worked for the Company, and again, the higher the person's position in the Company, the closer that person's house was to his or her job site. For example, the Costa Rican accountants who reported to the American Chief Financial Officer lived near the office building, and the Costa Rican nurses and orderlies who worked with the American doctors lived near the hospital. The houses here were not as big as those in the American Zone, and they were squeezed in more tightly.

This section of town also included two key buildings. The Gatehouse sat at the southern edge and actually included a large, metal gate across the road which restricted access. Only those who lived in these two residential sections or those who needed to visit were allowed to pass, and the Gatehouse was manned 24 hours a day. The Americans, after all, didn't want just anyone wandering through their neighborhood or the one that bordered it.

Saint Michael's Catholic Church and the Rectory where Padre Roberto lived were also located here, within walking distance of the Gatehouse. Thus, those who lived beyond the Gatehouse were allowed in on Sunday morning and on holy days, but they were expected to exit as soon as the services concluded. If the nearby residents detected a mild irony in the limited access to "God's House," they kept those thoughts to themselves or within their small circle of family and friends. Since the American Fruit Company was pretty much the only major employer in town, no one wanted to jeopardize his or her job or the allocated housing that accompanied it.

The fourth section of town was easily the biggest and the busiest. Just on the other side of the Gatehouse were the hundreds of small dwellings that housed the families of the blue-collar workers who toiled at the port and made it possible for the 50-pound boxes of bananas to slide off the railway cars and into the cargo holds of the huge ocean freighters that carried the bananas to North America and beyond.

This port section of town was anchored by the various facilities that made up the "downtown" area of Golfito: the import and export offices of the Costa Rican government, the storage facilities, the Club Latino restaurant and dance hall, the outdoor basketball court, the soccer stadium, the grade school and the high school, and the various stores and service shops that welcomed both the full-time residents of Golfito and the visitors who served on the banana freighters and the smaller boats that found their way to this tiny, key-shaped bay.

Perhaps the most popular structure in this downtown area, though, sat high above the town at the end of a winding road that climbed to a small plateau and offered the best view of the bay and the Pacific Ocean beyond. There, the "Vista" offered an open-air pavilion for dining, dancing, and socializing. Unlike the clubhouse and the recreational facility in the American Zone, which hosted smaller crowds and closed relatively early, this nightclub was packed during the week, overflowing on weekends, and busy some nights until sunrise.

The fifth and final section built by the Americans was about a half mile down the road from the port because the land area between the bay and the mountains dwindled down to a space that could only accommodate the train tracks, the road, and not much else. Where the flat land area opened up again, the Company built another neighborhood full of small homes similar to the ones in the port area, and this section included another grade school for the children who lived there.

The only other major structure in this section was the Company's sawmill and woodshop. Here, the trees that were harvested off the nearby mountains were cut, planed, and trimmed down to whatever sizes the Company needed to build new structures or to maintain those already in use. Naturally, the woodworkers and their families lived in this portion of town as did all the other manual laborers who were needed to harvest the bananas, pack them, and load them on to the train cars for transport.

The one small section of town that the Company ignored when planning this banana outpost was that narrow strip of land between the port section and the sawmill. This short strip of flat land suitable for building was so narrow that after accounting for the railroad and the main road through town, only about 50 feet remained, barely enough room for even a small house or a business. "Maybe we should let the locals fight over that little piece and see what they can do with it," one Company planner said in the early stages of development, and they never came back to it. Thus, when Rodrigo Gonzales noticed the availability of that small parcel once the port was up and running, he sprang into action.

A long-time opportunist who owned and rented out various buildings in the public section of town farther south, Gonzales bought the narrow parcel from the Company and began constructing buildings and nurturing businesses that wouldn't be adversely affected by the narrow footprint. At the northern edge of the strip, he built a long movie theater that included 240 seats, 20 rows with 12 seats per row.

Next, he built a series of six small storefronts with two small apartments over each one. He assumed some of the tenants would live upstairs over their establishments, but he also had an inkling that some of these apartments would be used for other purposes. Rodrigo had lived in this small, port city long enough to know that even when small boats entered the harbor, the men who piloted or worked on those boats were often looking for more than just basic supplies. So while the names and proprietors of these businesses had changed often through the years, by late 1973, this strip included four bars, a restaurant, and a vacant storefront, and only one of the second-floor apartments was occupied by a full-time resident.

After that fifth section of town, the public portion of Golfito grew up, and the contrast between the Company side and the public side was immediate and abrupt. While the structures on the Company side, both residential and commercial, were uniform in their design – like a boring, blue suit – the public side of town was more like Costa Rica itself: alive, colorful, and creative. The Company's wooden structures all stood straight and tall in subdued greens and yellows with black shutters around the window screens. The public structures, by contrast, provided a mix of slouching wood and metal, and their shapes and colors looked like a madras sports jacket with food stains here and there.

The layouts of the buildings also contrasted. On the Company side, most of the commercial buildings were situated near the main road, and the houses fanned outward in a symmetrical pattern that showed planning and foresight. The public side, however, mixed commercial and residential throughout, and the building sizes and lots merged like a Jackson Pollock painting, scattershot and haphazard. On the main road, for example, Enrique Vargas, the richest man in the southern section, owned the very plain general store that stood right next to his elegant three-story home which looked like an old, Spanish mansion. And on the other side of this mansion hid a small, simple, metal shack that housed a fisherman and his family.

Unlike traditional Costa Rican cities, which were centered around a large, Catholic cathedral with a park and a promenade nearby, this too-narrow portion of Golfito possessed no church or park. Instead, a one-story, cinder-block grade school with an open soccer field out front anchored the neighborhood. Padre Roberto from St. Michael's visited each Sunday and offered Mass in the school, but the service was later on Sunday afternoon. Padre Roberto's first priority, after all, was the Company employees who lived uptown and whose Company furnished his church building and his rectory as well.

Was there animosity between the poorer people who lived in the public section of town and the richer people who worked for the Company and lived at the other end of Golfito? Yes and no. On one hand, some residents of the public end of town resented what they viewed as the easy life on the Company dole, but others cherished their independence and swore they could never live or work in such a closed and regimented environment. And while many people there criticized the rich-to-poor layout of the Company side, they could also see a somewhat similar pattern developing in their own end of town. The people with skills and entrepreneurial abilities always found a place to live in the main *barrio*, but the unskilled and uneducated typically found themselves in the smaller and less sturdy *casas* that littered the main road leading out to the vast banana plantations that made life possible for everyone.

Chapter 3

Don Diego first visited Golfito during the early part of 1974. At the time, he was still simply Jim, a fresh-faced, recent college graduate and Peace Corps Volunteer who had heard President John F. Kennedy speak and had been inspired by him to try to save the world.

The inspiration occurred when Jimmy was a nine-year-old fourth grader at Saint Mary's Institute in Amsterdam, New York, during the autumn of 1960. At that point in his life, if Jimmy knew anything about a political topic, it was a rare occurrence. Typically, he was more concerned about Mickey Mantle's home-run count and batting average than he was about any politician. But Jimmy's teacher that year, Sister Anna Roberta, had a special fondness for candidate Kennedy, the senator from Massachusetts, and she talked to her students often during social studies class about this young man who offered new ideas and new programs for a new generation of Americans.

"He's a Catholic, too," she mentioned with obvious pride, "and the United States has never had a Catholic President before. You should learn as much about him as you can and maybe tell your parents about him."

Jimmy wouldn't go that far, of course, because they didn't talk about those things at his supper table, but he did get somewhat involved in the presidential campaign.

Every day after school, Jimmy and his best friends, Bernie and Larry, would walk downtown to Main Street before heading up Market Street to their homes. Yes, they were going a bit out of their way, but as fourth graders, they were finally old enough to explore the city a little bit on their own. "As long as you're with one of your friends," Jimmy's mom had told him before the school year began, "you can walk home any way you want – but don't be late for supper."

And in actuality, the boys weren't really exploring that much; they tended to take the same route every day. They would go immediately to Main Street by way of Liberty Street and head west toward "downtown." Sometimes, they ran through the alleyway between Grand Rapids Furniture Store and Sears and Roebuck, but usually, they avoided those dark and wet places where the junior-high kids smoked their cigarettes and harassed the "little kids" who dared to invade their territory.

The real attraction that fall was the Democratic Headquarters next to Sears and Roebuck on the north side of Main Street. This previously empty storefront that once housed a paint store was now occupied by a young cadre of recent college graduates who were swept up in the Kennedy candidacy. Unlike most Main Street shop owners who didn't want kids traipsing into their buildings, these New Frontiersmen eagerly invited everyone in to pick up JFK promotional materials, and the young people there were especially nice to these curious fourth graders.

"The Republicans have been in office for eight years now," a beautiful, long-haired redhead said to the boys as she tidied up the pamphlets and pins on the table before her. "Don't you think it's time for a change?"

"Yes, I do," Jimmy answered with fake sincerity, as if he really cared. What he really wanted was more "Kennedy-Johnson" bumper stickers. He thought it would be really cool if he could cut up the Democratic stickers and then use the letters to create his own brand of baseball bumper stickers. He figured he could sell them for at least a buck apiece to all the "ny-yenKees" fans in town.

Meanwhile, Larry and Bernie were busy working their own small-time con. They were trying to get as many political pins and brochures as they could, so they could sell them for a quarter each to the seventh- and eighth-graders who, as part of a social studies assignment, were supposed to visit not only the Democratic but also the Republican campaign headquarters, which was across the street. Those older students needed proof of their visits, and they were, naturally, too cool to actually make the visits themselves. Bernie and Larry had already made over three dollars each with their campaign sales.

After a while, of course, the newness and excitement of the campaign headquarters wore off, and the three friends moved on to more interesting endeavors. They explored the new department store downtown, they asked for old movie posters from the four movie theaters, and they felt much more confident about exploring the back alleys and shortcuts between the Chuctanunda Creek and Market Street. When Sister Anna Roberta announced that JFK himself would actually visit Amsterdam in the near future, however, Jimmy especially took a renewed interest in Kennedy's campaign and platform. Surprisingly, Jimmy actually began to read the brochures that he had picked up and the newspaper articles that explained what the Peace Corps was all about.

The Peace Corps, according to Kennedy's rough blueprint, would send ordinary Americans overseas to help the less fortunate in other countries. The program he outlined would differ from other foreign-aid programs in three key ways.

First, instead of simply sending American dollars, dollars that might never reach the intended beneficiaries, the Peace Corps would send people. These people would be teachers, farmers, technicians, engineers, nurses, and numerous other professionals who would share their expertise with those in need. This human investment in international relations would be so much more beneficial, Kennedy reasoned, than a mere financial donation.

In addition, the Volunteers themselves would benefit by learning about another country and another culture. They would learn the language, they would work with the natives, and they would gain a new appreciation for the America they may have previously taken for granted. As one who had grown up privileged and somewhat pampered, Kennedy knew how easy it was for many American kids to become spoiled and isolated from the rest of the world, especially during the decade of the 1950s when all seemed so good and so right in President Dwight D. Eisenhower's America. But Eisenhower's eight-year presidency was coming to a close, and Kennedy and the Democrats knew they needed something special and unique to attract this new generation of Americans who may have lived through World War II as infants but who didn't really remember the hardships and were ready, instead, to claim and shape an America that would be their own.

Finally, Kennedy and his advisors also saw the long-term benefit of the Peace Corps. Having served overseas in the Navy and having lived and traveled in Europe when he was young, JFK knew that living overseas gave him a broader perspective on world affairs. He wanted subsequent generations of Americans to look beyond their shores, to think not only nationally but also globally. After their two-year stint in the Peace Corps, Kennedy wanted these Volunteers to come home and tell other Americans what they had seen: the need, the poverty, the beauty, and the opportunity. He wanted the first Volunteers to come home and encourage the next wave, but he also wanted these forerunners to share the program with others in their communities: teachers, public servants, private tradesmen and women, business owners, and local politicians. If Americans could see themselves – and be viewed – not as the police force of the world but as big brothers and big sisters who wanted what was best for everyone, then John F. Kennedy could lead the United States into a new era of international cooperation and world peace.

Unfortunately, on the day of Kennedy's visit, Jimmy was a bit distracted. He had been playing ten-tag in the lot near the school before the first bell for homeroom rang, and he had been roughed up a bit. The physical pain and the emotional turmoil that followed had checked his excitement about the future President's visit.

Ten-tag sounds like a simple game, and in many ways, it is a simple game, but for a skinny, weak, nine-year-old boy who is trying to figure out who he is and what's important, ten-tag can be a daily challenge.

The cement-covered lot where the boys played was like a Roman arena of sorts. It sat between a house at the top of Grove Street and the school itself at the bottom of that same short street. The homeowner's wooden fence served as the top, northern barrier; the school wall acted as the barrier on the east side; and a shorter, wooden fence separated the bottom, southern end of the lot from another school wall. Thus, anyone who was too timid to play but wanted to watch had to stand to the west on the sidewalk and look over the iron rail that separated the participants from the bystanders. Jimmy was too afraid to not play and too timid to play well.

The boys who played ten-tag ranged from third grade to sixth grade, but most of the serious players were in the fifth and sixth grades. Jimmy never played as a third-grader, but when some of his fourth-grade buddies began to climb over or under the iron rail, they encouraged him to give it a try.

The game usually began with a sixth-grader in the middle and everyone else near the fence at the top. When this designated sixth-grader said "One, two, three, go," the mob rushed to the bottom fence and tried to avoid being caught. The goal of the boy in the middle was to grab one other boy rushing by and hold on to him up to the count of 10. If the captured boy broke free before the count of 10, he could run to the safety of the bottom fence, but if he did not escape, then he and the first boy would each try to capture another as the mob ran on the signal back up the slight incline. The game continued until most of the boys had been captured by the others and only the biggest and strongest were still running free. The last one captured by the mob "won" the game, and he became the solitary boy in the center of the next game.

As a classic, skinny weakling, Jimmy loved the early rounds because he could easily race across the far edges of the lot and avoid capture. As the number of boys in the center increased, however, he would inevitably be grabbed, and that's when his dilemma began. If he gave in easily to his capturer, his run would be over, and he'd have to attempt the even more difficult task: catching others as they ran by. However, if he resisted and tried to escape, the tussle could get physical and ugly. Jimmy wasn't good at physical and ugly, yet the same situation occurred once he was in the middle. He could try to catch a small kid who wouldn't resist, or he could try to go after someone his own size and struggle with him. Jimmy simply preferred the running and dodging part of the game to the grabbing and wrestling part of the game.

On this particular day, Jimmy miscalculated – twice. When a skinny sixth-grader grabbed him, Jimmy was all set to give up when he noticed the older boy's grasp wasn't that tight, and Jimmy wiggled free. As he did so, however, he got turned around and was facing the wrong direction. Jimmy's temporary confusion gave the surprised, older boy a chance to recover, and rather than simply grab Jimmy again, the boy banged Jimmy against the brick school wall, wrapped him in a bear hug, and quickly recited the game's prayer: "one, tw, th, fo, fi, sx, sev, eit, ni, ten, ten tag!"

Jimmy's shoulder ached from the bump against the wall, but he couldn't dwell on the pain because soon, he was in the center with the others rushing at him. Somewhat educated and emboldened by the pinning technique, Jimmy tried to force one of the smaller fifth-graders into the wall where he hoped to execute the same bear-hug maneuver that had just led to his capture. Once again, though, Jimmy was overmatched. When he bumped the kid into the wall, the kid bumped him back and used his strength to break Jimmy's grasp and escape. In the process, the kid had pushed Jimmy's right hand against the brick, and though his hand wasn't bleeding, the red burn stung, and Jimmy was ready to retire for the day. Fortunately, the bell for homeroom rang, so Jimmy grabbed his books and headed inside.

On the way to homeroom, he stopped in the boys' room to wash his scraped hand and splash water on his face. The game of ten-tag had quickly escalated, like football often did from two-hand touch to tackle, and Jimmy knew he would have to improve his game if he wanted to continue to play. A part of him feared the banging and the wrestling, but another part of him cherished that moment when he had initially escaped from the skinny sixth-grader.

As he sat through the brief homeroom period and his morning classes and as he listened to Senator Kennedy's short but inspirational speech that afternoon, Jimmy wondered about his willingness to fight, to struggle, to succeed. Did he have what it took to be a warrior, a conqueror, a survivor? Or would he be merely content to play and be captured easily by others, caught early in the game and destined to be a loser rather than a winner? He had read, of course, about heroes, and in his mind, he imagined himself to be one, but could he really make that transition from imagination to reality?

Chapter 4

On the same day that JFK visited Amsterdam, a young Costa Rican girl celebrated her fourth birthday with her mom and her mom's parents in their small home in the Saint Michael's Church neighborhood of Golfito. Lillianna, often referred to as Lilli, was without a father due to some unfortunate circumstances.

Her father, Jose, and her mother, Rosa, had worked together as young, single people in the Company store. Jose unloaded the supply trains and stocked the shelves, and Rosa worked in the bakery preparing the breads and desserts. Jose, who was 17 and three years older than Rosa, had been working at the store for two years when Rosa applied for a job at the age of 14. Somewhat reserved, Jose watched Rosa work for over two months before he finally found the courage to speak to her. Once they began speaking, though, their relationship blossomed quickly. He began to spend more time stocking the bakery's supplies, and he also began to walk her home at the end of each workday. At first, Jose walked Rosa straight home, a walk that took no more than five minutes, and he was extremely polite and respectful to Rosa's parents. Thus, Rosa's parents didn't really notice that gradually, the couple's trip home was taking more than five minutes; they were walking more slowly, holding hands, taking detours through the small neighborhood, and finding isolated spots along the way where they could really be alone. Three months later, Rosa became pregnant, and when her parents and Jose's parents found out, they all met with Padre Roberto and arranged a quick wedding. Rosa and Jose spent the first month of their marriage living with her parents until the Company found a small home for the newlyweds, just beyond the Gatehouse and less than two blocks away from the school where Lilli would eventually start kindergarten.

For the first six months of their marriage, as they walked to and from work each day, Jose and Rosa appeared to be so totally in love that some of the American residents began to refer to the couple as "Ken and Barbie." During the first year of Lilli's life, unfortunately, this idyllic relationship began to deteriorate. Due to medical issues related to Lilli's birth, Rosa was unable to return to work and unable to have sex for a while. Frustrated by their decrease in income and even more frustrated by Rosa's physical limitations, Jose began to spend more and more time in that lonely section of town between the port and the sawmill. At first, he went by himself to the movie theater once a week. Then, he began to frequent the bar next door, and, eventually, he found his way to the ladies on the second floor. One weekend, he failed to come home at all, and when his father-in-law found out what was going on, he moved Rosa and Lillianna back into the family home where Rosa had grown up, and he refused to allow Jose to visit.

Not surprisingly, Jose's drinking became even worse; he began to miss work frequently and soon was fired. Forced to move out of his own little house and unwilling to move back in with his own parents, Jose left Golfito altogether. After his firing, he knew he'd never be able to work for the Company again, and he was unwilling to try life at the other end of town. Yes, he probably could have secured a similar job with Enrique Vargas in the public *mercado*, but Jose felt both scared and scarred. Having grown up under the protection of the Company, he wasn't sure he'd be welcome in the public section of town, and even if he were to find his way there, he feared that he would always be viewed as an exile or an outcast. So, he used his last bit of money to buy a bus ticket to San Jose where he assumed he could find work and an opportunity to start his life over again. When Rosa found out through a friend what Jose was planning, she rushed to the bus stop with baby Lillianna in her arms and pleaded with Jose to stay – if not for their marriage then for their daughter's sake. And though Jose appeared to relent when he saw his child again, the bus driver's call to board – "*Dos minutos. Dos minutos.*" – startled Jose back to his own reality.

"*Lo siento, Rosa. Lo siento, Lillianna,*" Jose said over and over as he apologized to his wife and his baby girl. In his mind, he thought he might return for them one day, but two minutes later, Rosa's husband and Lillianna's father departed for San Jose – like many Golfiteanos before him – never to be seen again.

Chapter 5

When Jim finished the fall semester of his senior year at Siena College, he knew he finally had to get serious and get to work regarding his application to the Peace Corps. He had been thinking about it since the fourth grade when candidate Kennedy first intrigued him with the idea. During the dozen years since that initial exposure, Jim had sporadically been researching the topic by reading feature stories about Volunteers in various newspapers and magazines. In addition, when family members and friends began to ask him about his post-college plans, he had begun to admit to the possibility: "I'm thinking about applying to the Peace Corps."

"Really," they often replied in amazement. Then, the ensuing comments fell into four general categories. First, most people were truly impressed by Jim's ambition. "That is so cool," they might say, and, then, they followed up with a self criticism: "I could never do something like that."

Jim was both flattered and encouraged by these comments. These people could truly relate to what he was feeling, and he experienced a certain idealistic bond with them. He also tried to assuage their self criticism by offering some encouraging words such as, "Ah, I bet you could do it if you had to."

At the other extreme were those who had toyed with the idea themselves but for whatever reason had been unable to follow through. "I always wanted to do that," they said, "but . . . ." Then, their voices drifted off into nothingness as if they couldn't quite formulate the words to explain why they hadn't volunteered when they had the opportunity. Some, Jim thought, seemed truly sincere, and perhaps family commitments or work obligations had prevented them from signing up. Others, however, did not seem sincere, and Jim felt that they were just trying to make themselves feel charitable or noble. In either case, their comments also made Jim even more determined to follow through with his own decision.

On one hand, he knew this was his time – "It's now or never," he kept telling himself – and he didn't want to live the rest of his life wondering if he could have done it. Also, he felt that if he didn't go, he would probably sound just like those insincere folks who also didn't go, even if their intentions were pure. Jim wanted to be a man of action, so now he had to act.

The third type of reaction usually came from younger people who knew very little about the Peace Corps. "What is that exactly?" they might ask, and Jim would attempt to explain. Jim loved these conversations because he had a chance to tell the Peace Corps history as he knew it, and as he did so, he also enthusiastically explained his own optimistic and idealistic dreams. Like the teacher he wanted to become, Jim used the opportunity to not only inform these young people but also to motivate and encourage them. "My favorite Kennedy quote," Jim told them, "is from his inaugural address when he said, 'Ask not what your country can do for you; ask what you can do for your country.'"

Finally, Jim encountered the skeptics. "Yeah, you're doing that just to avoid going to Vietnam," they might say. Or the more subtle pessimists might ask, "Why do you want to go overseas to help when we have so many really needy people right here in our own country?"

The first comment was easy to address because by the end of 1972, most people were tired of the war in Vietnam, and Jim could easily and honestly admit, "You're right. I don't want to go to Vietnam. I don't know anybody who wants to go there, but that's not why I'm doing this." In fact, Jim probably would have gone to Vietnam had he been drafted – he definitely wasn't a draft dodger, and his father and almost all of his uncles had served in either World War II or Korea – but when Jim's Draft Lottery number was a lofty 212, he knew he wouldn't ever be called. Still, he tried to explain to these doubters that he actually wanted to serve his country but in a different way. Still, when he explained this to these inquisitors, they usually followed up with the "Why-not-volunteer-here-in-America?" question.

Jim wanted to answer that query with his standard JFK inaugural quote, but since most of the skeptics were also quite cynical, he also had to be more realistic: "I just have a feeling that the poor people in other countries need so much more help than the poor Americans. And since most Americans can't – or are unwilling – to go overseas to help, I would like to give it a try for two years. Then, maybe when I come home, I can do similar work over here too." Typically, Jim was so sincere and so serious with this response that even the die-hard skeptics began to believe in him.

Chapter 6

During the first few years of her life, Lilliana was a beautiful and perfect little baby. Her red cheeks contrasted vividly with her dark hair, and she rested peacefully whenever anyone held her. She cried only when hungry and took long naps after receiving her nourishment from her mother's breasts. Even after Lilli's mother returned to work at a small, non-Company restaurant, Lilli willingly drank the bottled milk from the Company store, milk that her grandmother warmed for her and fed to her. By the age of three months, Lilli was sleeping through the night, and she continued to take a long nap every afternoon. Lilli's mother and grandparents all marveled at how easily the child fit into their routine, and the four of them enjoyed a peaceful and calm existence.

For a few months after her husband left for San Jose, Rosa still expected Jose to return. Periodically, she saw his parents in the neighborhood, and she asked them about him and about his life in the Capital. Gradually, however, they began to avoid Rosa and her desperate pleas for information about him. Rosa thought she might keep them interested with stories of their newest grandchild, but they resisted. They already had eight grandchildren right there in Golfito, so another one, no matter how wonderful and beautiful she might be, did not matter. Thus, Lilliana seemed destined to grow up without her father and without her father's extended family.

Lilliana, of course, didn't even realize she was missing a father until the Christmas season of her kindergarten year of school: The man she often called "Grandpapa" treated her like a daughter, yet he was so much older than her classmates' fathers, and she seemed to have two "Mamas" while everyone else had only one.

"*Donde es mi papa?*" She finally asked on Grandparents' Day at school the following spring. Her grandparents said, "Your mama will tell you later." They wanted Lilli to simply enjoy that special day, but she couldn't stop wondering about him.

Later that night, Rosa explained to Lilli what had happened to her father. Rosa explained that Jose had to go to work in another city far away and probably wouldn't return to Golfito for a long time, if ever. She also pulled out three framed pictures of Jose and suggested that Lilli keep them on the small dresser near her bed.

One showed Jose alone, working behind the counter at the Company store. Another showed Rosa and Jose together; they were all dressed up in their best clothes, and Rosa said the photo was taken on their first Easter Sunday together as a married couple. The third one, naturally, showed all three of them in church for Lilli's baptism. Lilli's father was holding her tentatively with both hands and looking into the baby's eyes. Lilli's mom was looking directly at the camera and smiling brightly. Lilli's eyes were closed, and as the five-year-old Lilli looked at her younger self, her mom told her about the ceremony.

"You slept through most of the service, and you only awoke when Padre Roberto poured water over your head above the baptismal font. You cried for about thirty seconds, but once I dried your forehead and took you back into my arms, you closed your eyes again and slowly fell back asleep."

Little Lilli looked closely at all three photos and put them on the dresser as her mother had suggested. The picture of her father alone stood in the center, the picture of the newlywed Easter couple stood to the left and farthest from the bed, and the baptismal photo of all three stood to the right, closest to Lilli's bed. In fact, after Lilli's mom said evening prayers with Lilli, turned out the light, and said "*buenas noches*," Lilli always reached over, took the family photo, and held it over her heart as she fell asleep.

Chapter 7

When Jim actually filled out his application to the Peace Corps, four questions in particular helped him to clarify even further what he wanted to do and why:

"Where do you want to go as a Peace Corps Volunteer?"

Jim wrote that he would go anywhere. He didn't have a particular country or a specific area of the world in mind. He just wanted to help others in some way.

"What kind of work would you like to do as a Peace Corps Volunteer?"

As an English major in college, Jim knew that he was qualified to teach English, and he was wiling to do so. However, Jim also had an extensive athletic background: he played football, basketball, and baseball in high school; he played volleyball, tennis, and golf just for fun; and he even took a boxing class in college. As a result, Jim was also willing to teach physical education or to coach team sports. In summary, he admitted, "I am willing to do any job that needs to be done."

"Why do you want to be a Peace Corps Volunteer?"

For that most important question, Jim repeated some of the same information he had already shared with his family and friends: "I want to help people, I want to give what I can to those who are less fortunate, and I want to try to make a difference in the world. My long-term goal is to be a high-school English teacher in America, yet I don't want to go directly from a college classroom as a student to a high-school classroom as a teacher; I want to experience life outside the United States, and I want to bring that experience home with me to share it with my students."

"When can you begin work as a Peace Corps Volunteer?"

Technically, Jim could have begun immediately after his college graduation in late May 1973, so he was tempted to list June 1st as a potential start date. "But you'll miss my big day," his older sister, Kathy, interjected when Jim gave that date to his family. She and her fiancé had already reserved September 22 as their wedding date.

"Alright, I'll tell them I can start October 1st, instead," he added quickly and easily. Though Kathy assumed he changed his mind for her, Jim had an ulterior motive of his own. He really wanted to play one more summer of organized baseball, and the later availability made that possible. Jim knew he wasn't good enough to play professionally after college, so he would cherish one more summer playing the game he loved. Then, he would save the world.

At the end of the summer, just before the Labor Day weekend, Jim received his acceptance package in the mail. The Peace Corps officials had invited him to work in Costa Rica as a "Sports Promoter." His job, according to the packaged materials, would be to "teach sports other than soccer: sports such as basketball, baseball, volleyball, and the running sports among others." Since most children and athletes in Costa Rica played soccer year-round, the country's Sports Authority wanted to expand its array of offerings, and the Peace Corps Sports Promoters would live and work in communities throughout the country.

"That's perfect," Jim thought. "When can I start?" Wednesday, November 7, the package replied, and by the time November rolled around, he was more than ready. His summer baseball experience was finished. Most of his friends had either begun working or returned to school. And Bridget, his college girlfriend, a girl Jim had begun dating after he had submitted his application and one who knew all about his Peace Corps plans, was back in school as well. To pass the time, Jim took a job delivering flowers, and he exercised often to try to be in the best shape ever for this new adventure.

On the weekend before his departure, Jim experienced a trifecta of farewell parties. His college friends surprised him on Friday night, his Amsterdam friends did likewise on Saturday, and most of his extended family visited the house on Sunday afternoon or early evening. Some people gave him small traveling gifts, others gave him cash for the journey, and everyone said they would miss him, and they insisted that he take care of himself and return home safely. Some even cried, including Bridget, who promised to wait for him.

Jim cried, too, on the following Wednesday when his parents and sisters brought him to the Albany Airport. He had never flown before, so he was a bit nervous about that, but he was even more nervous about saying good-bye. Even though he had lived away from his family during his four college years, his college was only a 45-minute drive from home, and he had stayed in touch with regular Sunday-night phone calls. The Peace Corps, by contrast, was a faraway, out-of-touch, two-year commitment.

"Do a good job," Jim's dad said through his own tears, and, soon, Jim was flying to Miami, Florida, where he met his fellow Sports Promoters and other Volunteers for a two-day orientation. There, he also met nurses, teachers, foresters, farmers, and engineers, and these 40 new Volunteers processed their paperwork and received their inoculations before departing to Costa Rica. The in-country orientation also lasted two days, and during their time in a San Jose hotel, one of the Peace Corps executives suggested a name change.

"It's entirely voluntary, of course," the administrator said, "but if you want to fully immerse yourself into the culture, you can take on a Costa Rican or Spanish name. For example, if your name is 'Mary,' you could call yourself 'Maria,' or if you go by 'Joe' or 'Joseph,' you could call yourself 'Jose.' The name change isn't official or anything, and no paperwork is involved, but a lot of previous Volunteers have done it and have found it to be both enjoyable and beneficial. These Volunteers said the Costa Ricans seem to accept them more easily and more readily if they use a name that is familiar and easy to remember and pronounce."

"So, how do you say 'Jim' in Spanish?" Jim asked the speaker later that day.

"Jim is actually a good name to change," he answered, "because most Costa Ricans struggle with that name and mispronounce it as 'Jeem.'"

Jim laughed at the sound of it and hoped for a better sound in Spanish.

"So, as 'James' or 'Jim,'" the administrator continued, "you actually have two choices: you can be 'Jaime,' which the Costa Ricans will pronounce as 'Haime.'"

Jim made a face at that option.

"Or, you could be 'Diego.'"

"That's it. I love it!" Jim decided. And by the next evening, when he was driven to Hatillo, a small suburb of San Jose, to live with a Costa Rican couple – Carlos and Louisa – for his three months of language training, Jim greeted them with all the Spanish he knew: "*Hola. Como esta? Yo me llamo Diego.*"

Chapter 8

One of the more intriguing elements of Golfito was the cargo trains that brought the bananas from the fields to the port. Like a tide in some ways, the train cars rambled slowly as they entered the town, filled to the brim with cartons of bananas, toward the port on one track; then, a day later, empty, the train cars rolled out of town on the other track, more quickly this time, ready to be returned to the fields and re-filled and prepared for another journey.

Though they were not officially public trains, and though they didn't run at regularly scheduled times, these freight cars did help numerous people make the four-mile trip from one end of town to the other. The cars themselves were usually a deep red, and they contained huge sliding doors on each side, so the bananas could be easily loaded or unloaded. When the full trains lumbered into town – from south to north – the side doors were closed, but because each car included four ladders, two at the ends of each side, the natives often climbed aboard. Most riders simply hopped onto the bottom rung of a ladder and rode the train as far as they needed to reach their destination. Though the empty trains moved a bit more quickly as they left town, they were still easily accessible and, in fact, more accessible because the side doors were usually open, and the more nimble people could easily grab a door rail and hop inside.

So common was this activity in Golfito that riding a freight train was an unspoken rite of passage. The smaller children typically experienced it first as a passenger; Mom or Dad would scoop up a young child with one hand and use the other hand to grab the ladder and step aboard. Eventually, when the child was physically ready and up to the challenge, that same parent or an older sibling would train and supervise the child for his or her first solo flight.

Most often, the pair would choose the slower inbound train, and the two of them would carefully study the movement of the cars as the elder explained what to do. Then, they would run alongside to gauge the speed and observe the need to keep pace. "Keep your eyes on the ladder," the parent or older sibling yelled above the sound of the engine. "Push off the left foot, put your right foot on the bottom rung, and grab the ladder with both hands." Then, as soon as the child was comfortably aboard, the trainer would grab the next available ladder, and the two of them would ride, smiling and laughing, to their pre-planned destination.

Fortunately, getting off the train was even easier, especially since the train slowed down to enter the port. "Just jump," the coach yelled at the end of the trip, and often, he or she could jump first, and run quickly enough to catch up to and trot alongside the child to supervise his or her departure. Yes, a few children stumbled when they hit the ground and bruised their hands and knees, but most were able to maintain their balance and land safely.

Did any riders ever actually climb the ladders and ride on top of the cars? Yes, the male teenagers in town typically challenged themselves with this activity. At first, they climbed just because they could; then, they climbed for a better view; and later, they climbed to see if they were brave enough to stand on top and ride and, eventually, jump from one car to the next. For viewers on the road, the standing and jumping seemed terrifyingly difficult, but once these boys had accomplished the task, they quickly realized it wasn't that hard, and they soon became bored or did it only to show off. Thus, very few Golfiteños were ever seriously injured while riding the trains, and only one man ever died, a Panamanian tourist who had been drinking heavily beforehand.

Chapter 9

While Diego spent his evenings with Carlos and Louisa and their one-year-old son, Carlos Junior, in Hatillo, he traveled every day to San Pedro, another San Jose suburb, for his language training and his cross-cultural education. The Peace Corps officials rented space there and employed six Spanish teachers to work with the 40 new Volunteers, so they could begin their jobs in various communities near the beginning of February.

Since Diego had never studied Spanish previously, the teachers placed him in the lowest language group, and his particular teacher grilled him and the others on conversational basics: "What is your name? What time is it? How much does that cost? Where is the rest room? When does the next bus arrive?"

In addition, the instructors provided other activities to help teach the Volunteers the language and to assist them in understanding the Costa Rican culture. For example, Diego learned his numbers in Spanish by playing ping-pong, and he figured out the San Jose bus system by participating in field trips and city-wide scavenger hunts. Though tentative and nervous and self-conscious at first, he gradually became accustomed to – and comfortable in – his new surroundings.

At six foot, five inches tall, Diego may have been the tallest guy in the whole country, and he couldn't even stand up straight in most of the public buses. Initially, he was embarrassed in that situation, so he silently looked at the floor or out the windows when he traveled. As his Spanish improved and his comfort level increased, however, Diego began to make eye contact with his fellow passengers and engage them in small talk. And he laughed uproariously the first time he heard the Spanish versions of "How's the weather up there?" or "Do you play basketball?"

Christmas Day 1973 was the most unusual day in Diego's young life, not only because he was away from home for Christmas for the first time but also because of the unique adventure that Carlos had planned for him. Carlos wanted to show Diego the Costa Rican bullfights.

Carlos had begun to prepare Diego for this adventure about a month earlier. Since Diego's Spanish was still pretty weak at the time, Carlos had only told him the basics: around Christmas time, Costa Rica hosted a week's worth of bullfights in a place called Zapote, a small town outside San Jose. Carlos promised Diego that they would go together. Though Diego didn't appear to be all that excited about the idea, Carlos promised him that the experience would be special and that he would enjoy it. Carlos also explained that the Costa Rican bullfights were a bit more civilized than the bullfights in Spain because the Costa Rican matadors did not kill the bulls. Since Diego was having a hard time understanding the difference, Carlos actually visited the library near where he worked, and he brought home a book with pictures to show Diego how the two countries handled the bulls.

In both countries, Carlos explained, the matadors begin with merely a cape, their nerve, and their dexterity. They challenge the bull to charge, they evade the bull when he does charge, and they eventually wear the bull down to a point of exhaustion. In Spain, though, before the bull becomes completely exhausted, the matadors pull out long knives or spears, and they begin to stab at the bull as it rushes past. Eventually, of course, the combination of the physical activity and the bloody attacks wears the bull down, and it dies in the ring. The pictures that Carlos showed Diego were, indeed, a bloody spectacle. However, Carlos explained, "*en Costa Rica es differente.*"

In Costa Rica, the matadors never reach the point of attacking the bulls. Instead, they merely wear them down. While the Spanish approach may provide a more exciting duel because the matador takes more of a risk to get close to the bull while it is still quite active, the Costa Rican approach is much less violent, more like the difference between a rock concert and a classical symphony. The former is loud, intense, and visceral; the latter is calm, artistic, and soothing. Carlos tried to make the point that the Costa Rican tradition is much more civilized than its Spanish predecessor.

Once Diego understood the distinction, he was more interested and intrigued, and he conveyed that curiosity to Carlos, and Diego actually began to look forward to the event.

"*Cuando?*" Diego asked.

"*El dia de Christmas!*" Carlos answered proudly.

"We're going to a bullfight on Christmas Day?" Diego asked incredulously.

"*Sí, señor.*"

When Diego's silence and facial expression demonstrated his confusion, Carlos explained that while the bullfights lasted for over a week during the holiday period, he felt that the best day was the day of Christ's birth. The crowd was bigger, the excitement was more pronounced, and the experience was not to be missed.

"Okay," Diego agreed, though he would still need time to adjust to this foreign spectacle. It sounded so different from the solemn Midnight Mass, the early morning unwrapping of gifts, and the quiet family dinner to which he was accustomed.

And before Diego had completely adjusted his mind to accept this upcoming Christmas experience, Carlos began to explain the real surprise: Diego himself would enter the bullring.

"*Perdóname?*"

"*Sí, sí, Diego. Es muy emocionante.*"

"I'm sure it is exciting," Diego thought, "but I'm not sure it's a good idea."

Before Diego had a chance to verbalize his concern, however, Carlos was describing how this crazy component worked. In Costa Rica, once the professional matadors are finished for the day, the organizers open up the bullring to the amateurs, and anyone who is brave enough or foolish enough or drunk enough can enter the ring. Carlos explained that he did it himself for the first time at age 16, and he continued to do it every year for seven years until his wife, Louisa, became pregnant and told him "*no mas*."

Again seeing Diego's perplexed facial expression, Carlos described the scene as it would play out on Christmas Day. Instead of a solitary matador alone in the ring with the bull, hundreds of crazy and inebriated Costa Rican *hombres* would flood the center of the ring, hooting and hollering and waiting for the gate to open and for the bull to appear. Typically, the bulls provided for this portion of the day's activity were not as big or as fearsome as those that faced the professionals, but they still weighed over one thousand pounds, they still had horns that could maim, and they still possessed that animal quality that if provoked could gore, trample, and crush the life out of a man.

"*Sí, es posible*," Carlos answered, when Diego asked about the possibility of dying, "but it hasn't happened in a long time."

At that point, Diego laughed and shook his head, as if he could not see himself participating. Secretly, however, he was somewhat intrigued. For even though the possibility of a serious injury did terrify him, he had immediately seized upon another possibility. "It would be so cool," he thought, "if I could write home and tell my family and friends that I was actually in a bullring with a bull."

As he contemplated this new option, Diego knew he couldn't yet tell Carlos he was interested. Carlos would get too excited. Carlos would tell others. And Carlos would probably pressure him into doing it if he showed even the slightest bit of interest. Thus, Diego had to remain low key and uncommitted at least for the short term. He still had a good month to think it over, and he knew he wouldn't make a final decision until he had actually seen the arena and had a chance to view the complete situation before him.

During that month leading up to Christmas, Diego still had to deal with and adjust to his new home and his new culture. Naturally, Diego also became more animated with his host family. Instead of feeling ignorant and flustered when speaking to Carlos and Louisa and their extended families, he was beginning to feel at ease as he searched for words and tried to explain himself. Though Diego obviously still had a long way to go, Carlos could sense his progress, and he no longer felt like he had to shelter and protect this young and naïve American. Thus, Diego had more freedom to explore his new surroundings, and for the most part, he liked what he saw. The Christmas differences, however, did perplex him.

Intellectually, of course, he knew that he would not experience a "White Christmas" in Central America. Emotionally, though, he struggled, especially when he received Christmas cards from home with pictures of Frosty the Snowman or when he found himself silently singing traditional carols like "Silent Night" and "O Holy Night" as he waited at the bus stop.

The other aspect of the Costa Rican Christmas that bothered him was that the natives didn't seem to take church in general all that seriously. Diego had assumed that because Costa Rica was primarily a Catholic country, he would be going to Sunday Mass regularly with Carlos and his family, but they often slept in or scheduled other activities. "Maybe this is just Carlos' family," Diego thought at first, but his fellow Volunteers noticed this tendency too and conversed about it. Like many American families, these *Ticos* and *Ticas* focused more on Christmas shopping and on Christmas parties than they did on the Advent season. And while every church that Diego passed each day on his way to school had a beautiful and extensive manger scene – what they called a "*portal*" – out front, the churches themselves appeared desolate when Diego poked his head inside or less than half full when his family did attend Sunday service.

Fortunately, Diego was not alone during this adjustment period. He had the daily company of the other young American Volunteers who were experiencing similar feelings, and the Peace Corps staff – both Americans and Costa Ricans – who served as their hosts and were sensitive to their needs. As Christmas Day approached, the teachers eased up a bit on the language training, and they attempted to explain that the Catholic religion in Costa Rica over the years had become more of a cultural expectation rather than a firmly held religious belief. In addition, the staff scheduled activities that would not only increase the Volunteers' knowledge of the new culture but also ease the transition by incorporating American traditions. For example, the language teachers gradually taught the Volunteers the most popular Christmas carols in Spanish, and, a week later, they broke into groups and went caroling in the nearby neighborhoods. In addition, they hosted a Christmas party for the Volunteers with American foods and desserts and a pre-arranged gift exchange. Though Diego and the other Americans still longed for loved ones and recalled favorite Christmas memories, they were not overcome by sadness or loneliness, and most of them looked forward to their first Christmas away from home.

Chapter 10

Throughout her grade-school years, Lilli was usually the most animated and energetic student in her class. She greeted her teacher with a big smile each day, and she loved being involved in school activities. She always volunteered to read aloud, she constantly helped her teachers pass out papers, and she absolutely adored "show and tell," both the speaking and the listening. Though she wasn't necessarily the smartest student in her grade, she stood out among her peers, and most of her teachers assumed Lilli would become a teacher herself one day.

Lilli's grandmother walked Lilli to and from school each day, so Lilli's life outside school was strictly structured. She had to sweep the wooden floors in her home each day before school, and she was expected to do her homework at the kitchen table after school before she was allowed outside to jump rope with the few girls her age in the neighborhood.

Naturally, too, Lilli helped her mother and grandmother in the kitchen both before and after meals. Later in the evening, when all the housework was completed, the family gathered in their small living room to listen to Lilli read. Her mom had purchased an old set of story books from a family whose children were all grown, so Lilli read all of the classic fables.

When Lilli's mom tucked Lilli in at night, Lilli asked lots of questions about people and the world: "Why do people all look so different, Mama? Where are the stars during the day? How big is Golfito?"

Lilli's mom smiled lovingly when Lilli inquired in this way. She wished she could answer all of her daughter's questions, but since she had lived such a sheltered life herself and since she was normally exhausted after her own long day working at the small, house restaurant near the Mercado, she usually answered in the same way each night.

"*Yo no se, mi amor*, but we can ask Grandma and Grandpa tomorrow. They might know the answers to your questions." By the next day, of course, Lilli had moved on to other questions. Grandma and Grandpa answered some of them at breakfast and at dinner and afterwards; however, when they were unable to do so, if Grandpa were in a good mood, he would sometimes make up fantastic stories which made them all laugh.

Chapter 11

Early on Christmas Day, Carlos and his family and Diego exchanged gifts and enjoyed a leisurely morning, but they did not go to church. Instead, they walked over to Carlos' parents' house and dropped off baby Carlos for the day. Then, Carlos, Louisa, and Diego walked to the bus stop where they began their short pilgrimage to Zapote.

On the first bus ride from Hatillo to San Jose, Carlos tried to gauge Diego's intentions. Would he actually enter the ring or not? "*Yo no se*," Diego responded. "Maybe. Maybe not. I have to see everything first before I can make a final decision."

"*Pero, Diego* – " Carlos began his sales pitch again.

"Leave him alone," Louisa finally said to the shock and surprise of both Carlos and Diego. Rarely did this traditional, young woman interrupt or contradict her husband at home, much less out in public. Yet, she had heard the *macho* arguments so many times before, and she had also developed a sincere affection for this sensitive American giant in her home, and she did not want him to get hurt. "Let Diego decide. He is smart enough to make up his own mind."

Bolstered by this display of confidence in him, Diego relaxed a bit and knew that he would make the right decision. He wasn't stupid, after all, and he had only rarely caved into peer pressure since his ten-tag experience in fourth grade. Then, surprisingly, as he recalled that experience from over a decade earlier, Diego began to hear fireworks in the distance as the three *amigos* exited one bus and walked a short distance to the connecting bus bound for Zapote.

"*Sí, mucho* fireworks," Carlos explained. The promoters used early-morning fireworks to wake up the residents and remind them of the upcoming spectacle. And as the bus made its way closer to town and to the arena, Diego began to see the excitement and spectacle that Carlos had tried to describe earlier; the streets became more crowded with pedestrians and vendors selling food and souvenirs. The noise increased with music blaring from street-side stereos and groups of young men fueling their courage and challenging one another, just as Carlos had been challenging Diego. And the neighborhoods became more and more colorful as the bus approached its drop-off point. For just as American baseball teams decorated their stadiums with red-white-and-blue banners for the October World Series, the Zapote residents and the bullfights' promoters festooned their homes and their arena with colorful banners and flags to highlight their Christmas tradition.

The arena itself was not as big as Diego expected. Having attended a few Costa Rican professional soccer games with Carlos, Diego envisioned a structure similar to the soccer stadiums, but the playing field for this event was much smaller, just a little bit bigger than the infield for a major league baseball game. And the space felt even smaller because the stands were pretty much right on top of the action. When Diego took it all in for the first time, he saw this space as a smaller version of the Roman Coliseum he remembered from old films, and he began to wonder if he were about to be the Christian offered up to these Costa Rican lions.

"*Mira, Diego. Mira.*"

Diego's reverie was broken as Carlos pointed out all of the arena's special features. From their seats about 10 rows up from the infield, Diego could see the special gate from which the bulls would be released. Carlos also showed Diego the four-foot wall that circled the edge of the ring and the 10 yards of space between this small wall and the eight-foot wall that served as the beginning of the bleachers. Inside that small space, Diego could see various workers and emergency personnel busily preparing for the day's activities, but Carlos had previously explained to him the real importance of the smaller wall. For if a professional matador truly felt imperiled, he could run to the wall and hop over it to avoid disaster. Similarly, the amateurs could use the same escape route if they felt threatened or if they simply came to their senses once they found themselves inside the ring.

Finally, about a half hour later, the spectacle was ready to begin. Every seat in the arena appeared to be full when the first matador, Don Ricardo, strode to the center of the ring. Dressed all in white with a red belt and a red cape, this professional obviously enjoyed the spotlight, and in a grand display of showmanship and courtesy, he bowed to the various sections of the crowd and signaled for the first bull to be released.

The action began immediately. The bull charged out of the gate and directly at the matador. Undaunted, Don Ricardo stood his ground as the beast approached and deftly stepped to the side at the precise moment. The crowd roared. Don Ricardo was apparently one of the nation's best, and he was never in danger. Every time the bull charged at him, Don Ricardo escaped easily, almost too easily. The bull looked overmatched. Within 10 minutes of its entrance, the bull, indeed, collapsed at Don Ricardo's feet, and he placed his right foot gently on the bull's head to signal his victory. Again, the crowd roared, and two of the workers carried Don Ricardo aloft on their shoulders around the ring to receive his acclamation.

Most of the following matadors were not as good – or as fortunate. Some of them had to hop over the wall to escape injury, and others were run over or gored in the center of the ring. Fortunately, no one was seriously injured because just as the clowns enter the ring at an American rodeo to distract a threatening bull, Costa Rican cowboys also intervene, waving their hands and their hats, whenever one of the matadors needs to be saved.

Diego had to admit that he was impressed by some of the matadors. Previously, he thought bullfighting was similar to professional wrestling, more like a circus act than a true competition. As he watched these unique athletes, though, he acquired a better appreciation for this sport and its practitioners. These young men were all trim and fit and agile. Those like Don Ricardo could probably turn a double play in baseball if properly trained and given the chance, and even those who struggled with the bull in front of them showed a certain grit and determination. If knocked down or rolled over, they didn't immediately hightail it for the wall. No, most of them hustled to their feet, retrieved their capes, and prepared again to face the beast. Only a serious wound would drive them away.

After approximately two hours of excitement, all the matadors who had performed that afternoon appeared one more time for a grand finale of applause. As they promenaded through the arena, a certain rustling began in the bleachers. Everyone knew it was time for the real fun to begin. For if the Costa Rican professionals were really like a classical symphony, the rock concert of amateurs was about to start, with the greater possibility of human blood rather than the blood of the bull, and the crowd couldn't wait to see what would happen.

"*Listo, Diego? Listo?*"

"No, Carlos. I'm not ready yet. I still want to see how this works before I try it."

As soon as the line of professionals exited the ring, Diego watched as another line entered, this one much different in so many ways. Unlike the real matadors, who dressed stylishly and maintained a reserved air about them, these wild *borrachos* ran into the ring yelling and jumping as if they had just been freed from prison when, in fact, they had just entered a cell of sorts. Obviously, most of them were liquored up and ready, oblivious to the possible danger that awaited them.

As Diego continued to observe, he noticed that not everyone in the ring was drunk. A few of them had actually dressed up and brought their own capes, obviously intent on becoming professionals one day themselves. Others, meanwhile, ambled in after the initial horde, and they displayed a bit of common sense. Instead of gathering near the bull's entrance, this sober portion of the crowd purposely walked away from the entrance and gathered near the wall – just in case – or at the other side of the arena altogether. "If I do go into the ring today," Diego thought, "I'll be hanging out with those guys."

Finally, with 200 to 300 *hombres locos* gathered in the ring, the first bull was released. Instead of charging out into the arena, though, as all the previous bulls had done, this bull appeared startled and confused by the scene in front of him. He didn't move at all until one of the aspiring professionals approached him and waved his red cape. Then, the bull charged forward a bit and began kicking at those near him. At that point, the bull was about 15 yards into the ring and surrounded on all sides, and the chaos ensued.

One of the drunken idiots raced up to the bull and slapped it in the face. Another one in the rear began pulling on its tail. And a third actually tried to climb aboard American style. The bull went nuts. It charged directly at those in front of him, and two men went down. The bull stumbled over them and began chasing those in front who had not yet scattered. Diego had never seen anything like this in his life. While Carlos and many others laughed at the chaos and the foolishness, Diego worried a bit for those who were down and searched for the emergency personnel he had seen earlier. Unfortunately for the fallen, the emergency personnel, like Carlos, were also pointing and laughing uproariously.

"Perhaps being drunk is an advantage in this situation," thought Diego. Those who had fallen scampered somehow to their feet, and the adventure continued. The bull was obviously outnumbered and didn't know which man or men to attack. They came at the bull from all sides, and in his quest to protect himself, the bull quickly exhausted his energy and tumbled to the ground. At that point, those near the bull piled on top of him, and many of the others did the same until the pile was three and four bodies deep. Soon, the cowboys entered and shooed everyone off, so they could rescue the bull and coax it out of the ring. The process took a while, so Carlos bought *cervezas* for Louisa and himself, but Diego settled for a cola; unlike most of those in the ring, he wanted to remain sober. In fact, as Diego watched these foolish, young men, he began to wonder if they might be even more dangerous than the bull.

After that first bull, Diego watched four more before he finally decided he could take on this challenge. Only two or three men had been injured, none seriously, and only those who had been extremely foolish needed to be carted off. Diego had formulated his plan, and he told Carlos he was ready.

"*Muy bueno, Diego. Muy bueno,*" Carlos congratulated him while Louisa silently shook her head, knowing she could do nothing to stop Diego. Then, Carlos told Diego to hurry because the announcer had just mentioned that the next bull would be the last bull of the day.

As Diego hustled downstairs from the bleachers to the arena's entrance, he went over his plan in his head: "Stay as far away from the bull as possible at all times. If the bull goes left, you go right; if the bull goes right, you go left; and if the bull somehow gets too close, just go over the wall." After all, Diego reasoned, the purpose of this adventure is to write home and, later, tell the story about actually being in the ring with a live bull; the ultimate intent is to exit unscathed.

When Diego found his way into the ring, he felt a bit like Gulliver in the Land of the Lilliputians; at six-foot five inches, he towered over his Costa Rican contemporaries who were all at least six inches shorter. And Diego's pale skin made him look sickly in the midst of this brown mob. The only thing that could make him look even more out of place were if he wore wire-rimmed glasses, which he did. The overall impression was that of a lost librarian, who had somehow stumbled out of the book he was reading and into a surreal experience.

Fortunately, Diego didn't let any of these differences bother him. And even though he heard some of the crowd members pointing out the tall *gringo* to one another, he was focused on his game plan, and he situated himself directly across from the bull's entry point, as far away as he could be while still remaining in the ring. Unfortunately, Diego was missing one key piece of information that Carlos purposely neglected to pass along to him: they always saved the biggest and the baddest bull until the very end of the day's festivities. And this bull did not disappoint the crowd.

While the previous bulls allotted to the amateurs appeared overweight, slow, and out of shape, this bull was in tip-top condition. And unlike the previous five, this one did not stumble out of the gate and stand transfixed before being antagonized by someone in the crowd. No, indeed, this one came charging out of the gate at top speed, and he headed straight for Diego, as if this idealistic Peace Corps Volunteer owed him money.

"Wow," Diego thought as he witnessed this surprising development. "He looks like he has me in his sights," and the mass of humanity in front of him split like the Red Sea. Momentarily frozen because the bull was bearing down on him and not veering either left or right, Diego finally remembered his back-up plan and quickly hoisted himself over the wall.

"That was a close call," he uttered in relief once he found himself on the other side, but his safety was short-lived, for an amazing – and extremely unlikely – event had occurred. This bull was charging so fast and so hard that when it reached the wall, it was unable to stop. Thus, the bull simply lifted up its front legs, and his momentum carried him over into Diego's safety zone, that 10-yard space between the two walls that was now full of cowering cowards.

"Oh my God," Diego prayed aloud. This mountain of breathing, angry flesh – much like the cartoon images Diego remembered from the Saturday mornings of his youth – was within striking distance and stabbing and kicking at anyone in his vicinity. Diego's entire life did not flash before his eyes during those milliseconds of fear, but his death or his disfigurement did. In his mind, Diego saw one of the bull's hooves kicking out his front teeth, or, worse yet, he imagined one of the bull's horns piercing his heart. "I better get out of here."

Diego's only escape, though, was to hop back over the four-foot wall and return to the main ring, and he had a small army of Costa Ricans in front of him with the exact same thought. Normally a polite and well mannered, young man,

Diego understood for the first time in his life the meaning of the phrase "every man for himself." Rather than let his cohorts precede him, Diego climbed on the backs of three different Costa Ricans in his haste to hustle to safety.

When he reached the inside arena again, Diego quickly looked back at his pursuer and was relieved to see that the bull was trapped. In that small space, he could not get enough momentum to climb the wall again and chase down the only American brave enough to enter his kingdom. The bull would have to be led around by the cowboys to the opposite end and the normal entry point. And by the time they did that, Diego, who was no longer feeling brave at all, would be long gone. Though his heart was pulsating with accumulated fear and though he could barely breathe as a result of the sudden and unrelenting tension, Diego watched as his assigned assassin was led away, and as soon as the beast entered the ring again, Diego exited. He hopped over the short wall one more time and found his way to the nearest exit. There, he sat and waited for his heartbeat and his blood pressure to return to normal and for Carlos and Louisa to bring him home – to peace and quiet and safety. His career as a matador was over.

Fifteen to 20 minutes passed before the spectators exited the arena, and Diego's guardians arrived.

"Diego!" Carlos exulted when he found him outside the stadium. "*Hombre mas bravo*," he added, and he gave Diego a congratulatory hug. Though Carlos was only five years older than Diego, he treated his North-American guest with fatherly pride and offered to buy him a celebratory beer.

"Quiere una cerveza ahora? Esta listo?"

"*Sí*," Diego responded. "I am definitely ready now."

Even Louisa had to laugh at Diego's response, and she, too, hugged him, more in relief for his safety, though, than in celebration. Then, the three of them found a nearby *cantina* where they all toasted Diego's accomplishment and sang "*Feliz Navidad*" to the one Christmas Day that Diego would never forget.

Chapter 12

As Lilli moved from her grade-school years into her middle-school years, she found herself alone often. The girls in her neighborhood no longer jumped rope, and, instead, they were allowed to walk to the Company store or to the Saturday afternoon movies together. Not surprisingly, Lilli's mom and grandparents did not allow her to accompany them. They remembered all too well how Rosa had gotten herself into trouble on unsupervised walks, and they were all determined to make sure that Lilli did not find herself in a similar predicament.

When Lilli politely asked why she could not join her classmates on their walks, her mom explained merely that "Sometimes bad things can happen to young people when they are left alone. You will understand better one day when you have children of your own."

Lilli didn't fully understand. Her little section of Golfito seemed so safe. What could possibly happen?

Fortunately, Lilli did have one diversion that tempered her isolation and her disappointment. One of the women who lived nearby had a two-year-old boy and a set of six-month-old twin girls, so she asked Lilli's mom if Lilli could help her once in a while. Rosa knew this would be a good experience for Lilli, so Lilli spent many hours at this neighbor's house playing with the two-year-old while also learning how to care for the babies.

Initially, Lilli merely watched as the mom dressed the babies and changed their diapers. As the months passed, however, and as Lilli demonstrated her gentle care and her attention to detail, the mom allowed Lilli to perform some of those same chores, and Lilli loved doing so. She spoke gently to the girls when she cleaned them or when she pulled their shirts over their heads. Then, she read to them and sang songs to them as she prepared them for their naps. She especially loved the warmth of the babies in her arms in the old rocking chair and the gradual transition that occurred as the babies moved from fidgeting to settling in to finally falling asleep in Lilli's arms. Lilli's mom had previously told her that she would understand so much more about parenting when she had children of her own, and this experience with the neighbors' three young children allowed Lilli to see and appreciate her mom's wisdom.

Lilli was so good with the children that what started as a regular and unpaid activity gradually turned into a daily and paid position. Each day after school, Lilli went to the woman's house and worked for two to three hours. The woman, whose husband worked as an apprentice accounting clerk for the Company, gave Lilli a small amount of money each Friday. Lilli gave this money to her mom and grandparents, and they allowed her to keep half of it. The other half, they explained, would be divided between the family's budget and her college education fund, and they commended her for her work and for her contribution to both. Lilli could see the pride on their faces, and she noticed that they were no longer treating her as a simple child. Yes, she still had to perform all of her normal chores, and, no, she still could not go out with the girls her age, but she suddenly felt so much more like a young adult because she finally had some money of her own.

Initially, Lilli kept all of her *centavos* in an old shoe box under her bed. She wasn't yet sure what to buy, and she didn't want to waste her money on something foolish. In fact, she secretly feared that her position would end shortly when the twins became bigger and needed less care or supervision. Gradually, though, Lilli realized what she wanted to buy: books and magazines.

Her mom wasn't surprised by Lilli's desire to buy books. In fact, Lilli's family had all assumed that Lilli would spend some of her money in that way, and they all looked forward to hearing Lilli read the stories she chose from the limited collection at the Company store.

"But why do you want to buy magazines?" They asked her.

"No, I don't want to buy magazines," she answered. "I just want to buy a subscription to one magazine. Our social studies teacher receives a news magazine each week in the mail, and she tells us a little bit about what's going on in the world. I would like to receive that magazine as well, so I can learn more about the world and see lots of pictures too. Please, Mama, will you help me use my money to buy that magazine?"

Her mother agreed quickly and easily, and before the week was over, Lilli's mother spoke to the teacher who provided the information Lilli needed, and together, all three of them arranged for the purchase. The teacher gave Lilli and her mom the subscription card, Lilli provided the cash, and Lilli's mother purchased the bank check and the stamp needed to mail the order. The card indicated it would probably take six to eight weeks before Lilli would receive her first issue, and Lilli was already bubbling over with excitement. In fact, she was so excited and eager to start reading and learning that Lilli's teacher let her borrow a few of the school's older issues until Lilli's first issue arrived.

That night at home, Lilli began reading to her family from the magazines. Naturally, she didn't read every single article. Instead, she chose articles that she thought her family would enjoy or find interesting, and she avoided any articles that she thought would displease them in any way. She was still a young girl, after all, and she feared that if somehow they found the magazine to be inappropriate for her, they would prevent her from receiving it even though she had provided the money. Thus, she read from the international section any articles that mentioned Costa Rica or Central America, and she avoided articles about the war in Vietnam. She also read to them articles about education or medicine or new inventions, and she avoided the articles about race relations in the United States or anything about drugs or the so-called "sexual revolution."

Chapter 13

Once Christmas and New Year's Day had passed, Diego and the other Sports Promoters knew their time in San Jose would soon be over. They knew because those in charge began talking more and more about locations and start dates. In fact, Bill, the official who supervised the dozen Sports Promoters, had set up various sports clinics and visits, so the Volunteers could see some of the targeted communities, and so the local leaders could watch the Volunteers in action. Though Bill had tentatively matched the Volunteers and the cities – based on a combination of factors such as skills, personalities, fluency in Spanish, and the needs and the wants of the communities themselves – he was flexible, and he wanted to make sure the Volunteers and the cities they were assigned to were a good fit.

The city of San Jose, for example, was trying to improve its premier basketball league, and they wanted two Americans to serve as player coaches in the league. As a result, Bill chose Dennis and Charley, two of the best hoopers in the group of 12, to remain in the capital city. For the town of San Ramon, which was northwest of San Jose, he chose Albert because volleyball was his best sport, and the people of San Ramon had fallen in love with the game. And since Diego had the most baseball experience, Bill chose him to serve in the Atlantic port city of Limon because that town already had an old baseball stadium that wasn't getting much use.

Not everyone was pleased, however, with the initial designations. "I don't really care for San Ramon," Albert admitted to his peers after the group visited one afternoon. "I think it's too small, and I think I'd go crazy there. In fact, I think I might ask for another country altogether," Albert added.

These comments didn't surprise his fellow Volunteers because Albert had privately bragged earlier that he'd never complete two full years as a Volunteer. "I'm just here to see the world, and when they say I have to actually start working," he said with a wink, "I'll tell them about my sick mom back home, and I'll be on my way."

Diego couldn't believe it when he had first heard Albert's words. Diego had assumed, of course, that his two-year commitment meant a two-year commitment, and he was locked in. He had assumed, too, that every Peace Corps Volunteer would be a wide-eyed idealist like himself, so Albert's attitude and his willingness to take advantage of the program shocked him. Diego was shocked again and pleasantly surprised when Bill calmly addressed Albert's concern and put the young whippersnapper in his place: "Albert, you have to realize that Costa Rica and the sports promotion program are probably the most coveted assignments in all of the Peace Corps organization. So if you say you can't work in Costa Rica, they won't send you anywhere else."

Properly chastised, Albert's bluster diminished during his last month of training, and he did, in fact, serve as a volleyball instructor in San Ramon for six months before his mother "was stricken with a serious disease," and Albert went home to California to care for her.

During that last month of training, Diego and the other Sports Promoters also visited Limon and Golfito for baseball and basketball clinics respectively. They visited Limon first, and while the prospect of coaching baseball in the old stadium appealed to the tall first baseman/outfielder, he didn't fall in love with the town. The man who would be his supervisor there was a bit aloof, and the turnout at the clinic was small and unenthusiastic. This was in direct contrast to the trip to Golfito the following weekend. There, Padre Roberto would be the supervisor, and he was over-the-top excited to bring a Volunteer to his community. Though he himself was a native of Costa Rica, Padre Roberto had attended college and seminary school in Pennsylvania, and he had participated in college athletics and knew well the benefits of sports for young people. In addition, he had come to know several Peace Corps Volunteers through the years – like Steve, the engineer, who had departed just a few years earlier – so he was thrilled to secure a Volunteer who would work exclusively with sports and young people.

In addition to Padre Roberto's enthusiasm, Diego was impressed with Golfito because every session of their weekend clinic was packed with kids of all ages – both males and females – who wanted to play basketball. "Boy, I really like this place," Diego said to the other Volunteers on Saturday night.

"Really?" Nick, who had been tentatively assigned to work in Golfito, asked Diego with a hopeful tone. "How would you like to switch?"

"Seriously? You'd rather go to Limon?"

"I think so. Let's talk about this."

In their conversation, Nick revealed that Golfito felt too small and too isolated to him, and he preferred Limon because it was a bit bigger and also closer to San Jose. "I'm more of a city boy," the Chicago native revealed, "and Golfito seems too much like a one-horse town with just that one main street."

"Alright, let's talk to Bill," Diego agreed, "and see what he says."

Bill approved the switch rather quickly. "Okay," he told them the following Monday once the decision had been approved by Bill's boss. "We want you guys to be happy with your assignments, and since you're both pretty well rounded sports wise, we think this can work. We'll let the local supervisors know, and you'll probably start work in about two weeks." Both Diego and Nick were eager to begin.

Chapter 14

During that same time, as Lilli was growing intellectually and beginning to have some freedom and some time away from her mother and her grandparents, she began to take an interest in boys. Her interest, however, was not so much in the boys her own age, for they seemed foolish and immature. Instead, she noticed the boys who were two or three years ahead of her in school. In fact, they were easy to notice because they called out to her often in a way that was common in her culture. "Hey, *Bonita*," they would call to her softly, or "*Qué linda*" to compliment her beauty. Others would hiss at her as if she were "*caliente*," like a steaming dish of tortillas.

Like a good girl, of course, Lilli ignored them, but her fair complexion and her long, dark hair contrasted beautifully, and she was aware that soon, her mother and her grandparents might begin to look for a husband for her. Lilli's family never actually said anything about an arranged marriage to her, but Lilli, as a quiet observer of life around her, understood what was going on. In addition, because one of her high-school teachers had required all the students to keep a journal of their thoughts, Lilli began to record not only what was going on in her life but also her thoughts about what was going on nearby.

The Costa Rican families of that era did not specifically arrange marriages between their children. They did, however, talk to one another about possible matches once the children reached high school. This was especially true in a small, rural, and isolated town like Golfito where the local opportunities for further education were nonexistent. The parents of the young females assumed that their daughters would graduate from the local high school and marry a local boy who would get a job with the banana Company. Then, the two of them would raise their children in that community.

Lilli was intrigued by all of this. She herself had grown up with this same expectation, but she had also observed another possibility. For she had learned about the American school near the airport, a school that only provided instruction up to the eighth grade.

"Where do those children go to high school?" She asked her classmates.

"Why, in America, of course," they answered, and they laughed at her ignorance. Then, they explained to her that when the children of the American employees were ready to attend high school, these children went with their mothers to America or were sent to live with relatives. The American children did not attend the small, Spanish-speaking high school in Golfito. Lilli pondered this revelation for a long time. On one hand, the idea of leaving Golfito to live in a faraway country at the age of 14 was frightening and overwhelming. Yet, on the other hand, she was intrigued with the idea, and she pondered it often. Even though she knew she would never have that particular opportunity, she wondered often why some people have more options than others. She considered it even more so when she learned of a local girl who had left Golfito to study at the University in San Jose.

"How is that possible?" Lilli wondered, and she began to ask her friends about Cecilia Mora, this girl who had lived nearby. Cecilia's father worked as an admissions receptionist in the Company hospital, and she had a brother who lived in San Jose. Though Cecilia's father enjoyed his job and his life in Golfito, he wanted something better for his six children. So when his oldest boy, Angel, graduated from high school in Golfito, he arranged for Angel to move to San Jose to attend college there. Like his father, Angel wanted to work in a hospital, but he hoped to work as a doctor.

Cecilia, the eldest daughter in the family, also wanted more than what Golfito could offer, and she took advantage of a unique opportunity that opened up for her. When Cecilia was in grade school, her teachers noticed that in addition to excelling in her normal subjects, she was exceptionally fluent in her English studies. She had perfect pronunciation, and whenever she saw or heard a new word in English, she memorized it immediately. When her fourth-grade teacher mentioned this fact to the bilingual fourth-grade teacher at the American school, that teacher and the principal of that school asked Cecilia's parents if they would allow Cecilia to interview to attend the school for grades five through eight.

"We can't afford to send our daughter to your school," Cecilia's father answered when first approached, for he knew that the American school was the only school in town that charged tuition.

"According to Cecilia's current teacher, your daughter has unique language abilities, and as a result, we would like to offer her a scholarship," they responded. Though the school officials had never offered such a scholarship before, they realized that their students were a bit too isolated in their English-speaking cocoon, and these officials wanted their students to have at least some exposure to a typical Costa Rican student. A few of the teachers there were skeptical at first; they didn't think a 10-year-old fifth-grader could keep up academically with all the instruction in a second language. However, once those same teachers interviewed Cecilia, entirely in English, they realized that she was, indeed, a special and unique student. Thus, Cecilia completed four full years at the American school, and by the time she completed eighth grade and graduated, her English was practically flawless. Unfortunately, Cecilia couldn't follow her classmates to attend high school in America, but during her high-school years in Golfito, she was able to work part-time as a translator for the American supervisors in the banana Company, and she knew she could do similar work in San Jose after high school when she joined her brother and also began her studies at the university.

As Lilli learned more and more about Cecilia's situation, Lilli gradually realized that she wanted a similar opportunity for herself, and she would not be content to simply marry a boy from Golfito and raise a family there. "I want to attend college in San Jose too," she told herself. Not surprisingly, she was not yet ready to share these thoughts with her family, but she did begin to take her studies even more seriously, and she decided she needed to talk to Cecilia when she next visited Golfito. Then, Lilli could find out what else she had to do to make her university dream a reality.

Eventually, when the two girls sat and spoke, both in Spanish and in English, under the giant tree near Cecilia's house, Lilli realized quickly that she would never have the same opportunity as Cecilia. Lilli's English was nowhere near as strong as Cecilia's, and Lilli did not have any relatives in San Jose. Still, Cecilia reinforced the importance of academics to Lilli, and she also strongly encouraged Lilli to do whatever she could to improve her English. Cecilia had seen so many opportunities open up to her because of her language skills, and she felt confident that Lilli, too, would have a much better chance of escaping Golfito if she became even more fluent in English.

Thus, Lilli periodically purchased a copy of the weekly English newspaper called the *Tico Times* and read as much of it as she could. In addition, she decided to try to converse with any Americans she met in her daily routine. This was an unusually bold step for Lilli because she was normally quite shy and reserved, even in Spanish among her Costa Rican neighbors. Lilli's new goal was especially difficult to achieve because her family didn't want her to talk to strangers and even more so to strangers from another country. Lilli became pretty resourceful, though, to accomplish her mission; she relied on God to help her.

No, she didn't actually pray to God for help; she merely used God's house to facilitate her task. Sunday Mass at Saint Michael's was the one place that Lilli could go to by herself. At times, her mom or her grandmother did accompany her to the

10:00 a.m. Mass, but often, they failed to attend either because they were too tired from a busy week or because they simply wanted a complete day of rest, one when they did not have to get up early and prepare to go out.

Since Lilli always enjoyed church and since the church was so close to their home, Lilli was allowed to attend by herself, but she had to return home immediately after the Mass. "*Sí, Mama*," she said excitedly the first time she was allowed out on her own. "I promise to go only to church and back." And that's exactly what she did, quietly sitting near the front of the church and keeping pretty much to herself both before and after the service. That all changed, however, once she decided she needed to really practice her English.

Lilli had previously observed that some of the American families also sat near the front. Previously, she had kept her distance, but with her new goal in mind, she made sure that she sat near them, so she might have a better opportunity to speak to them. At first, she waited until that point in the service just before Communion when the priest says to the parishioners, "Peace be with you," and they respond, "And also with you." Then, the priest spoke the following words: "And now let us offer one another a sign of peace."

At that moment, each person shook hands with those nearby and said, "Peace be with you." Lilli usually only greeted her fellow Golfiteños in Spanish with the words "*Pax contigo*." With her new determination, though, she also began to reach out and greet the Americans in her vicinity, and she did so in English: "Peeece bee weeth you." Like most Costa Ricans and without intending to do so, she overemphasized the "eees" in her words, and the Americans smiled at her effort. And the effort sometimes paid off after the Mass ended. While the American children her age were too cool to speak to Lilli and the dads too oblivious, one or two of the moms were kind enough to engage Lilli in conversation.

"What is your name?" they asked, or "Where do you live?"

Lilli answered these initial questions quickly and easily because they were so similar to the questions in her school's English textbook. During subsequent weeks, the questions became more difficult and the conversations more in depth. These conversations simultaneously frightened Lilli and thrilled her. She had to stop and think before she replied, and at times, she had to admit, in Spanish, her inability to translate her ideas. As she became more comfortable, though, she worried less and less about making a mistake, and she began to take chances with vocabulary and verb endings.

Each week after Mass, too, Lilli rushed home not only to appease her mother and grandparents but also to look up new words in her Spanish-English dictionary and to compare what she had said to what she should have said. Gradually, Lilli became more proficient and more confident in English, and she developed new friendships. In fact, these American women became so impressed by Lilli's willingness to converse with them that they wanted to get to know her even more.

"Would you like to come to our house with us and have lunch?" one woman asked Lilli after a few Sunday conversations with her.

"Yes, I would like that," Lilli replied, "but my mama and my *abuelos* will not permit me. I must return home immediately after church. But thank you so much. You are so kind."

Lilli had not expected the woman to be so generous. Lilli had only wanted and only expected conversation. Anything else was amazing.

"Well, why don't I walk home with you and meet your family. Perhaps your mother and your grandparents would like to come for lunch also," the bold American woman persisted.

"Well, um, um . . . ." Lilli mumbled as she fidgeted in the pew and suddenly began twirling her long, dark hair with her left hand. "Ah, I don't know. No. No, I don't think that's a good idea."

Though Lilli actually loved the idea, she knew she would have to prepare her mother and grandparents for such a visit or, at the least, her family would need to meet this woman and her family in church before they allowed Lilli to go to their home.

Sensing she had crossed a cultural line of some sort, the woman backed off. "Well, okay, but please know that you are welcome at our home at any time. We would love to see more of you."

Lilli was trembling a bit when she left the church that day. She was so excited and flattered because she had made such a good impression on them, yet she was so frightened about what her family would say if they knew how she was expanding her horizons and planning to leave them and their little town. They would need to be gradually prepared for that departure as well.

Since Lilli wanted to interact more with the Americans, she began to encourage her mother and her grandparents to attend Mass with her again. If the families met and if Lilli's family liked these Americans, Lilli might be able to visit their homes to learn more English and learn more about American ways and American culture.

Soon enough, Lilli's gentle encouragement brought her mother and her grandmother back to church. When they entered three weeks later, Lilli steered them toward her American friends by saying, "I usually sit over here."

During the service, Lilli's family was a bit surprised to see her offer the sign of peace in English to the Americans, and they were even more surprised after the service when the persistent American woman appeared to go out of her way to meet them and to address them in Spanish. Even Lilli was somewhat surprised by the woman's fluency.

"You must be Lilli's mother," the woman said. "We have gotten to know your daughter through conversations with her here in church. You have raised a fine, young lady. She is so sweet and so well spoken."

The woman also greeted Lilli's grandmother and complimented her as well. Lilli was nervous that the woman would invite all of them to lunch. "It was too soon," Lilli thought.

Fortunately, the woman must have had other plans for that day because she left church immediately after their short conversation, and Lilli was left to explain how she had become so familiar with this woman and her family.

"They always sit in the front like I do, and one day, I decided to try out my English with them. Most of the family was polite and friendly, but, as you can see, Mrs. Dugan is extremely friendly. Since that first Sunday we met, she usually talks to me after Mass."

Lilli's family was not suspicious at all. Despite all the years of Americans living alongside Costa Ricans in the banana Company in Golfito, the two groups never really mixed in a social way. They co-existed in a professional way at work and in a respectful way outside work, but most of the Americans who worked for the Company had never been in a Costa Rican home and vice versa. As a result, Lilli's mother didn't expect anything to happen between the two families.

As a naïve and innocent young person, however, Lilli still wanted more. She thought she would meet one family after another, and somehow, opportunities for social and educational advancement would open up for her, and some opportunities did present themselves, but they weren't exactly what Lilli wanted or expected.

"Do you ever babysit for young children?" Mrs. Dugan asked her one day after Mass.

"Yes, I do."

"Well, I don't have young children myself any more, but a few of my friends in the American Zone do need a babysitter once in a while, so if you'd like, I can give them your name."

"Yes, that would be fine."

Though somewhat disappointed that the connection had become more professional than personal, Lilli also realized that the American families would probably pay her much more than the nearby Costa Rican families could afford. In addition, she gradually realized that her family would be much more likely to approve a babysitting relationship with an American family than a friendly relationship. And although these babysitting opportunities didn't materialize as quickly as Lilli thought they might, Lilli did meet another American who, surprisingly, was moving right into her neighborhood.

Chapter 15

The first time Diego approached his new home in Golfito, he was accompanied by Padre Roberto who had previously arranged for Diego to stay with the Mora family. Though this family already had six children of their own, the family typically rented out space in their home to help pay for their expenses. As Diego and Padre Roberto walked up the narrow, winding sidewalk to the Mora home, Diego noticed a mother, Rosa, and daughter, Lillianna, walking in the opposite direction toward them.

The mother walked with her eyes down, and Diego guessed that she was a bit older than he. The daughter, by contrast, had her eyes up and wide open. She had never seen such a tall man before, and she opened her mouth as if to speak, but no words would come out.

Padre Roberto stopped for a second as if he wanted to introduce Diego, but the girl's mother did not stop. She politely said, "*Buenos tardes, Padre*," and moved quickly along. Lillianna, the daughter, who Diego estimated to be about 16 or 17, hesitated for just a bit before silently following her mother's example.

Somewhat intrigued by the young girl, Diego turned around to look at her, and she had done the same. Smiling, Diego waved at her, and Lilli flashed her beautiful white teeth and waved back.

Five seconds later, Diego met another beautiful, young *Tica*, Susanna, the three-year old daughter of the Mora family. Like Lilli, Susanna was also silent, and, in fact, she hid shyly behind her mother as Padre Roberto introduced Diego.

"*Es muy grande!*" Doña Marcella exclaimed as she met the big *gringo* for the first time.

"Yes, he's definitely a big man," Padre Roberto echoed, and "we're hoping he will have a big, positive effect on all of our young men, including your boys."

Doña Marcella then explained that her three youngest boys would be home soon, and she was more than happy to show Diego his room and the rest of the house. As she did so,

Padre Roberto explained to Diego that Doña Marcella's two oldest children – Angel and Cecilia – lived and attended college in San Jose, so the Moras had an extra room to rent to Diego.

The room was simple and empty, with only a single bed as furniture. Two windows surrounded the closet in the left corner. One window looked out over the front yard, and the other looked out over the side yard. Though not attached to one another, all the houses were near each other, and from those windows Diego would be able to see all his neighbors coming and going.

"*Es muy buena*," Diego said. "*Gracias*."

Then, together, Padre Roberto and Diego negotiated the conditions for Diego to stay there. He would pay the family 200 *Colonnes* a month, and this price would include not only his room but also three meals a day with the family, and Doña Marcella would also do his wash on a weekly basis.

Diego thought the arrangement was wonderful. He would have the privacy of his own room, but he would also have the opportunity to really get to know the family and also work on his Spanish – and he wouldn't have to cook or clean. What could be better for a young American man who was still a boy at heart?

Doña Marcella asked Diego when he would move in, and Diego said if it were okay with her, he would check out of his room at the hotel the next morning and, then, move in. She agreed, and everyone was pleased with the arrangement.

Chapter 16

"Mama, who is that man with Padre Roberto?" Lilli whispered almost immediately.

"He must be the new Peace Corps Volunteer Doña Marcella was telling me about."

"What is a Peace Corps Volunteer?" Lilli asked.

"I don't know exactly," her mother admitted, "but Golfito seems to get a Peace Corps Volunteer every couple of years. I remember there was a Peace Corps nurse at the hospital when I was pregnant with you, and before that, I remember people talking about a Peace Corps Volunteer who was trying to help some farmers at the other end of town."

"Where do Peace Corps Volunteers normally live?" Lilli asked next.

"I don't know," her mother answered again, "but it looks like this one is going to live with the Mora family."

"*Qué excitante!*"

"What is so exciting about that?"

"Oh, I don't know. Has an American ever lived in our little neighborhood before?"

"Not in my 31 years of life."

"So, isn't that exciting?"

Lilli felt it was an omen of some sort. If she weren't going to get to know the Americans who attended church as she thought she might, perhaps she would get a chance to talk to her new neighbor, the Peace Corps Volunteer who was going to live with Cecilia's family.

Chapter 17

Later that day, as Diego prepared his belongings to move from his hotel to the Mora house, he realized he was leaving one end of town for the other. He was leaving the non-Company part of town for the Company section, and he wondered if he were doing the right thing.

On one hand, Diego realized that it was Padre Roberto in the Company end of town who had arranged for him to work in Golfito in the first place, and he knew, too, that the northern Company end of town had much better facilities for athletics. On the other hand, however, Diego wondered if perhaps he were needed even more in the non-Company southern end because of what it lacked.

The Company end had four outdoor basketball courts: one at the high school, one at each of the two grade schools, and one more in the public square near the port; these courts also all had volleyball nets and sideline pipes, so that game could be played there as well.

The high school and one of the grade schools also had wide open areas nearby for soccer, and the port area included a public stadium that was used primarily for soccer. As a baseball guy, Diego hoped to see the youngsters of Golfito playing the American pastime on these fields as well.

Finally, though the Company's club facilities were private and available to only members and their families, these facilities included a nine-hole golf course, two tennis courts, an outdoor swimming pool, and an indoor space that was often used for volleyball.

By contrast, the other end of town had an open field for soccer near the grade school, but that was it. Yes, that end of town included other open spaces, but . . . .

Diego's mind wandered off at that point. He wasn't even sure how he was going to work with the Company facilities, so working without facilities would be even tougher.

Thus, as he prepared to leave the southern end of town, he resolved to get back there somehow and try to do something. "Do something – even if it's wrong," Diego's dad had always said to him when he was young. Though Diego was now 22, he felt so much younger, perhaps younger than ever, because of this new adventure that awaited him.

The next morning, as Diego carried his three bags from the hotel to the bus stop, an older man offered to carry the bags for him. Diego often froze in these situations previously. The man had to be close to 60, and Diego assumed by the lines on the man's face, by his bare feet and dirty clothes, and by the unwashed quality of his hair that he was a homeless alcoholic. Obviously, Diego didn't need help carrying the bags, and the man probably wanted to earn some loose change to later buy another beer.

Diego usually froze in these situations because he was never sure how to handle them. He couldn't give money to every man, woman, and child who asked for a handout, and he didn't feel equipped to help them in any other way. As a result, he usually put his head down, said, "*Lo siento*," and walked away. This situation, though, was different.

This old man wasn't asking for a handout; he was offering his services to Diego, much like a valet might at a fancy hotel. All Diego had to do was say "Yes," allow the man to carry the bags about a hundred yards to the bus stop, and then give him a small tip. There were no other beggars in the area, and since Diego assumed this man lived in this public section of town, the man wouldn't often see Diego at the Company end of town and pester him frequently. So Diego nodded his head and handed the old man his three bags. Amazingly, the man showed tremendous strength as he easily lifted and carried the suitcase, the duffle bag, and the gym bag to the bus stop. He moved so quickly, in fact, that for a moment, Diego imagined the old man running off with his stuff. Fortunately, that didn't happen, and when Diego caught up to the old man, he handed him all the coins he had in his pocket, probably about 80 or 85 *centavos* – enough perhaps for a small glass of beer.

Diego assumed that this man would disappear once he had his money, but that didn't happen. Instead, the man placed Diego's bags next to the bench near the bus stop, and he sat down to rest. Unsure what to do, Diego thought about the situation for a few seconds, and he did what he would have done if the man had disappeared; he sat down on the bench and waited for the bus.

During the first half of the 10-minute wait, both men were silent. Diego had never spoken to a homeless man before, even in English, so he had no idea what to say to this man in Spanish. The older gentleman seemed content to sit in silence, and he gazed off toward the water in the Bay of Golfito.

Diego expected other passengers would arrive shortly, but when that didn't happen, he decided to start a conversation after all. He knew he needed to practice his Spanish, and he realized he should probably begin his work. After all, many of his Peace Corps supervisors had emphasized that the Volunteers were really American ambassadors to the Costa Rican people, so even though his primary job was to teach sports to the young people, Diego decided he should actually be reaching out to people of all ages in all situations, and so he began.

"*Mi nombre es Diego. Como se llama usted?*" And he reached out to shake the man's hand.

The old man, pleased to be addressed in this way, smiled and responded: "*Mi nombre es Cundo. Mucho gusto,*" and he shook Diego's hand in return.

Pleased by the response, Diego continued the conversation to the best of his ability and discovered the following. Cundo did not live in the southern section of town but in the northern, Company end of town. At least, that's what Diego understood. Since his Spanish was still a bit shaky, Diego wasn't confident that he understood everything perfectly, but rather than ask questions to clarify any confusion he might have, he often nodded in agreement, instead, as if he understood.

Finally, when the bus arrived, Diego stood and prepared to carry his own bags to the bus. Cundo, however, intervened, quickly and efficiently. He also stood and grabbed all three bags and carried them onto the bus. Once on board, he deposited Diego's bags in the open space across the aisle from the driver, and he took a *peseta* that Diego had given him earlier, and he placed it in the fare box. Then, he sat in the first seat, next to the luggage.

Since Diego had previously given Cundo all of his change, he had to pull a bill out of his wallet and ask for four *pesetas*, so he could put his own fare in the box. Then, once his transaction was complete, Diego hesitated for just a second before sitting right next to his new friend.

Cundo had correctly grasped that Diego's Spanish was not that strong, so he began miming his words when possible to make sure that Diego understood him. First, he pretended to be fishing, and he asked Diego if he were a fisherman. Diego shook his head "No" as Cundo pointed out a small inlet where three old men were sitting on rocks and holding their lines.

Then, when the bus stopped near the grade school, Cundo noticed the children playing on the outdoor basketball court, and he asked Diego if he played. "*Sí, sí,*" said Diego. "*Y usted?*" He asked in return.

Cundo laughed, and using his hands, he pointed out the huge discrepancy between his height and Diego's, as if to say "No way!" Together, the two of them laughed, and as the new passengers entered the bus, they were all quite mystified by this odd pair who seemed to be having such a good time.

"*Donde vive?*" Diego asked next, and Cundo said he lived near the Catholic church.

"*De verdad?*" Diego replied in disbelief. Diego had assumed that all the residents in that neighborhood had to be Company employees, but Cundo explained otherwise. Apparently, a family that did live legitimately in that section of town allowed Cundo to live with them.

"*Mi lugar es muy pequeño,*" Cundo said, "*y detras de la casa.*"

As Diego translated Cundo's words, it sounded like Cundo's place was small and outside the house. "Must be some sort of shed," Diego reasoned. Diego was about to ask the family's name, but Cundo had moved on to another subject as they approached the thin strip of buildings that included mostly bars and the town's only public movie theater.

"*Le gusta peliculas?*" Cundo asked.

"*Sí, sí,*" Diego answered again. "I love movies." And from that point until they reached Diego's stop a few minutes later, they compared their favorite movie titles.

When the bus finally arrived at Diego's stop, Cundo again rushed into action. Before Diego could reach for his own bags, Cundo had retrieved them and began carrying them off the bus.

"*Es okay, Cundo,*" Diego said, and he tried to carry the bags himself, but once more, the old man was too quick. He was already out the door and walking up the sidewalk toward the Mora's house. Diego assumed Cundo was trying to earn another tip, and that was definitely the case, but something else was going on as well. Diego realized this when he noticed all of the neighbors began addressing Cundo as if he lived nearby.

"*Hola, Cundo. Qué tal?*" one of the women said.

"*Qué pasa, Cundo?*" said another.

"He must live around here somewhere," Diego reasoned. Then, when Doña Marcella Mora opened her front door and warmly greeted and thanked the old man, Diego realized Cundo probably lived with the Moras, and Cundo probably knew all along that the new American might be willing to pay him to carry his bags.

Sure enough, Cundo did live with the Mora family. He didn't actually live inside the house, and he didn't pay rent, but the Mora family allowed him to sleep in a small, covered enclosure on the back of the house. Doña Marcella later explained to Diego that Cundo had no family of his own and no real job, so they allowed him to have at least a clean, dry place to sleep at night. During the day, Cundo traveled around town doing small chores for people, and they would pay him with food or tips. Doña Marcella assured Diego that Cundo was "*una buena persona*," but he just never fit in like everyone else.

After Cundo dropped off Diego's bags in his room and after Doña Marcella returned to her housework, Diego took an even closer look at his new home. The bedroom was approximately eight feet by eight feet with a small closet, probably three feet wide by two feet deep, near the left, rear corner.

The bedroom door opened inward to the right, and Diego's bed was against the door on the left. There was also a small shelf on the left side just below the window. The window opening was a screen only, rather than glass, and had shutters on the inside, so Diego could close them for privacy at night and also against the rain that apparently came every day during the rainy season. Diego hadn't noticed the lack of glass before, but as he looked at the nearby houses, he could see that they were all the same in that regard.

Naturally, Diego would keep all of his clothes in the closet, but he would have to keep all of his possessions there too because besides the bed, the room had no other furniture: no nightstand for his glasses, no bookcase for his books, and no dresser for his socks, his shirts, and his underwear. He would either have to hang everything in the closet or put it on the shelf or on the floor in the closet. At first, Diego was disappointed, but when he looked at the large open space on the opposite side of the bed, he realized he could stretch out there each morning and do his pushups without anyone watching.

So he began getting settled by tossing his blue suitcase on the bed. When he opened it, he first pulled out the five-by-seven picture of Bridget and him at his college's Senior Ball. Diego stopped for a second, sat on the bed next to the suitcase, and stared at the photo: Diego was smiling proudly in his black tuxedo, and Bridget was smiling beautifully in her long, blue gown. That night, which was oh so special, seemed so far away, and Diego wondered what Bridget was doing at that moment back home.

She was probably sitting in class, the spring semester of her junior year in college. As he imagined her sitting in a Siena Hall classroom, he knew she was not thinking of him. She was too serious as a student. She'd be listening attentively and taking notes. By contrast, if the roles were reversed, he'd be far away, daydreaming or doodling in his notebook. Like a lovesick, high-school boy, he'd be drawing small hearts and inside writing "Jim loves Bridget."

Gently, Diego placed the photo on the small shelf near his bed and continued unpacking. He put his pants and shirts on hangers and everything else – underwear, socks, handkerchiefs, etc. – on the shelf above the clothes bar. His shoes and sneakers, he placed on the floor in the closet along with his luggage and his books. He kept the suitcase open there and decided he would use that as his dresser, a place where he could toss his wristwatch, his wallet, and his loose change at the end of the day.

As Diego was just about finished unpacking and organizing everything, he heard laughter outside, and he looked to see three boys walking toward the house. They must be Doña Marcella's sons, he assumed. And sure enough, within a minute, Diego was downstairs in the kitchen meeting Ernesto, age 13, Felix, 12, and Antonio, 11. They were in grades eight, seven, and six, respectively.

Felix was the most outgoing of the three, and he eagerly shook Diego's hand, welcomed him, and started asking him questions: "*De donde eres? Por cuanto tiempo estarás ahi? Le gusta arroz y frijoles?*"

"*New York. Dos anos. Y sí,*" Diego answered quickly while laughing.

Felix's mother scolded him gently for being so curious so soon, and she ushered Felix off to the side, so the others could say "Hello."

Ernesto, though the oldest of the three, was easily the most shy, so he stood back while Antonio introduced himself with a big smile, and in his best English, he asked Diego the same three questions Felix had asked earlier: "Where are you from? How long will you be here? And do you like rice and beans?"

"New York," Diego said again, and then "two years," and "yes," as everyone laughed at Antonio, the young comedian. Even Doña Marcella had to smile at her little clown, though her dark face had turned a mild shade of red.

Finally, Ernesto stepped forward and seriously apologized for his two younger brothers. "I am so sorry, Diego, *para mis hermanos son muy loco*," he said in a perfect combination of Felix's Spanish and Antonio's English.

Diego bonded with the boys immediately, but when they asked him if he played "*fútbol*," he hesitated.

"*Fútbol Americano, sí*," he said, "*pero fútbol Costa Riccense, no mucho*."

"*Venga, venga, venga*," shouted Felix and Antonio. "*Te enseñaremos*," they added, and by the time they finished encouraging Diego to play, Ernesto had already retrieved the family soccer ball from the hall closet, and the four of them headed outside to play in the small open space between the back of the house and the slight incline that led to the mountains beyond.

Diego's first week with the Mora family in their home went extremely well. The house itself was a simple, two-story, wooden structure with a metal roof. The main entrance to the house was on the far right, and as Diego entered, he saw the main dining room to his left, a smaller enclosed room to his right, and the kitchen in the middle of these two rooms. Beyond the main part of the house was a small section that was open to the outdoors but still underneath the second floor. This area was similar to the open space underneath the outdoor deck of some American homes. Here, the Mora family kept their extra furniture and their gardening tools. This section served like an American garage, but no families in this section of town owned cars, nor were there any driveways to the houses. Here also, the Mora family had installed a small, extra bathroom with a shower, so that any boarders would not have to use the main family bathroom on the second floor.

The stairway to the second floor was near the front door, and the second floor included three bedrooms: Diego's small bedroom in the left, rear portion, a bigger room near the right rear, where the three boys slept, and a large master bedroom and bath off to the right. Naturally, Señor and Señora Mora slept in the master bedroom with three-year-old Susanna.

The head of the Mora family was Don Francisco. Like many Costa Ricans, he was short and thin and also soft spoken and extremely kind. He worked nearby at the hospital in admissions.

Doña Marcella was actually slightly bigger than Don Francisco. She was about the same height, but because of her stout build, she appeared bigger. At home, she was always cleaning or preparing food or washing clothes – by hand – or hanging them out to dry. She and Don Francisco enjoyed the classic, old-fashioned marriage where he worked exclusively outside the home, and she worked exclusively inside the home and with the children. They appeared to get along well, and the children appeared to love and respect them both. Since the Moras did not own a television, a rare luxury in this small town, the family spent a lot of time around the table after a meal, and they continued to talk and enjoy time together even after the dishes had been cleared and cleaned. All this interaction was sometimes hard on Diego, who really wanted some quiet time, reading alone or writing letters in his room, but he knew that these dinner-table conversations and story-telling marathons afterwards would be good for his fluency in Spanish.

One of the main reasons the Mora family took in boarders was to help support their other two children who lived in San Jose. Their oldest boy, Angel, was 21 and married and studying at the University for a medical career, and their oldest girl, Cecilia, who was 19 and bilingual, worked at the telephone company and also studied part-time at the University. The three of them, including Angel's wife, Patricia, rented a small home in the San Jose suburbs. Naturally, Don Francisco and Doña Marcella wanted their four other children to go to college as well. Though neither of the parents ever attended college, they saw education as the only way out of Golfito and away from the Company.

Don Francisco especially wanted something better for his children. He himself had worked for the Company for over 25 years, and the Company had generally paid him well and treated him well, but he was well aware of what could happen. If he were unable to work for any reason or if he retired, he would have to move out of his Company home. Otherwise, his children might feel locked into Company employment, so their parents wouldn't have to move and could continue to live in Company housing. Thus, he wanted more individual freedom for himself and his family, and he desired to move his entire family to San Jose and buy a home there, one he could own and live in until the day he died.

Doña Marcella, meanwhile, was especially intent on taking care of not only her family but also this new, giant *gringo* in her home. In fact, she made a special trip to the Company market on the day Diego arrived to make sure that he would have an American treat for breakfast: Corn Flakes. She had never purchased them before for her own family, and her children were not permitted to eat them; these were for Diego alone.

Diego, however, didn't particularly care for Corn Flakes. As a kid, he had always preferred Frosted Flakes or Sugar Smacks. Fortunately, Diego, at age 22, was smart enough and mature enough to simply smile in amazement and say "*Muchas gracias.*" As an unofficial ambassador of the United States, he knew he could not be a spoiled brat. He had to appear to be a grateful American even though by then, he had truly come to enjoy rice and beans for breakfast and would have preferred *arroz y frijoles.*

"*Le gusta?*" Doña Marcella asked as he ate the Corn Flakes, and Diego replied, "*Sí, sí.* I love Corn Flakes," and he piled on a mountain of sugar in a vain attempt to try to make them taste more like Frosted Flakes.

Chapter 18

Once Diego settled into his new situation, he set about trying to figure out the best way to start "promoting sports." Since the schools in Costa Rica had their "summer vacation" during late December, January, and February and wouldn't be open for another few weeks, he felt he should start spending his evenings at the town's lighted basketball court next to the soccer stadium. So every night after supper and before the family storytelling went into high gear, Diego excused himself, retrieved his trusty basketball from his bedroom, and dribbled his way downtown to go to work.

At first when he arrived, he was alone on the court. Undaunted and unperturbed, he began by shooting jumpers from the top of the key, rebounding each shot, and following up with an easy lay-up. Then, he dribbled to the other end of the court and repeated the procedure.

As Diego dribbled from one end to another, he accentuated each bounce rather than glide easily and dribble lightly. As a longtime neighborhood hooper, he knew that the heavy sound of a bouncing basketball penetrated deeply and traveled far. He knew it was only a matter of time before the young people in the surrounding homes, those who were just finishing dinner themselves, would hear the sound, glance down toward the court, and follow their hearts to the sound of the bouncing ball.

Sure enough, within 10 to 15 minutes, some young children began to wander down to the area near the court. Rather than enter the court, however, they stood and watched, or they sat on the benches or picnic tables nearby.

Diego saw them, of course, all of them, but he played it cool. He pretended to be intently working on his own game: spinning, faking, and shooting as if he were being guarded. Naturally, he wanted someone, anyone, to join him, but he didn't want to single anyone out; he didn't want to make a bad first choice. Instead, he wanted some of them to take the initiative. He wanted it to be their curiosity, their hunger, their passion that motivated them.

Finally, Diego got a break when one of his shots ricocheted oddly off the rim and bounced near a young pair of boys walking by the corner of the court. The older boy, who appeared to be nine or 10, retrieved the ball for Diego.

Instead of picking up the ball and passing it back to him, though, the boy let the ball roll over his right foot, and then using that foot, he lifted the ball up into the air where he began to bounce the ball first off one knee and then the other. Finally, after a brief display of his soccer skills, the boy allowed the ball to drop below his knee, and he deftly kicked it to Diego who had moved a bit closer to watch. The kick was clean and crisp, and Diego caught it at chest height as if it were a perfect basketball pass.

"*Muy bien*," Diego said to the young boy. "Very good," and Diego applauded for him.

The boy bowed his head lightly, and said "*Gracias*," and he and the other boy, who appeared to be his younger brother, began to walk away.

"*Pero una problema*," Diego said loudly before the boys left.

"*Problema?*" the boy stopped and asked, confused. "*Qué es la problema?*"

"*Esta bola no es fútbol; es una basketball.*" Then, Diego performed some magic of his own.

First, he held the basketball up with both hands, and in a flash, he spun the ball with his right hand while balancing it on his left index finger. The boys watched with wide eyes as the ball rotated quickly. Then, before the spinning ball had a chance to slow down, Diego slapped it repeatedly with his right hand, so the ball spun even faster. Next, he lowered his left hand, with the spinning ball, from eye level to his waist and drew a big circle in front of him, so the ball was revolving in front of the boys' faces as it rotated on Diego's finger. He made three counter-clockwise revolutions before he slapped the ball again, so it would pick up speed before he transferred it to his right index finger and made three similar revolutions. After the third revolution, he transferred the ball back to his left index finger, slapped it again for speed, and motioned with his right hand for the boys to follow him as he walked toward the basket.

Obediently, the boys followed, and Diego could tell by the surrounding silence that everyone around the court was watching him now. Still spinning the ball and walking, Diego waited until he was under the hoop and just a bit to the right, and, then, he began counting backward from the number 10.

"*Diez*," he said slowly and at a normal pitch. Then, with each succeeding number, he spoke more loudly: "*Nueve. Ocho. Siete. Seis.*" Naturally, he kept spinning the ball, but he also spun his empty right hand in small circles to encourage the boys and those in the nearby audience to join in the countdown. They obliged.

"*Cinco. Cuatro. Tres. Dos. Uno.*" And at blastoff, Diego pushed the ball upward with his left index finger, so that it approached the rim as if he were taking a shot.

Naturally, everyone expected the ball to go into the hoop, but it didn't, and the crowd was momentarily disappointed by Diego's apparent failure. But the Caucasian Globetrotter from Amsterdam, New York, knew exactly what he was doing. For just as the ball fell and reached Diego's eye level again, he punched the ball in mid-air with a closed right fist, and the ball shot upwards again, kissed off the wooden backboard, and swished through the hoop.

The two boys jumped up and down and yelled, like the soccer players they were, "*Goallllllll!*" And the onlookers on the perimeter applauded as if Diego had just won the World Cup for his new country.

Within seconds, Diego was showing the two brothers how to shoot, and minutes later, five other children had joined in, some of whom addressed Diego directly and said they remembered him from the basketball clinic he and his fellow Volunteers hosted just weeks earlier. Not surprisingly, all the children wanted to shoot, so Diego quickly showed them how to run layup lines. He divided the group of eight, including himself, of course, into two lines.

Diego positioned himself at the front of the line on the right, and he put the brothers at the beginning of the line on the left. Next, he dribbled in and shot a layup and moved to the end of the opposite line, all the while explaining to the older brother how to rebound the basketball and pass it to the next person in the line on the right. Since this was a new experience for some of the kids who had not attended the clinic, Diego needed a few minutes to get everyone correctly coordinated. When it finally happened, though, five more children joined in, and with the longer lines, Diego had a chance to watch and enjoy, and as he did so, he remembered his own initiation to the joy of basketball so many years earlier.

Eventually, of course, Diego arranged for the children to play an actual game. And because the game included so many newcomers who had never played before, it was often full of chaos and confusion, and Diego had to step in often as the referee and instructor. Still, the court, which was empty just a half hour earlier, was finally throbbing with life and excitement, and Diego knew that Golfito was definitely the right choice, his new home.

By nine o'clock, most of the children needed to return to their homes, but Diego's night was not quite over. As the youngsters began to depart, Diego noticed a new wave of hoopers had appeared. The older boys, high schoolers and beyond, had gathered near the benches and picnic tables, and when only two of the young kids remained, one of the older boys approached Diego.

"*Hola. Como esta? Mi nombre es Juan.*"

"*Hola, Juan. Yo estoy Diego. Mucho gusto.*"

"*Mucho gusto también.*"

"*Qué pasa?*"

"*Nosotros,*" and Juan pointed back towards his friends near one of the picnic tables, "*queremos jugar. Es possible?*"

"*Sí, sí,*" Diego said excitedly. "Of course you can play," he thought. "That's why I'm here. Get down here. Immediately."

"*Venga, venga,*" Diego called out, and he waved to the boys, to invite them to play. Diego knew from his previous clinic experience that the court lights would go off automatically within the hour, at about 10:00 p.m., but he wanted to squeeze as much basketball into that hour as he could. And by the time that hour was over, Diego had set up a nocturnal precedent. Every night at around 7:00 p.m., he dribbled from his house to the court, and there, he oversaw the younger children for at least an hour and a half. Then, somewhere between 8:30 and 9:00, he gradually transitioned the game to the older group, depending on the size of the group and their patience. This tentative schedule worked well for a week or so, and Diego was thrilled with his early success.

Chapter 19

Meanwhile, Diego had to figure out the best use of his daytime hours. Since the schools were still on vacation, he thought the morning hours would be the best time to organize an activity because most Costa Ricans would not venture out during the hot afternoon hours. In fact, they all thought he was a little bit crazy when they saw him working out in the afternoon.

"*Diego, estas loco?*" they might ask if they saw him jogging. Or, "Diego, geet out of the sun. Eats too hot," they might say in their best English.

At first, Diego was oblivious to their suggestions because having come from a New York November, he was determined to soak in as much sunshine as he could. Gradually, however, he began to see the wisdom of their advice. His nose was starting to reach Rudolph proportions, and his light, Irish-Italian complexion was becoming surprisingly close to the light brown, Costa Rican shade.

Since Diego assumed he could get basketball or volleyball games going under the lights at night, he wanted another sport for his daytime adventure, and what better sport than the American pastime itself: baseball?

In the back of his mind, Diego seemed to recall that Padre Roberto had once said something about a bag full of old baseball gear in his garage. When he first mentioned it, Diego didn't take it that seriously because he didn't think there would be enough equipment or enough interest to actually play a full game with two teams, but then he remembered the self-organized ball games of his youth, and he figured it was worth a try.

So what if he didn't have an actual baseball field. And so what if he couldn't gather nine players to a side with a glove for each fielder. And so what if he only had one or two bats and the same amount of baseballs. He remembered all too well the sunny, summer mornings when he and Larry and Bernie and all the other kids on Wilson Avenue and Bunn Street and Glen Avenue would gather in their neighborhood and walk or ride bikes together to their nearby field for a game. Some days, they had enough for nine on nine, but on many other days, they played six on six or five on five, and they adjusted the rules accordingly. Heck, at times, they even played three on three or two on two. When the numbers were that low, though, they often argued about what was in play and what wasn't, but sometimes the arguing and the teasing were just as much fun as the baseball.

So right after breakfast the following morning, Diego went to visit Padre Roberto to check out the baseball equipment. And Diego was pleasantly surprised when they searched through the back of the church garage and found a large, dusty, dark green, canvas bag very similar to those Diego remembered from his own ball playing days in Amsterdam. And inside, he found five bats, six baseballs, and nine gloves – including a catcher's mitt and a first baseman's glove. He even found one glove in the group that was left-handed. Diego was amazed. In addition, the bag contained a full set of catcher's safety equipment: a mask, a chest protector, and a pair of shin guards.

"Wow! Where did all of this equipment come from?" Diego asked. "And when was the last time anyone used it?"

"I think the Company donated it to the church a while back, but I don't think anyone has used it in years."

"*Por qué?*" Diego asked.

"Baseball seems to go in spurts here. Sometimes, when the sailors from the ships start a game on the soccer field, the Costa Ricans get all excited and want to play. But, then, their excitement fades after a week or two, and they go back to soccer. They always go back to soccer, which, of course, is the reason you're here. Maybe you can get the young boys interested and, who knows, they might keep playing. They'll never give up soccer, of course, but it would be nice if we had more than one sport around here."

Diego prepared to load all the equipment back into the bag, but before he did so, he pulled the bag inside out to thoroughly empty it, and as he did so, he poured a quantity of dirt and bubble-gum wrappers and empty cigarette packs onto the garage's dirt floor. Naturally, he threw away the garbage and began to clean up the dirt when Padre Roberto stopped him.

"*Diego, por favor.* It's dirt on dirt, a floor made of dirt. *No problema.* Get out of here. Go play ball."

Diego laughed, and the two of them put all of the equipment back into the bag. Rather than go home and procrastinate, though, Diego decided to go immediately to the soccer field and see if anyone wanted to play baseball. Since it was already another extremely hot day, Diego wasn't surprised to see an empty soccer field, but he was pleased to see the two young brothers again. They were sitting on one of the benches between the basketball court and the soccer field, so Diego went right up to them this time and formally introduced himself.

"*Hola, mi nombre es Diego. Como se llama usted?*"

"*Hola, Diego,*" the older boy said quickly and confidently as he stood and reached out to shake hands with him. "*Yo soy Alphonso.*"

"*Mucho gusto, Alphonso,*" Diego said in return as they shook hands. The younger boy was much more reticent, and he waited, seated, with his head down, kicking his legs back and forth beneath the bench.

"*Este es mi hermano, Jose,*" said Alphonso.

"*Mucho gusto, Jose,*" Diego said as he offered his hand, and they shook, though Jose remained seated.

"*Qué es eso?*" Alphonso asked, pointing to the green bag.

"*Quiere jugar beisbol?*" Diego asked.

"*Beisbol?*" Alphonso asked in return.

"*Sí. Sí,*" Diego answered. "*Beisbol. Venga. Venga,*" and he motioned for the boys to follow him.

They quickly walked from the basketball court to the entry gate for the adjoining soccer field, and Diego put the bag down in the nearest corner of the field and reached in for three gloves and a ball. When he pulled out the gloves, Diego noticed that the younger brother, Jose, was no longer with them. He had retreated to the shade of the covered bleachers, determined to merely watch from afar.

Rather than make a big deal out of the boy's reluctance, Diego concentrated on the willing and eager boy in front of him. Diego handed Alphonso a glove, showed him how to properly insert his thumb and fingers, and, then, he walked about 20 yards away and tossed the ball to Alphonso. Alphonso reached to catch it, and the ball hit the glove but fell out.

"Gotta squeeze it a bit," Diego said in English because he wasn't fluent enough yet to know how to say that in Spanish.

"*Qué?*" Alphonso asked, though he pretty much understood what the big first baseman was trying to say to him. Alphonso picked the ball up and easily threw it back to Diego as if he'd been playing baseball forever.

"Wow! He's a natural," Diego thought, and the game of catch was on.

Diego and Alphonso played catch for less than five minutes before two other boys arrived. Again, the sound of the game – leather on leather this time – called out to those nearby.

Diego quickly grabbed two more gloves and a ball for the newcomers, introduced himself, and all four of them played catch side by side just as if they were in a major-league bullpen. And though Diego didn't understand everything the boys said to one another as they played, he recognized it immediately as the international language of baseball banter with a good dose of laughter thrown in as well.

As the newcomers threw, Diego noticed that they were both throwing too much with their arms and not enough with their bodies behind their throws. Thus, he stopped them a few times to, first, show, and, later, reinforce the correct throwing motion.

"*Necesitas girar* your shoulder," Diego said in a mix of Spanish and English as he showed the right-handed boys how to turn their left shoulders toward their target and how to shift their weight from right to left to maximize their throwing power and their accuracy. Both boys were receptive to Diego's instruction, and Diego encouraged Alphonso, too, by having him demonstrate his natural motion as the correct way to throw.

Then, Diego began throwing with Alphonso again, and he watched the two new boys practice. Knowing that all three boys would tire soon of simply playing catch, he interrupted them a few minutes later.

"*Bueno, muy bueno*," Diego said as he caught the ball from Alphonso and then reached across and also caught the other ball to let the boys know they were moving on to another activity.

"*Ahora, nosostros vamos a jugar* 'pepper.'"

"Pepper? *Qué es* pepper?" the more animated of the two new boys exclaimed.

Diego led the boys back to the green bag of equipment, he reached in, and pulled out the biggest bat he could find, and he stationed himself up against the fence. Then, he lined up the three boys about 10 yards from the fence, and he tossed the ball in the air and hit a soft liner to Alphonso who stood between the other two boys. Alphonso caught it easily, and Diego motioned for him to throw it back. He did so, and this time, Diego hit a grounder to the animated one. He, too, caught the ball, and he and the others all caught on quickly. Within seconds, Diego was peppering all three of them with soft grounders and line drives, and Diego waited for the deep, throbbing "thud" of bat on ball to bring even more players to the field. The 1974 Golfito baseball season was officially under way.

After a few minutes of pepper, Diego gave up the bat and let Alphonso hit next. At first, he hit the ball too hard, and one of the three fielders – now including Diego – had to chase it down.

"*Suave*," Diego told him. "*Suave*."

He wanted the boys to learn bat control and contact first, and then they could focus on power later. Alphonso actually figured it our quickly, but the other two struggled. They struggled to hit the ball in the first place, and they struggled again to hit it gently.

As he worked, Diego forgot for a moment that he was a young, American Peace Corps Volunteer who had traveled over a thousand miles to another country to demonstrate American goodwill. Instead, he felt like a missionary of baseball who was visiting a nearby sanctuary to share the good news of Abner

Doubleday. Though Diego was only 22 years old, he felt like an old, cagey veteran. He knew his own career as a player was effectively over because he was not good enough to play professionally, but he also knew his 12 years of experience – from Little League at age 10 through the end of his college years at age 22 – would be more than enough to show these young and eager athletes how to play the game, even if he didn't know the language very well.

By the time all three boys had the opportunity to hit for a few minutes, six or seven additional boys had arrived to play. Since Diego didn't yet have an assistant to show these new boys how to play catch and also teach the game of pepper, he simply moved on to the next stage of the game, real batting practice, and he worked the new boys into the rotation.

Diego placed Alphonso at an imaginary home plate, and he told the next two boys they would hit soon, but one would be "on deck," and the other would stand behind home plate and retrieve any balls that Alphonso failed to hit. Then, he let all the newest arrivals choose gloves, and he placed the boys in the various baseball positions, both infield and outfield.

"Each *batador* will get *diez* hits," he told them. "*Diez*," he repeated. Then, to make sure they understood, he asked them: "*Cuántos?*"

"*Diez*," they repeated. "*Diez*."

Once they were all settled in, Diego began to pitch to Alphonso, and he swung heartily and lined a drive right back at Diego who ducked out of the way.

"*Bueno, Alphonso! Muy bueno!*" Diego exhorted, and then he also yelled "*Uno*," as he waited for the centerfielder to retrieve the ball and toss it back to the infield.

Again, Diego asked his charges, "*Cuántos?*"

"*Uno*," they answered in unison.

"*Dos. Tres. Cuatro*," they yelled soon enough as Alphonso quickly and easily hit pitches two, three, and four.

When Alphonso completed his 10 hits, Diego moved the on-deck hitter into the batter's box and the catcher into the on-deck circle. Next, he rotated the infielders from third to short, short to second, second to first, and first to catcher.

Naturally, too, he rotated the outfielders from right to center and center to left, and he brought the leftfielder in to play third.

"*Es como* volleyball," one of the infielders said as they all rotated positions, and Diego's heart lifted to hear that boy make that connection.

"Maybe there's hope for these soccer players after all," Diego thought aloud, and he laughed alone at his own little joke.

The next 30 minutes proceeded smoothly as most of the new boys all had a chance to hit. Naturally, some failed to pick up the hitting part of the game as easily as Alphonso, so Diego relinquished his pitching duties to the easy throwing Alphonso. Then, Diego stood next to the batter's box to physically help these novices with their holding of the bat, with their swing, and with their weight shift.

If a boy appeared to grasp the game easily, Diego retreated to the shade of the nearby grandstand for a bit and let the boys play. During one of these interludes, however, he had to step in and explain one of his favorite unwritten rules of baseball. This opportunity to teach occurred when Ricky arrived and wanted to hit.

Chapter 20

Ricky was a year or two older than all the grade-school boys who were already playing, and he was at least a head taller and 20 pounds heavier than all of them as well. So when he arrived and walked right up to home plate and demanded to hit immediately, the diminutive boy at bat instantly and willingly handed the bat over to Ricky.

"*Un momento, un momento*," Diego said loudly and clearly as he exited the shade and returned to the field. Alphonso had anticipated this confrontation between Ricky and Diego, so he refrained from pitching, and Ricky looked behind him to see who was causing this delay.

"*Hola*," Diego said to the older boy. "*Mi nombre es Diego*," and he offered his hand.

"*Ve, viejo. Quiero golpear.*"

"I can't believe he just called me an 'old man,'" Diego thought aloud and laughed.

Noticing Diego's laugh, Ricky swung the bat at Diego, not so much to hit him but to move him out of the way. Stunned momentarily by the boy's aggression, Diego nonetheless recovered quickly and reached behind the boy and grabbed the bat before he had a chance to swing it again.

"*Estas loco?*" Diego screamed at the boy. "*Si usted quiere golpear, tiene qué* play the field first."

Somewhat stunned and confused by the quick turnaround of events and by Diego's Spanglish, Ricky looked at Alphonso for help.

"If you want to hit, you have to play the field first," Alphonso said in clear Spanish, so Ricky could understand.

"Who says?" Ricky asked.

"Diego says," Alphonso replied. And added, "He's our coach." Naturally, Alphonso used the word "*entrenador*," and Diego's chest filled with pride at the sound of it in Spanish, but Ricky wasn't so quickly persuaded.

Temporarily perplexed by his loss of control, this bully stared at Diego and considered his options. He looked around, and when he saw other bats nearby, he walked over as if to choose another weapon. Everyone froze, including Diego, but before Ricky picked up another bat, he stopped, paused, and looked again at the situation before him. Then, he slowly turned, and instead of grabbing a bat, he retrieved a nearby glove and ran off to the outfield.

Diego and everyone else sighed, and Alphonso pointed Ricky toward right field.

"Wow!" Diego exhaled. He had never seen that happen before, and he made a mental note to try and connect verbally with this young rebel before they all went home for lunch.

Fortunately, by the time Ricky's turn to hit rolled around, he had settled into the routine and appeared to be having fun chasing batted balls and throwing them back to Alphonso who was still pitching. Like Alphonso, Ricky had a certain athletic grace about him, and he caught the ball easily and threw fluidly. He had even begun to tease some of the other players when they struggled to catch the ball or to throw accurately.

When it was Ricky's turn to hit, all of the other boys backed up a bit at their positions without having to be told to do so. His bigger body was partly the reason, but his aggressive stance and his ferocious practice swings, plus the one he had demonstrated earlier, also appeared intimidating, and everyone could tell easily that if he hit the ball, it would probably go a long way. But as the infielders retreated just a bit and as the outfielders moved back a good 10 to 20 yards, Diego noticed a hitch in Ricky's practice swings, and he doubted Ricky would actually be able to make contact.

And sure enough, Ricky struggled. His stance looked good as Alphonso threw the ball to him, but just as Ricky was about to swing, he dropped his hands below his waist, and he tried to hit with a swing that was low to high, much like a tennis player who was trying to hit the ball with topspin. Ricky didn't look like a tennis player, so Diego wondered if perhaps Ricky had played some golf on the course near the airport; that might explain why Ricky's swing was more golf-like than like that of a baseball player.

As Ricky swung heartily and missed badly on his first two swings, Diego was seriously tempted to let Ricky experience the humiliation of striking out. A big part of Diego, in fact, wanted to get even with the boy for his *macho* attitude earlier. However, since Diego had not let any one of the other boys swing and miss three times before offering some instruction, he felt that as the "*entrenador,*" he had to be fair to Ricky too, so he told Alphonso to wait a second. Then, Diego stepped in to offer Ricky some assistance.

"Ricky," he said gently to this burly boy who was almost six feet tall and who had to be close to 200 pounds. Your stance is "*excellente, muy excellente.*" From his education courses at Siena, Diego knew the value of positive re-enforcement before offering constructive criticism, and Ricky beamed at the compliment. In Ricky's eyes, though, Diego could also see fear, for despite Ricky's manly form and attitude, Diego knew Ricky was still really a boy, a boy who desperately did not want to fail publicly, especially since the other boys were both younger and smaller. So Diego cautiously showed Ricky what he was doing wrong and showed him how his swing had to be more level and how, in fact, he should keep his hands above the ball and try to swing downward a bit.

Ricky appeared a bit confused by that instruction, but rather than swing and miss again, he was willing to try what Diego suggested. Happily for both of them, Ricky hit a ground ball right back through the mound, and when Alphonso couldn't catch it as it scooted by him and also by the middle infielders into centerfield, Diego proclaimed, "Base knock, Ricky. Base knock. Way to go."

Encouraged by his success, Ricky hit two more sharp grounders through the infield before he really caught on to the art of hitting. Then, he totally mashed the next three pitches, and the balls traveled well beyond the reach of the outfielders who had backed up earlier.

"You're hitting ropes now, Ricky. Way to go. *Muy bueno*," Diego exclaimed. Ricky smiled with uncontrolled enthusiasm and pride, and all the other boys laughed at Diego's excitement and language.

"You're heeeting 'rrrrropes,' Ricky. 'Rrrrropes,'" they said, and they used their rolling 'r's to accentuate this new English word from Diego's baseball vocabulary. The boys laughed even harder as Diego tried to roll his 'r's and failed miserably.

Finally, after all the boys had a chance to bat, Diego called everyone in. He really wanted to conduct some fielding practice, both infield and outfield, just like he would have done if this were his team back in the States. This wasn't his team back in the States, though; this was a bunch of young kids who had only minimal exposure to baseball, and he could tell that some of them were getting anxious to play a real game. So Diego decided to save fielding practice for another day, and he prepared to split the boys into two teams for a scrimmage.

Wanting the boys to be able to do this on their own in the future, he chose Alphonso and Ricky to be the captains, and with the handle up, he threw a baseball bat vertically at Ricky, knowing that he would be able to catch it easily. Yes, Ricky was surprised to see a bat coming at him, but before he had a chance to react, Diego brought Alphonso over and placed Alphonso's right hand on the bat just above where Ricky had caught it with his right hand. Next, Diego placed Ricky's left hand above Alphonso's right hand, and they took turns placing their alternating hands on the bat until Alphonso's right hand held the handle of the bat.

"Alphonso, you win. You get to choose first," Diego said in English before trying to communicate that same message in Spanish, and, eventually, the two boys figured out what was going on. Soon, they chose their teams, and Diego explained that since Alphonso had the first pick, Ricky and his team would bat first. Diego also explained a few basic rules to those who were playing the game for the first time, he answered a few questions, he helped Alphonso figure out the positions for his players, and, finally, the game began.

The first two innings were a bit rough because some of the boys still weren't sure what to do defensively when they caught the ball or what was happening on the base paths. Soon, though, with Diego's help, they figured it out, and Diego again retreated to the shade of the grandstand. Yes, he was still called upon periodically to umpire a close play or to explain a rule, but for the most part, they competed without him. And as they did, like before, Diego again recalled fondly his own youthful days on the baseball fields near his home. He and his friends had needed no adults to organize and supervise them because they all had their own balls, bats, and gloves. Since these Costa Rican children had so little of their own, however, Diego was pleased that he could re-live his own youth with them and give them the gift of baseball.

In the midst of inning five, with the score tied at seven, with two runners on base, one out, and two strikes on the batter, the game ended abruptly and immediately. Diego didn't see it coming, nor had he orchestrated it.

The game ended when the 12:00 noon siren screamed through the port and the surrounding area indicating that it was lunch time, time for the laborers to go home and eat and rest, and time for their ball-playing sons to join them.

Diego, of course, had heard that noon siren every day, but it had never registered for him before how it affected the children. Apparently, they were all under strict orders to return home as soon as the siren beckoned. No matter where they were or what they were doing, they had to either go directly home or meet their father on his way home from the port and walk with him to the house.

"*Hasta luego, Diego,*" one boy said.

"*Gracias, Diego,*" said another.

"*Manana también?*" a third boy asked.

"*Sí, sí,*" Diego answered. "We will play again tomorrow."

Only Ricky stayed behind as the other boys threw their gloves toward Diego's green bag and rushed off. Ricky gathered the gloves and began putting them in the bag with the bats and balls.

"*Muchas gracias,* Ricky," Diego said to this man-child as he worked silently. Then, Diego asked him if he had fun playing.

"*Sí, sí. Mucho,*" Ricky replied without looking up.

Diego could sense the boy wanted to say more, so Diego waited – silently. Finally, when all the equipment was packed away and Diego himself was ready to leave, Ricky spoke.

"*Lo siento.*"

Diego remained silent, not because he was unwilling to forgive Ricky for his earlier mistake but because he couldn't come up with the right words in Spanish.

Ricky, meanwhile, thinking Diego was still mad at him or didn't understand him, tried to apologize in English.

"I sorry. Bad. Very bad. What I do. Sorry. Sorry."

"It's okay, Ricky," Diego finally said in English and quickly repeated in Spanish: "*Es okay.*"

Ricky looked up and smiled. "*Gracias, Diego. Gracias.* Thank you. *A mi me gusta mucho beisbol.* I reeely like beisbol. *Yo voy a estar aqui también manana.* Tomorrow."

"Yes, Ricky. We'll play again tomorrow."

"Okay. Okay. *Hasta luego. Hasta manana.*" And Ricky ran off quickly – and happily.

"Wow," Diego thought. "That was amazing." Earlier, he thought he might have to pull Ricky aside to talk to him after the game, but because the apology all happened so quickly, Diego was stunned. Pleasantly so, of course, but stunned nonetheless. Then, Diego hustled home himself. For even though he didn't have to find his own father and walk home with him, Doña Marcella did remind him that lunch would be served at about 12:15 when Don Francisco returned from his morning hours at the hospital.

As Diego walked home with his green canvas bag of equipment draped over his shoulder, he could see Don Francisco walking up the road from the other direction. Diego's first thought was to simply wave to Don Francisco, walk up to the house, put the equipment away, and get ready for lunch. Then, he reconsidered, and like the boys he was just working with, he decided that he, too, should wait for his Costa Rican father and walk up to the house with him. And since Don Francisco's three young sons were not running out to greet him on this particular day, Don Francisco was pleased to be welcomed by his newest tenant, his American son, Diego.

"*Hola, Diego,*" he said with a warm smile. "*Como esta*?"

"*Muy bien, Don Francisco.Y usted?*"

"*Muy bien, también. Gracias. Y qué tiene aqui?*" Don Francisco asked, indicating the giant green bag with the baseball bats protruding.

At that point, Diego began to share the details of his morning baseball game, and together, they walked up the path from the main road to the house. When they arrived, Diego excused himself to walk behind the house to put the baseball equipment in the storage area and to wash up. Don Francisco, by contrast, entered the front door, greeted his wife and children, washed his hands in the kitchen sink, and sat in his chair at the head of the table to eat.

When Diego entered the kitchen from the other door, he offered to help Doña Marcella serve the food. "No, no, *Diego*," she declined. "*Muchas gracias. Sientase. Por favor.*"

Diego did as he was told, and he sat between Ernesto and Felix on one side of the table facing Antonio, who sat closer to Don Francisco, and Susanna, who sat closer to her mother at the other end.

When everyone was seated and all the food was on the table, everyone became silent and looked to Don Francisco. He made the sign of the cross, bowed his head, closed his eyes, and prayed a traditional Catholic grace, but in Spanish: "*Bendícenos, oh Señor, estos son regalos que estamos a punto de recibir a través de Cristo nuestro Señor, Amen.*"

Like most Costa Rican families, lunch for the Moras was the primary meal of the day. On this day, they began with a bowl of black bean soup, followed up with a small salad, and then ate rice and beans with a small piece of fish. For dessert, they ate some grapes and a small piece of cake.

The lunchtime meal was so filling that Diego wanted to simply go upstairs and go to sleep, and that's exactly what he did. Since the post-lunch siesta was commonplace in most Costa Rican homes, and especially in the warm, low-level areas near the coast, Diego fit in perfectly.

Before dozing off, Diego tried to read, but it was hopeless. He was asleep before finishing one paragraph, and he slept solidly and serenely for over an hour. Even when he awoke, he couldn't get out of bed. He was so thoroughly spent after a morning in the sun, a full meal, and a comforting nap that he wondered if he would ever work again.

When Diego finally arose 30 minutes later, he decided to study his Spanish quietly in his room. He knew that he needed some quiet time alone to re-energize himself for the very social work he was called to do. And though the many Spanish conversations he was having were definitely helping his language skills, he felt so much more confident when he compared what he heard in the streets to what he saw in his dictionary and his textbook. The language really came together for him when he combined the verbal and the visual, and he was determined to be fluent, so he could be clear and understood when he spoke in his new language.

Chapter 21

Over the next few weeks, this became Diego's daily routine: baseball practice in the morning at the soccer field, a big lunch with the family, a siesta followed by reading and study, supper with the family, and basketball afterwards at the court near the center of town. Diego felt as if he were doing good work, and he was surprised at how easily everything had transpired. His quick and easy success, however, pretty much disappeared when the new school year began in early March, and the morning baseball games and the evening basketball games deteriorated. The baseball stopped, naturally, because the young boys were in school in the morning, and the evening basketball games stopped for pretty much the same reason. The parents of these children wanted their young ones home after supper, doing their homework and preparing for the next day of classes. As a result, Diego had to reconsider his strategy and his schedule.

Diego knew he had to get into the schools somehow, so he met with Padre Roberto early one morning to figure out how to do that. Padre Roberto, as a longtime resident of Golfito, also knew this was necessary, so he was ready to spring into action when Diego approached him.

"I think you should try to volunteer at the high school in the morning and then do the same at the grade schools in the afternoon. I can definitely introduce you to the school principals, and you can take it from there."

Diego was more than willing to give this idea a try, so Padre Roberto said, "Let's go."

"Now?" Diego asked. "Right now?"

"Right now," Padre Roberto repeated. "*Immediamente!*"

"But don't we need an appointment?"

"No. This is Costa Rica; they're pretty flexible and easy going about that stuff." Then, checking his watch, he added, "Besides, it's still early, and classes for the day haven't even started yet. We'll just drop in, say 'Hello,' and see what happens."

"But shouldn't I get dressed up?" asked Diego who was dressed in sneakers, shorts, and a short-sleeve, button-down shirt."

"You look great," Padre Roberto assured him. That's probably similar to what you'll wear when you go to teach, right?"

"I guess so."

"Okay, so let's go," and off they went in Padre Roberto's green, four-wheel Jeep.

As Diego walked through the high school, he recognized some of the kids from the basketball court and the baseball field, and they greeted him or waved to him from a distance. He was also aware of the other kids staring at him and wondering why this tall, thin American with glasses was walking through the covered passageways that connected the various, small buildings that served as classrooms.

"*Hola, Diego!*"

The big guy was startled when he heard his name, and he was mystified, too, because he didn't initially recognize the smiling face of the young girl who greeted him. Fortunately, Padre Roberto recognized her and addressed her by name.

"*Hola, Lilli. Como esta?*"

At that point, Diego remembered Lilli, the girl who lived just a few houses away from Diego and who had smiled at him the day before he moved into the Moras' house.

When Padre Roberto asked Lilli about school, she happily offered that she was a junior, and she was thrilled to be back in school and away from the confining and somewhat isolated environment of the home she shared with her mother and grandparents. Diego noticed that her smile lit up the area, and her enthusiastic conversational style was contagious. This was a side of this young girl he had not seen that day when she walked quietly and obediently behind her reticent and reserved mother.

Padre Roberto responded by mentioning that Diego might be helping out with the physical education classes or coaching the basketball or volleyball team – or both.

"*Que bueno,*" Lilli replied with a big smile.

"Do you play?" Diego asked.

"Ah, no," Lilli replied, and her smile and her enthusiasm softened a bit. "*Mi mama no me permitte jugar.*"

Padre Roberto and Diego both nodded knowingly, for they had previously discussed the matter of girls' athletics in Costa Rica. A few parents were enthusiastic and supportive, but a majority still held to the traditional customs that young females should remain at home and learn to perform their expected duties: cleaning, cooking, washing clothes, and caring for children. Obviously, Lilli's family was a traditional family.

After Lilli left them to go to her class, they found Don Mario, a grizzled, older man with a grey mustache, and Padre Roberto introduced Diego and explained why Diego was living in Golfito.

"*Ah Cuerpo de Paz*," Don Mario said knowingly. "I remember Steve. He was a good man, and he spoke to our students once or twice about engineering."

As they talked, Don Mario led them past several classrooms to his own physical education classroom which was twice the size of the traditional classroom, and Diego could see balls and mats and other exercise equipment on the perimeter of the main space. He also saw a small group of young boys who silently waited for their professor to unlock the door, usher them in, and take attendance. "These must be freshmen," Diego assumed because they were so small and so well behaved. No one said a word or even picked up a ball after they entered until Don Mario said it was okay to do so.

"Well, I should go," said Padre Roberto once he felt that Don Mario and Diego could work together. "Is it okay if Diego stays for a while?"

"*Sí. Sí. Absolutamente*," Don Mario responded, and before Padre Roberto was out the door, Don Mario was introducing Diego to the class. Diego didn't quite understand everything Don Mario was saying about him, but he did catch some key words: "*deportes, ayuda, emocionante*" (sports, help, and exciting).

And sure enough, within 10 minutes, Diego was participating in the activities right alongside the students. Don Mario had decided to start the school year with a lesson on gymnastics, and after he showed the boys how to do some of the basic movements and tumbles, he asked Diego to demonstrate. Though Diego had no formal instruction in this sport back in the States, it reminded him somewhat of the football drills he had done in high school, so he eagerly participated and encouraged those who seemed unsure and tentative. At that moment, he wasn't exactly sure why taking a freshman gym class was part of what he was trying to do as a

Sports Promoter for the Peace Corps, but he was working with kids and he was working out, so he figured it fit his job description somehow.

In fact, Diego participated in all four of Don Mario's morning classes that day – both male and female and from various grade levels – and he felt both welcome and helpful in all of them. Some of the younger females were a bit hesitant and shy at first, but within 10 minutes, Diego's enthusiasm and his broken Spanish made everyone smile, and the morning passed quickly.

"*Yo tengo irme*," Diego said to Don Mario as the lunch hour approached.

"*Bueno. Gracias. Muchas gracias*," Don Mario said in return and then asked: "*Hasta manana?*"

"*Sí. Sí.*" Diego replied. "I'll be here tomorrow. *Hasta manana*," and off he went.

The following days were much the same. Diego was essentially serving as a teacher's aide or as a student-teacher because Don Mario was more than willing to let Diego do as much as he wanted. On one hand, Diego realized this experience could be a good thing because once the gymnastics unit was over, he could probably convince Don Mario to teach sports that were much more in line with what Diego knew and what he really enjoyed: basketball, volleyball, and baseball or softball.

On the other hand, however, Diego felt like the much older Don Mario was taking advantage of him. Midway through the class or the lesson, for example, Don Mario would wander off without saying a word and return with a coffee. On another occasion, Diego actually saw Don Mario sneak off to smoke a cigarette while Diego was overseeing a class of 26 young boys. Since Diego wasn't quite sure how to handle this dilemma, he decided to continue temporarily until he could figure out what to do or say to Don Mario.

Meanwhile, Padre Roberto had taken the initiative to set up work for Diego at four different grade schools. On Monday and Wednesday afternoons, Diego was scheduled to work at the Company school in the port area; on Tuesday and Thursday afternoons, he would work at the Company school near the sawmill; on Friday afternoon, he would work at the American school near the airport; and on Saturday morning, he would work at the only public school in town, down near the poorer, southern end of town.

Here, too, Diego was perplexed. Yes, Padre Roberto was being helpful but perhaps too helpful. Diego had assumed he would have some freedom in deciding how best to go about his work, yet the schedule Padre Roberto set up for Diego hadn't left him much time to pursue his own ideas. Again, since Diego was young, naïve, uncertain, and inexperienced, he decided to give Padre Roberto's schedule a try.

Initially, the busy schedule appeared to be a real positive because Diego didn't have much time to miss family and friends and his girlfriend back home, and he felt like he was really educating the young people of Golfito on the importance of regular physical exercise. Gradually, however, over a period of about two months, exhaustion and doubt began to trickle into Diego's frame of mind.

Since he was working at the high school every morning and at one of the grade schools every afternoon, Diego was pretty whipped by the end of a typical day. After supper with the Moras, Diego really wanted to just relax or do something fun for himself, like go for a walk or go see a movie or even just stay at home and read. However, the basketball court near the port always called out to him, and he felt that the work to be done there was probably even more important that what he did in the schools.

Yes, he knew that his work in the schools was a good thing, but outside the schools, he could potentially reach those who had already dropped out or who had completed school, and they probably needed sports more than anyone. Otherwise, they could easily fall into a common port life of alcohol and drugs. Diego wanted something better for them. He wanted them to have experiences similar to what he enjoyed as an athlete back home. He wanted to see recreational leagues in various sports, so that the young people could continue to work out and stay in shape. He knew that occasional pick-up games were definitely fun for the average athlete who enjoyed playing, but that athlete might not work out at all between pick-up games; thus, those unscheduled games were not quite as productive long-term. By contrast, if that same athlete knew that more games were already planned, he was more likely to work out once or twice beforehand in preparation for those games.

After pondering his ideas for almost two months, Diego realized he might burn out completely if he kept up this morning-high school, afternoon-grade school, and evening-basketball schedule. Thus, he finally decided that he would continue with the grade schools because these schools did not have a physical-education teacher, but he had to get out of the high school. He needed to let Don Mario do his own job, and he needed his mornings to be free, so that he could better prepare himself and try to organize his evening activities.

Naturally, Diego was a bit worried. He wasn't sure how to explain it to Don Mario, and he worried that his decision would be misinterpreted by the students and by others. After all, most of his Peace Corps peers were struggling to find work to do, and here he was giving up what was currently a third of his workload.

Fortunately, he was able to run his ideas by Padre Roberto, and he agreed with Diego's decision. After all, the high-school kids still had Don Mario to instruct them while the grade-school kids and the older kids at the park had no one at all. Padre Roberto admitted that he saw it coming, and Don Mario must have seen it coming too because when Diego explained his decision, Don Mario was more than understanding. He thanked Diego for the two months he had given to the high-school kids, and he asked Diego if he would be interested in helping to coach the high-school basketball teams when they began playing later in the school year. Diego quickly and confidently said "*Sí*," and he immediately felt that his decision to give up the mornings at the high school would pay off in other ways. Little did he know that another educational opportunity was about to present itself.

Chapter 22

About a week later, as Diego was coming home from a session at the grade school down near the port, Doña Santiago called out to him as he walked by her house. The Santiago family lived just down the path from the Mora family, so Diego had to pass by their house each day as he walked to the main street and again as he returned home. Señor Santiago also worked in the hospital with Don Francisco Mora, and Doña Santiago stayed at home with their two small children. So even though Diego had said "*Hola*" to Doña Santiago many times, and she always seemed friendly, this was the first time she had ever called him aside to have a conversation.

After the initial greeting and the customary questions, Doña Santiago asked Diego if he would like to have dinner with her family. Diego was a bit surprised, so he said, "*De verdad?*"

"*Sí.*"

"*Cuando?*"

"*Manana.*"

Thursday night was normally a basketball night for Diego, so he felt torn between his work obligation and this welcome invitation. Not sure what to do, he asked another question: "*A qué hora?*"

"*A las seis.*"

Six o'clock was a bit later than when the Moras usually ate, so Diego explained that he would love to have dinner with the Santiagos, but that he would also have to leave to get to the basketball court.

"*No problema,*" Doña Santiago reassured him with a big smile.

Using his best manners and trying to be a good American ambassador, Diego also asked if he could bring anything. Doña Santiago insisted that he did not have to bring anything, just himself.

Naturally, Diego brought something anyway. He purchased a bottle of red wine and offered it to the Santiago family when he arrived. Together, they enjoyed a pleasant meal, and since it was raining heavily that night, Diego decided he did not need to leave early. The pace and the tone of the meal was slow and a bit crazy because of the young children, ages six and four, but they all enjoyed the food – steak with onions and, of course, rice and beans – and one another.

The real surprise, however, came later. Diego helped to clear the table, and he actually prepared to leave because he assumed that the parents would need to put the kids to bed, but Doña Santiago insisted he wait a bit longer and stay for dessert once the kids were all settled into their bedrooms.

So, Diego, again the good ambassador, looked through their collection of old magazines for about a half hour before they returned with dessert and a request. "Diego, I have a favor to ask you," Doña Santiago said as they enjoyed sweet, fried *plantains.*

"*Sí,*" Diego said, even before she had specified what it was she wanted. "These fried bananas are so tasty that I'll do whatever you ask."

She laughed and said, "*De verdad?*"

"*Sí, sí, sí,*" Diego repeated. "May I have more? *Por favor?*"

"Diego, would you be willing to come here one night a week to teach us English?"

"Really?"

"Really."

Despite his earlier exuberance, Diego had to actually stop eating his dessert to give this question some thought.

"Hmmm," Diego pondered aloud. "Who would I be teaching?" He asked finally.

"Just Señor Santiago and me," she answered quickly.

"But not the kids?"

"Oh, no. This is for adults only."

Again, Diego paused, and Doña Santiago anticipated the question in his mind, and she explained their motivation.

"I have always wanted to speak better English, and we know that Samuel would do so much better at work if he could speak English too. And don't tell anyone else around here, but," and she paused for dramatic effect, "we would really like to move to America some day."

"Wow!" Diego reacted. "That's exciting."

"Isn't it?" She responded, excited herself just from verbally sharing their idea with this young American.

"Why is it a secret?" Diego asked.

Samuel finally chimed in: "Everybody here says they want to move to America some day, so we're trying to keep it quiet until we can seriously consider it, and we feel like improving our English is a good first step."

"Well," Diego responded, "since everybody in town is telling me that the rainy season is about to begin and may prevent some of my basketball nights, let's give it a try, and see how it works out."

Doña Santiago gleefully clapped her hands like a schoolgirl and gave Diego a hug and a second helping of fried *plantains.*

Chapter 23

Approximately three months after Diego's arrival in Golfito, another Peace Corps Volunteer descended on the small town. Christina came from Boston, and she had been assigned to work as a nurse. Previously, the Peace Corps supervisor of the medical Volunteers, Don Hector, had asked Diego to welcome her, so Diego was at the airport when Christina arrived.

Christina was the only American who exited the plane that day, so Diego knew it was she as Christina walked down the portable stairway and shielded her eyes from the midday sun.

"*Hola. Bienvenido a Golfito. You soy Diego,*" he said and offered her his hand in greeting.

"*Hola Diego. Mucho gusto,*" Christina responded. Instead of shaking his hand, however, Christina reached up both of her arms and gave Diego a warm embrace. "It's truly a real pleasure to meet you, and thank you for coming to greet me."

Christina smiled brightly, and her straight, brown hair reached to her shoulders. Diego estimated her height at about five-foot five. Though she didn't appear athletic, she walked with confidence as her flip-flops echoed her steps. Dressed in modest, blue shorts and a white blouse, she immediately peppered Diego with questions while they waited for her luggage to be unloaded.

"How long have you been here?"

"What kind of work do you do?"

"Is it always this hot?"

Diego, recalling his own initial nervousness and excitement, laughed at her intensity and encouraged her to slow down, to relax. "Christina, take a breath. You're in Golfito now. The pace of life is very slow here, even slower than it is in San Jose, and nothing like whatever you experienced in the States."

She laughed, too, at her excitement at finally arriving at her destination. "I'm sorry. I couldn't wait to get here. I can't wait to start work."

Since Diego lived close to the airport, he had walked there to meet Christina, but he had also arranged for a taxi to drive them to her apartment at the other end of town. Though her position had been vacant since Diego had arrived, Christina's job was to work in a government-owned medical clinic serving the poorest people in town. Prior to Christina's arrival, Don Hector had visited Golfito, and with Diego, they had found a modestly furnished apartment for Christina just three blocks away from the clinic. The apartment's owner had agreed to a three-month lease for the new American, and Christina could decide at that time if she wanted to renew for a longer period or seek another place elsewhere in town. With her housing already set up, though, she could start work the day after arrival, which had been Don Hector's goal all along.

Since Don Hector had previously explained all of this to Christina in San Jose, Diego simply shared his version of the story as the old Volkswagen bus that served as a taxi carried them and three other passengers through the descending layers of town. Like all visitors to Golfito, Christina was intrigued by the deteriorating conditions as the bus moved from north to south. She began to worry about how desolate and decrepit her own place might be. Thus, she was pleasantly surprised to see that it wasn't as bad as she had imagined.

"Okay, this is not a grass hut, and, wow, it does have running water," she said in relief when Diego unlocked the front door and allowed her to view and walk through the small living room, the kitchen, the bathroom, and the bedroom beyond. "This is actually bigger than the place I rented in college with a friend," she continued. "Thank you, Diego. You and Don Hector did a great job."

The apartment was situated almost directly in the middle of the public, commercial section of town. Christina's place was three blocks up from the main street and three blocks away from the mountains behind it. The building was made of wood, and Christina's apartment was aligned with another apartment next door. The building was nicer than some of those nearby, which were mostly metal and tin, but it was much smaller than some of the other wooden houses in that same neighborhood. Don Hector had liked it because it was modest enough for a Peace Corp Volunteer, and Diego liked it because it was nice enough for a female. In fact, during the time after Don Hector had departed Golfito and before Christina arrived, Diego visited the apartment twice: once to remove the cobwebs, sweep the floors, and thoroughly clean the furniture; and once to deliver a new box spring, mattress, and bed sheets he had purchased himself for the old metal frame with Don Hector's prior approval and cash. "If she doesn't get a good night's sleep," both Diego and Don Hector agreed, "she won't last long."

Christina quickly unpacked a few items from her big suitcase, clothing items that she wanted to hang up immediately, and she explored the few nuances of her apartment like the small window frame that was covered over with plywood, an old rocking chair that sat in the corner, and the picture of a sunset that sat on the dresser in her bedroom. Within five minutes, though, she was ready to walk through her new neighborhood and to see what the clinic looked like.

Diego had given her the key to the clinic along with her apartment key, and the two of them exited the apartment and began walking. Diego assumed Christina would head directly to the clinic, but she surprised him. She stopped to say "Hello" to children on the street, and she walked into every store she passed along the way. Diego could see that she, like most women, was much more social than he, and he felt confident that she would fit right in and do great work.

When they finally arrived and opened the door to the clinic, Christina felt a mix of emotions: pleased again that the facility was better than she expected but disappointed by the lack of equipment and supplies. "They told us in San Jose," she said to Diego, "not to expect much, so I tried to keep my hopes modest, but this is even more modest than I imagined."

The storefront building was wooden, much like Christina's apartment, and about the same size with a wall separating the small entrance from the big room behind it. Like the apartment, too, the facility was clean only because Diego had done what he could to prepare it for Christina. The only furniture, though, consisted of an old examining table, three sturdy, wooden chairs, and a single glass storage case for medicines and supplies. As Christina looked over its contents, she wondered aloud how she would help anyone. "I hate to be pessimistic on my first day here, but this is really sad. These supplies won't last more than a week: band aids, gauze bandages, aspirins, cough syrup, and liquid soap. That's it?"

Diego tried to cheer her up by moving toward her on the set of wooden crutches that was leaning against the opposite wall. "*Por favor, Doctor. Por favor ayuda me. Yo soy en* pain."

Christina laughed at Diego and returned quickly to her more positive nature. "Yes, you are a pain. Here, swallow two of these," as she handed him two large gauze bandages, "and call me in the morning."

Before their laughter had subsided, Diego and Christina heard a small child crying outside. Christina reacted more quickly than Diego, and within seconds, they were both out front, looking to help.

Two small girls, about five or six years old, had been running down the street, and the smaller of the two girls had tripped on the uneven sidewalk. Her right knee was scraped and bleeding, and her tears watered the street.

"I'll get the soap and the band aids," Diego said as he rushed back inside.

"There, there, *mi niña*," Christina said soothingly as she sat on the sidewalk and comforted the child in her arms. "It's going to be okay. You're going to be okay."

The other young girl looked nervously at the pale *gringa* who had appeared from nowhere. "*Cual es el nombre de tu amiga*," Christina asked her.

"*Bonita*."

"*Hola, Bonita. Mi nombre es* Christina. *Y tu*," she asked the friend.

"*Flora*."

Christina smiled and said, "*Hola*, *Flora*. You are a good friend to wait here with *Bonita*."

By then, Diego had returned with the supplies, and Christina gently spread some soap on the gauze and spoke to Bonita while cleaning the scraped knee. "This may hurt just a bit at first, but then it will feel better." The fallen girl shivered just a bit when Christina applied the soap but then relaxed as Christina washed away the blood and dried the wound with another piece of gauze and applied the band aid. Bonita had stopped crying and looked admiringly at the band aid. When Christina finished, Bonita touched it gently and smiled. Flora reached out to help Bonita rise, and when standing again, Bonita reached up to Christina and gave her a warm hug.

"*Gracias. Muchas gracias*."

"*De nada, Bonita. El gusto es mia*."

Flora also extended her arms to hug Christina, and the two girls departed, walking slowly this time down the street.

"You were awesome, Christina. Your first emergency. Way to go!" Diego exulted. "And I was here to help. Maybe I should work as your assistant."

"Maybe," she agreed. "Maybe."

Diego and Christina spent the next few hours together. First, they walked a bit more through the neighborhood. Then, they shared a traditional Costa Rican meal of rice and beans and soup with a soft taco at a small house restaurant on the main road. And afterwards, they returned to Christina's apartment. Diego sat in the old rocking chair while Christina unpacked, and the two of them traded stories of growing up in the United States, their decision to join the Peace Corps, and their experiences up to that point in Costa Rica. Diego hadn't enjoyed that much extended conversation in English since his move to Golfito, and he felt like he didn't want to leave her. Eventually, of course, he said good night, and as he took the bus back to the Moras' house, he wondered about Christina. For even though he had a girlfriend back home, he hadn't heard from her in a while, and he wondered if he and Christina might really develop a relationship together or if that day's experience were merely a one-time, shared pleasure of two like-minded people.

Chapter 24

During the next month, Diego set aside every Thursday evening to meet with the Santiagos, and from her bedroom window on the opposite side of the Santiago's house, Lilli noticed this new development. Why was Diego going there every week, and why was he carrying what looked like a notebook and some sort of textbook?

Finally, Lilli was curious enough to find out, so one day after school, she made sure she was sitting outside when Doña Santiago came out to retrieve the items on her clothes line before the late afternoon rains arrived.

"*Hola, Doña Santiago,*" Lilli called to her, and she also walked toward her. "*Qué tal?*"

"*Muy bien, gracias. Y tu?*"

"*Muy bien, también. Gracias.*"

At that point, Lilli began to help Doña Santiago take her laundry off the clothes line, and as she did so, she began the conversation. "May I ask you a personal question?"

"*Sí. Por supuesto.*"

"*Por qué estuvo Diego en tu casa anoche?*"

"Oh, Lilli. I am so excited. I invited Diego to come to dinner a while back, and we asked him if he would give us some English lessons, and he said 'Yes.' "

"*De verdad?*"

"*Sí. Es muy excitante. No?*"

"*Sí. Es muy excitante.*" Lilli agreed. "Can I come too?" Lilli then blurted out without even considering whether it was appropriate for her to do so.

"It would be okay with me," Doña Santiago replied. "It would be fun to have you in class with us. But I think I should ask Diego first. So when I see him today, I will ask him."

"Is he teaching you today?"

"No, only on Thursdays, but he walks by our house every day on his way to the Moras, so when I see him, I will call out to him and ask him."

"*Sí, sí. Absolutamente*," Diego said later that day when approached by Doña Santiago. "Does Lilli already know some English?" He asked.

"*Sí, sí.* She probably knows more than Don Santiago and I do."

"Okay. That's great. Tell her to come next week then."

Diego was really pleased when he heard that Lilli wanted to be in the class. She appeared to be a sweet, young girl, and Diego felt sorry for her when he heard from Doña Santiago the sad story about Lilli's dad leaving Golfito when she was still a baby. Diego himself had a classmate in school whose father had died when the classmate was young, and Diego couldn't even imagine how difficult it would be to grow up without a father. Diego's own father had been such a strong presence in Diego's life, and if he could serve as a father figure or even a big-brother figure in someone's life, he wanted to do so.

So on the following Thursday, Lilli was sitting directly across from Diego at the Santiago's dinner table when the 90-minute class began. She had purchased a red, spiral-bound notebook and two blue-ink pens specifically for this class.

"Good evening, Diego," she said to him, and she also stood when he entered the room. "Should I call you 'Professor'?"

Diego really liked the sound of that title, but he laughed and said, "No. 'Diego' will be fine." And thus began the learning process for both of them, Lilli learning English, and Diego learning about this beautiful and eager, young *Tica.*

"What's your name?"

"My name is Lilli."

"How old are you?"

"I am seventeen."

"Where do you live?"

"I live in Golfito."

After a few sessions with his three students, Diego realized that each one was at a different point in the language, and each one also fit into one of the three different learning styles he had studied in his college education classes. Doña Santiago was the auditory learner who grasped the spoken language easily. She heard the words perfectly, pronounced them flawlessly, retained everything, and asked lots of questions. Like Diego, Lilli was a visual learner. Though she had the most formal schooling in English, she needed to see most of the words in written form before she could understand them and say them properly. So while Doña Santiago never took any notes, Lilli wrote down as much as she could, even when she wasn't sure about a word's spelling or meaning. And Don Santiago was the kinesthetic learner. He needed to be active to truly understand, and Diego realized he would need to devise something special for him. Otherwise, Don Santiago would simply sit passively at the table without taking notes, without asking questions, and speaking only when called upon. Unlike his wife, he didn't really want to be there at all, but she had convinced him that improving his knowledge of English would help him in his career and in their plans to move to America.

During the actual classes, Diego tried to do just as his Spanish instructors had done when he was in his three-month training period in San Jose. Each week, he focused on a certain aspect of life, and their conversation revolved around it. At first, for example, he had his three students talking about themselves and their families; then, they gradually began to talk about simple everyday matters and, later, current events.

As a result, Diego gradually learned about Lilli's upbringing and her educational dreams; he also learned in more detail how the Santiagos met and fell in love and, again, how they dreamed of one day moving to America. This dream did not really surprise young Diego because practically every person he met in Costa Rica either asked him about life in America or described their hopes of moving there one day.

"Wow!" Diego pondered. "This vision of America as a paradise or as the dream destination of the world may actually be true." Yes, he had always heard America portrayed as the "Land of Opportunity" in his middle-school classes, but experiencing that sentiment first-hand in another country was another matter altogether.

Consequently, while the English classes were a wonderful experience for the Santiagos and for Lilli, they were also a great benefit to Diego because he was able to gain some experience as a teacher, the career he planned to pursue when he returned to the States. He also was able to enjoy their warm Costa Rican hospitality and fellowship, and he gradually developed a better appreciation for the life he had left behind in his own country. His Thursday evenings became the highlight of his week. That small group for Diego later became even more important for Lilli when she experienced an unforeseen event that would drastically change her life forever.

Chapter 25

A few weeks later, Mrs. Dugan approached Lilli after Mass and told her about a short-term babysitting opportunity in the American Zone, and with her mother's permission, Lilli followed up on it the next day.

The Wilsons had lived in the American Zone for almost five years, and they were about to return to America. In fact, the father of the family, Jerome Wilson, had already returned to Boston to start working in an administrative position. As a result, his wife, Susan, needed a bit more help, especially with her youngest child, Martha, who was only two years old and not yet potty trained.

In addition to the baby, Susan also had four older children: Tom, who was 16; Mary, 13; Sara, 10; and Willie, 6. On the surface, the children appeared to be friendly and kind, but, unfortunately, like some of the other American children who had spent a long time living in the American Zone, they had become a bit too spoiled, a bit too self-centered. They viewed themselves as special, superior to the Costa Rican children who lived outside the borders of the American Zone. Thus, when

Lilli showed up on Tuesday of that week to help Susan prepare for the move that was only two weeks away, the children were not that helpful or welcoming. Instead, they treated Lilli like they treated the Costa Rican cleaning lady who came in twice a week to wash their clothes and tidy up their rooms. Basically, they ignored Lilli. She tried to initiate conversation with Mary and Sara, who were somewhat close to Lilli's age, but they were too busy to bother with her. They had their nearby American friends to play with, and they didn't have time for the *Tica* girl who was there to take care of the baby while Mom packed up their dishes and their clothes. Even little Willie ignored her while he ran about the house with his friends playing tag or hide-and-seek. So Lilli often found herself alone with Martha playing peek-a-boo and patty-cake and also teaching Martha her numbers, her letters, her colors – all in English, of course, which was one small consolation for Lilli.

Even Mrs. Wilson seemed to take Lilli for granted. When Lilli arrived at the house to help, Mrs. Wilson handed the baby off to her and set about accomplishing her own agenda for the afternoon. The only family member who paid any attention to Lilli was Tom.

At age 16, Tom really should not have been in Golfito. He was supposed to be living with his aunt and uncle in New Orleans and completing his second year of high school. However, when he got into a few too many fights at school and when he also struggled to fit in with his aunt, uncle, and cousins, everyone agreed – both the entire family and the school authorities – that Tom should be with his own family for a while before they all moved to Boston for a fresh start.

Since Tom had attended the American School in Golfito for grades six, seven, and eight, he was very familiar with the community, and during the weeks leading up to Lilli's arrival, he and a friend, Dave, who was in a similar predicament, began to explore the parts of Golfito they had never known before. They began to walk around near the port. Though none of the bartenders would sell beer to the two young Americans, the boys were allowed to sit at tables in the bar and drink soda and order food. So they spent their evenings watching some of the Costa Rican laborers drink away the monotony of their jobs,

jobs that required them to move 50-pound boxes of bananas all day long – boxcar after boxcar after boxcar and ship after ship after ship.

These impressionable boys also watched as the crew members from the ships ventured into town. Mostly Europeans, they, too, struggled with the monotony of their work. For once their ship's hold was filled with bananas bound for America, they began the long journey from Golfito: south to the Pacific entrance to the Panama Canal, through the Canal to the Atlantic, and, then, up the coast – past Central America and the Southern and Mid-Atlantic states – to New York or Boston where they would empty their hold and start the process all over again.

These foreign sailors were a bit more entertaining to Tom and Dave. The sailors spoke different languages – French, Italian, German, Swedish – they spent their money more freely on mixed drinks instead of beer, and they talked more loudly, sang more often when the juke box was playing, and danced even when no women were present, which was often. Often, too, were the fights that typically began when a sailor bumped into a *Tico* – sometimes accidentally and sometimes intentionally. The fights were usually only a two-man boxing match or wrestling feud that served as entertainment for the others. Sometimes, though, an all-out brawl would ensue, and the Port Authority *Policia* would have to be called in before someone got killed. Then, the foreigners were ordered back to their ships, the Ticos were ordered to return to their homes, and the bars and the port were closed for the night.

Once the foreign sailors realized there were no women in the bars near the port, bars which were tightly controlled by the banana Company, the sailors migrated away from the port to that thin strip of land between the port and the sawmill where certain women were present and available and entertaining. And like little black ants following the ants in front of them, Tom and Dave followed these foreign sailors and, in fact, were encouraged by them. Since some of the sailors spoke English, Tom and Dave felt much more comfortable with the sailors than they did with the Costa Rican laborers who mostly ignored them. Again, Tom and Dave were still prevented from buying beer, but they were tolerated by the bar owners because they were with the sailors who spent lots of money. So Tom and Dave sat on the periphery as these men and women interacted in a way that the boys had never seen before. And when the sailors went upstairs with the girls, the young boys were left alone in the bar, sipping sodas and munching on pretzels; sometimes, though, the boys secretly followed the men and women up the back staircase, and they caught glimpses of the adult activities. Later, they returned home, and they talked about and pondered all they had witnessed.

As a result, when Tom spoke to Lilli for the first time, a wide chasm existed between their words, their worlds, and their expectations.

"*Hola, como se llama usted?*" Tom said to Lilli, trying to impress her with his willingness and his ability to speak her language.

"Hello, my name is Lilli," she replied in his language, always eager to speak English.

"It is very kind of you to help my mother with the baby."

"I love little children."

"Would you like to have your own children some day?"

"Maybe. I want to move to San Jose and study at the University there."

A short silence followed. Tom hadn't really expected this Costa Rican servant in his home to have any aspirations beyond serving him and his family. During the silence, Lilli gathered some of the blocks Martha was playing with and tried to think of a similar question to ask Tom about his future.

"Will you go to a university in America?"

"Probably. My parents say Boston has more good colleges than any other city."

"What will you study?"

Tom hesitated again because his thoughts about college had only concerned parties and girls. An actual field of study hadn't yet entered his mind. Falling back on his father's example, he finally replied, "Business. I think I would try to figure out how businesses work and maybe start a small business of my own some day."

"Really?" His answer surprised her because she expected him to say he didn't yet know. As a result, she responded by asking, "What kind of business?"

Again unprepared, Tom responded with a joke: "I thought I'd start a banana company in Costa Rica."

They both laughed at that one, and thus began their daily routine. Around 4:00 p.m., each day, when Tom's mother was busy preparing dinner and when his siblings were enjoying after-school play time with their friends, Tom would find his way to the baby's room. There, he and Lilli would talk, mostly in English, which she enjoyed and which was much easier for him. At first, Tom only stayed for five minutes or so; gradually, though, he stayed longer, and they talked more.

As they talked, they played with the baby together, and Lilli imagined that their time together was like what a marriage would be: enjoying one another and a child they created together.

Tom's thoughts were much different. Though he found Lilli easy to be around and to talk to, he didn't really see her as an equal. He was attracted to her for other reasons. He wanted to sing with her and dance with her and be physically close to her, just as he had watched the sailors in the saloons on the strip. He couldn't do this in his own house, however, especially in the baby's room, so he kept trying to figure out a way to meet with Lilli secretly, away from his family and hers, some place where the two of them could really be alone.

"Can I take you to the movies?" Tom asked about a week later.

"Oh, no. I don't think so. My mother will not let me go on dates."

"But we could go to the afternoon show – when it's still daylight."

Lilli laughed. She was so pleased to be invited, and she was even more thrilled that Tom was being persistent. "My momma won't even let me go to the movies with my friends yet."

Lilli could see the disappointment on Tom's face, so she added, "But thank you so much for inviting me. You're the first boy to ever ask me out."

Tom thought for a bit and, then, asked: "Can I at least walk you home some day?"

"No. My grandfather gets nervous even when I'm just talking to a boy in church."

"But maybe – "

Lilli stood and picked up the baby. "Excuse me, please. I think your sister soiled her diaper. I will have to change it now, so she doesn't get a rash."

"Okay," Tom said with his head down. He sensed he needed to back off temporarily and try to come up with a new plan – and fast. His family was scheduled to leave in less than a week, and he knew he would probably never see Lilli again.

Naturally, Lilli knew this as well, and though she was somewhat disappointed that her babysitting job and her English conversations would soon end, she was just glad that a boy had taken an interest in her. She wasn't disappointed because she knew she would not miss Tom when he left; she did not like him in that way. Their short time together was nothing more than a cool, refreshing lemonade on a hot summer day.

Meanwhile, as Tom's family made their final plans for departure, Tom heard his mother say something that really intrigued him.

"On Thursday afternoon, they're having a small, going-away party for our family at the school." Then, she spoke directly to her oldest son: "Tom, I expect you to be there too. I'll have Lilli stay here while Martha naps."

"Alright," he replied, trying to appear as disinterested as possible. Yet, he viewed this as his opportunity, his one final chance to be alone with Lilli. He would go to the party, of course, but then he could easily slip away and hustle back up to the house. After his token appearance at the school, his mother would never notice his absence. She would be so busy saying good-bye to her friends and taking pictures of the little ones that she would forget about Tom completely.

Chapter 26

One night prior to his English class, Diego realized he had failed to prepare a lesson. Normally, he prepared on Thursday morning, but he had helped one of the neighbors move some furniture on that particular day, so he was forced to recover quickly. Fortunately, he was pretty good at improvising and last-minute planning, so when he walked into the Santiago's home later that evening, he started with a question – in English.

"What is your favorite movie?"

"*Love Story*," answered Doña Santiago quickly and easily.

"Me too," Lilli echoed.

"And you too, Don Santiago?"

"No way, Diego. *Love Story* is a movie for women. I like movies with car chases and explosions and good guys and bad guys. I like *The Godfather* and *The French Connection*."

Diego was pleased that all three of them talked excitedly about their favorites and about so many other movies. They did so for a good 10 to 20 minutes before Doña Santiago interrupted and said politely, "Pardon me, Diego, but shouldn't we be doing our lesson?"

"This is our lesson. You need to take a break from the exercises once in a while to just practice your conversational English, so that's what we're doing."

"Really?" Lilli asked. "Seriously?"

"Yes," Diego replied. "Yes."

So, they spent the entire 90 minutes talking: first, about movies; then, later about sports; and after that, politics. Diego was surprised to realize that most of them knew more about what was going on in the world than he did. He was especially impressed by Lilli's knowledge of the United States. For even though they both subscribed to the same magazine but in different languages, it was obvious that Lilli was reading and retaining much more than Diego.

"I better take more time to read each week," he said to himself when class ended that night, and he returned to his home.

When Lilli returned to her home, she thought about her future. She felt confident and competent. Her English skills were improving. She was learning so much about the world, and she believed that Tom liked her. Even though he was leaving soon and even though she didn't really care for him in a romantic way, she enjoyed her time with him, and she liked to imagine what it would be like if she were really in love with an American boy like him. She wrote about Tom often in her journal.

She imagined the two of them exchanging letters after he returned to the States. She imagined his mother sending her a plane ticket and arranging a work visa, so she could be a nanny for them in America. Then, instead of attending the University of San Jose, she would go to one of the really prestigious schools in Boston. Eventually, she and Tom would marry and raise beautiful children together. With her degree in teaching, she could work the same school schedule as her children and have the same vacations as well.

Chapter 27

On the following Thursday, their final day in Golfito, Tom did exactly as he was told. Intentionally, he arrived at the school 10 minutes before the party was scheduled to begin, and he made sure he spent those 10 minutes near his mom and his siblings. They waited near the front of the gymnasium together as all the other families arrived carrying casseroles and breads and plates of vegetables and desserts. Tom hadn't realized that a pot-luck supper was part of the party. "This will last even longer than I thought," he murmured.

Consequently, he didn't feel the need to leave as early as he had anticipated. He hung around as the school principal and a few of the teachers thanked his mom for all of her volunteer activities and as his siblings' classmates sang a farewell song and presented them with going-away gifts: souvenirs from Golfito and tee-shirts with the school's name on the front.

Once the ceremony itself was over, Tom gradually made his way toward the exit. Since many of the children and some of the parents also used that same exit to move toward the playground and the picnic tables, no one noticed when Tom disappeared around the corner and began striding toward his house.

When he entered through the back door, he found Lilli walking in the hallway with Martha sleeping in Lilli's arms. Lilli was somewhat surprised to see him, but she was even more concerned that Martha would wake up before she set the baby gently in her crib. "Shhhh." Lilli whispered softly to Tom, and she also quickly raised her index finger to her lips, so Tom would be sure to get the message. Tom nodded in understanding and walked into the kitchen as if that were his destination all along.

He quietly pulled two Coca-Cola bottles out of the refrigerator and waited for Lilli to return. She did so within 30 seconds and asked, "*Qué pasa?*"

Without answering immediately, he opened one of the Cokes for Lilli and handed it to her. Then, he opened the other for himself and sat down at the kitchen table. Lilli normally read or cleaned up the house when Martha slept, so sitting at the table and drinking a soda was a rare pleasure. Tom told Lilli about the going-away ceremony and party and explained his departure from the party as simply wanting to say "Good-bye" to her in private before the rest of the family returned.

"I'm going to miss you," he said to Lilli.

"Really?" She asked, both surprised and flattered.

"Really," he repeated. "You're so different from all the other girls I know. You're so much more mature, and . . ." he paused for effect. "You're so pretty." Then, he pulled his chair closer to hers, and he reached over and took her two hands in his.

Lilli looked down as the word "pretty" echoed in her brain. She knew she was pretty because so many people – her mom, her grandparents, people in the neighborhood and at school – had always described her as "*bonita*." But she had never before heard that word, either in Spanish or in English, from a boy approximately her own age, especially an attractive American boy.

His hands felt warm and large and even a bit sweaty as they enclosed her hands, and she finally looked up at his face. He was looking directly at her and moving closer. She froze as he kissed her gently on the lips. Her first kiss.

She pulled away slightly, but he pushed forward and kissed her again, still gently and lovingly. She relaxed just a bit, enjoying the moment, one she had dreamed of often. That moment escalated out of control quickly, however, when he hugged her tightly and tried to kiss her more passionately.

She tried to resist – to no avail. When she tried to stand up to escape, Tom pushed her, and together, they tumbled to the floor. There, he held her down and put one hand over her mouth. Frightened beyond belief and no match for his size and strength, Lilli froze. As if dead, she closed her eyes, gritted her teeth, and only hoped that someone would return to save her.

Within minutes, he was off of her and gone. When she heard the back door slam shut, she rose quickly, straightened her dress, and staggered to the bathroom. She locked the door, lifted the seat cover off the toilet, knelt down, and vomited.

When finished, she rose slowly, again rearranged her clothes, and tried to wash away her tears. They kept coming, and she shook nervously. Feeling faint as well, she covered the toilet seat, flushed, and sat down.

"Leave now. Go home," her mind told her. "Tell your mom what happened." Yet, she couldn't move. She couldn't get up.

"Why did he hurt me? I thought he liked me. He said I was 'pretty.' I don't understand. I don't understand."

After Tom left the house, he walked quickly back to the school. A few people were walking away from the school, but most were still at the party, either playing or talking outside the gym or eating dessert inside.

Rather than go inside himself, Tom sat at a picnic table near the playground and watched as his little brother played soccer with his classmates. Tom, too, was frightened. Though he had just acted like the men he had seen in the saloons, he was nervous, and he didn't know what to do next. A few of the older boys motioned for him to join their soccer game, but he waved them off. Like Lilli, he sat and waited.

Finally, after a half hour or so, Tom's mother appeared with her other children. They carried their gifts with them, and Mrs. Wilson was pleased to see that Tom was watching out for his little brother. They would all go home together.

"Did you get any food, Tom? I don't think I ever saw you during the meal."

"Oh yeah. I grabbed some food and ate outside. What they did was really nice," he said to distract her. And as he expected, she began talking non-stop about how wonderful everyone was and about how much she would miss all of them.

When Tom and his family finally arrived at their house, Martha was still napping. Lilli sat at the kitchen table, speechless.

"I hope we're not too late," Mrs. Wilson said, oblivious to Lilli's condition and intent on moving forward with her own preparations for the move to the States. "Here, I have a special gift for you," she added, and she retrieved a business envelope from the small desk near the dining room and handed it to Lilli. "It's your payment for today plus a little extra because you've been so kind to our family. Thank you."

Lilli stood up, took the envelope, and quietly and politely said, "*Muchas gracias.*"

At that point, finally, Mrs. Wilson noticed that Lilli looked pale and weak. "Are you okay, sweetheart?" She asked Lilli.

"I don't feel very well today," Lilli responded feebly. "I should go home."

"Of course. Of course. I understand," Mrs. Wilson said without understanding at all. She was so focused on tying up loose ends on her final day in Golfito and on all she still had to do to get her family to the airport the following morning that she was just as relieved to see Lilli go as Lilli was to depart.

After what Tom had done to her earlier, Lilli had wanted to go home immediately, but she couldn't bring herself to leave the baby alone there in the Wilson's house; in addition, Lilli couldn't yet form the words to tell anyone what had happened.

"Well, let me give you a good-bye hug at least," Mrs. Wilson said, and she gently put her arms around Lilli. "I sure hope I find a babysitter half as good as you in Boston. You are the absolute best."

"Thank you," Lilli said, anxious to leave. "Thank you for everything." Then, she exited quickly, afraid that if the other children came into the kitchen, her departure would be delayed. Moving slowly and gingerly, Lilli walked out the back door and headed home.

From the backyard, Tom watched her go. He had been hiding outside the kitchen window, listening and trying to discover if Lilli would say anything to his mom about what he had done. Relieved that Lilli said nothing, Tom continued to watch her until she was out of sight. He still worried, of course, that Lilli might tell someone once she got home.

Fortunately for him, when Lilli arrived at her house, her mother and grandmother were standing outside talking to a neighbor, and her grandfather was working late. So Lilli remained silent. She waved at her mom and walked inside her house and went upstairs immediately to her bedroom. There, she crawled under the thin blanket on her bed, curled up into the fetal position, closed her eyes, and tried to sleep. She didn't actually fall asleep, but she pretended to do so because she wanted to be left alone. "I'll tell them tomorrow," she thought. "After he's gone."

When Lilli's mother entered the house, she checked on her daughter. "Are you okay, *mi amor?*" She whispered into Lilli's room. When Lilli failed to respond or move, her mom let her be. "She must be really tired," her mom thought, "to miss her English class. I'll let her sleep."

And that's pretty much what Doña Santiago said when she stopped by later to ask if Lilli were okay. "It's not like her to miss class; she's usually ten minutes early."

"*Sí, sí, es verdad,*" Lilli's mom echoed. "But I think she's just exhausted from all the babysitting she's done lately. That family leaves tomorrow, so Lilli can get back to her regular schedule again."

Lilli heard the entire conversation going on outside her window, and she wondered if perhaps she should get up and tell Don and Doña Santiago and Diego what had happened. It would be so much easier to tell them than to tell her own family.

Her grandfather especially would yell. He would yell at Lilli for wanting to be with the Americans, and he would yell at his wife and daughter for permitting Lilli to babysit for them. Her mother and her grandmother would try to calm him down, and then they would all be yelling. Lilli had seen it many times before, whenever they disagreed about something.

And then what would they do? Would they call the *policia?* No, that would bring too much shame on the family. Would they tell Padre Roberto? Probably not. Again, too much shame. Would her grandfather go after Tom himself? Lilli couldn't even imagine that. Her grandfather could be a loud, angry man at home, but outside his home, Lilli had never seen him confront anyone. He typically deferred to his wife when problems arose: when the Company-owned house needed a repair and a Company employee needed to be called in, when they had to talk to Lilli's teachers at school, even when they received the incorrect change at the market. No, Lilli could not tell her family what had happened.

And if she told the Santiagos or Diego, they would probably go to the other extreme. They would call both Padre Roberto and the police immediately. Then what? Her family would find out. The whole town would find out. She would be labeled a "*puta*," a whore.

And Tom? What would happen to Tom? He would lie, of course. He had lied to her already. He said she was pretty. He said he would miss her. And then he hurt her. Why? What did she do?

Lilli decided she could not tell anyone. She wouldn't even write about it in her journal. She did not want a record of what Tom had done to her. She felt so alone with her secret, yet she could not imagine a good outcome. "I can keep a secret," she told herself. "He hurt me, but I don't need to hurt anyone else. When he leaves tomorrow, my problem will leave too. I will never see him again. I will forget all about him, and I will forget what he did to me. I just have to get through tonight. Then, tomorrow, he will be gone."

By morning, Lilli was exhausted. Despite going to bed early, she had slept only fitfully and only after lying awake for so long. "*Mama*," she cried out when she heard her mother in the kitchen preparing breakfast.

"*Qué es, mi amor?*" Her mama asked when she entered Lilli's bedroom.

"May I stay home from school today? I still feel tired, and my stomach hurts too."

"Oh, my poor baby," her mama said as she hugged her daughter and touched her forehead to check for a fever. Since Lilli had never before faked an illness and was rarely sick, her mother readily believed that something was wrong. "Yes, you can stay home today if you need to, my child. What can I get you? Something to eat? Something to drink?"

"*No gracias, Mama.* I just need more rest now. I just want to close my eyes and sleep."

"Okay, my child, my darling. You rest. You sleep. I'll tell Grandma you're staying home today, and you can call downstairs to her if you need anything."

Left alone, Lilli did close her eyes, and she did sleep – finally. And as she slept, a LACSA airliner left the Golfito Airport bound for San Jose, and later for a connecting flight to Boston.

Chapter 28

By Saturday, after resting almost all day on Friday, Lilli felt strong enough to go to school. She rose at the normal time and dressed and then went downstairs and sat at the kitchen table. She ate her food in the normal manner, and she was her normal, polite self as she answered questions about her health.

"*Sí, Papa*, I do feel better today. Thank you," she said to her grandfather. "I feel rested, and my stomach does not hurt anymore."

"Here, drink some extra juice," her grandmother added, "and eat an extra piece of fruit, too. You didn't eat much yesterday, and I don't want you to pass out in school."

Physically, Lilli knew she felt fine, yet her morning demeanor was somewhat different. As she walked to school, she kept her eyes down and breathed deeply. When she arrived at school, instead of greeting her classmates and asking about what she had missed, she sat alone on a bench and pretended to read, for unlike every other day in Lilli's young life, she did not look forward to going to classes that day. She was apprehensive. She felt different, almost as if she had been scarred or tattooed. Though none of her classmates or teachers would be able to see what had happened to her, Lilli knew she would never be the same. That boy, that American boy – she could no longer even say his name – had changed her. He had robbed her not only of her virginity but also of her confidence, her enthusiasm, and her pride, and she wondered if she would ever truly recover.

During classes, she convincingly continued the charade of not feeling well. "We missed you yesterday," her teachers said, and her friends expressed similar sentiments saying, "I hope you feel better today."

Though their greetings helped somewhat, Lilli had to drag herself through the morning. She didn't raise her hand to answer, and she didn't say much to anyone as she walked from one class to another. And when one boy offered to carry her books for her, she surprised herself by saying "No" and rather brusquely at that. She had known this boy since kindergarten, and he had always been polite and friendly and helpful. On this day, though, she viewed him differently. "Would he ever do that to me or to another girl?" Lilli asked herself. "Is this what boys are really like?"

By the end of the school day, Lilli was exhausted again. But she had persevered. She could rest up at home after lunch because Saturday classes were only in the morning. Then, she would rest again on Sunday and prepare for a new week.

The following Thursday, when Lilli returned to her English class with Diego and Don and Doña Santiago, they all asked her how she was feeling, and Lilli put on a good act for them, just as she had done at school. She pretended to be still a bit tired, so she wouldn't have to be her usual happy and outgoing self. Despite her acting, Diego noticed something, as did Doña Santiago, and they spoke about it afterwards.

"Why did she miss our class last week?" Diego asked.

"She said she was real tired and also had a stomach ache. She missed school on Friday too."

"You sound like you don't believe that story."

"I don't know what it is, but something is different, something that has nothing to do with her health."

"I know what you mean," Diego agreed. "I noticed that she didn't make eye contact with me tonight. Every time I looked at her to see if she understood what I was saying, she would look down or away, almost as if she were afraid of me."

Doña Santiago laughed at that comment. "Afraid of you? You don't scare anybody."

Diego laughed too at that description of him because he knew it was true, but then he was serious again. "Maybe you should talk to her. Maybe something is going on at school, or maybe she's having a hard time at home for some reason. She likes you. She'll talk to you."

"Okay, Diego," Doña Santiago reassured him. "I will talk to her soon."

Chapter 29

Meanwhile, Diego was struggling to get any work done. The rainy season had begun which meant that his main time to promote sports was dwindling. For every day at around 4:00 p.m., the afternoon rains moved in from the mountains. In fact, the Golfiteños could hear and see the rains coming each day. If someone were walking on the main road during the late afternoon, the soft sound of the rain would arrive first as the water sprinkled the trees on the mountains. Looking to the mountains, one could then see the rain moving westward from the inlands toward the port and the bay. The gentle rains moved slowly and methodically, and those who carried umbrellas had plenty of time to open them, and those who did not had just enough time to sprint home or to seek temporary cover in a store or on a porch. During the early part of the rainy season, the storms passed quickly and tapered off within 10 to 15 minutes. A few weeks later, though, the rain persisted throughout the late afternoon and into the evening, destroying all possibilities of an outdoor game of basketball or volleyball. As a result, Diego had to be a bit more creative during this season to somehow promote sports.

One of his ideas was to promote a race from the public end of Golfito to the soccer stadium in the Company end, a distance of about three miles. This would be completely new and different to Golfito; Diego had never even seen anyone in town jogging, an activity that had become quite common in the United States. Yes, the soccer players would often run wind sprints to build up their speed and their stamina, but these wind sprints usually covered only the width of the field – about 50 yards – and only rarely the length of the field – over 100 yards. Most soccer players, after all, were only responsible for a portion of the field, so their training runs typically involved short bursts of activity rather than the endurance runs of a miler or a cross-country runner. Diego was hoping to introduce a new type of running to Golfito, and he began by introducing it to the youngsters in the grade schools.

"Let's run a lap around the entire basketball court," he would say before he began the normal layup drills and passing exercises.

"Let's run two laps today," he said the next time they got together, and "Let's go for three" the following time. In this way, he gradually built up their strength and conditioning, and he noticed that some of the smaller and thinner children, the ones who normally struggled in the typical soccer or basketball games were suddenly enjoying this activity and enthusiastically leading the way.

"Why do we have to run so far?" asked the others who were more accustomed to the shorter distances.

"These longer runs will strengthen you," Diego explained, "so that you have more energy at the end of the game when your opponent is starting to get tired." Later, once they had worked their way up to five laps around the basketball court, Diego moved them to the soccer field and began the same routine. Based on his own running experience around the football fields back home, Diego estimated that four laps around the soccer field had to be about a mile. He hoped to get the younger children up to one mile and the older ones up to three miles, which Diego recalled as the normal distance for a high-school cross-country race.

"Why are you making them run so far?" one of the male teachers asked when he observed what was going on.

"Distance running is not only great exercise," Diego replied, "but it's also a great discipline. If we can encourage these kids to gradually work up to longer distances, we can also encourage them to work on other long-term goals that require a firm commitment over a longer period of time.

This particular teacher, Don Martin, was so impressed with Diego's answer that he, too, when free and able to do so, began to run with the children. In fact, once he began running on his own on a regular basis, Don Martin became Diego's biggest encourager for the big race. And while initially, Diego thought Don Martin would help him organize the race, he really only wanted to run the race because he was hoping to be its first winner. In a town and country that was soccer crazy, Don Martin knew that he himself was a mediocre soccer player at best, and he was hoping to find a small slice of athletic fame in another way. When he realized that he was pretty good at running and that he enjoyed the peace and solitude that it offered, in addition to the workout, he talked to Diego whenever he could about the race.

"When will it be, Diego?" He asked often. Also, "Will there be a prize for the winner? Do you think many people will run?"

Secretly, of course, Don Martin didn't want too many participants because that would reduce his chances of winning. But too few participants would also cheapen his victory. And since he was only accustomed to running with his students, whom he could beat rather handily, he wasn't entirely convinced that he was the best runner in town. He worried often: "What if some of the really strong soccer players decide to run?" In reality, though, he didn't actually need to worry that much.

Most of the soccer players in town thought Diego's long runs were foolishness, merely a way to deplete the energy and stamina that should be reserved for the soccer field. So although Diego was hoping for a big turnout for his cross-town event, he realized that if he got 10 runners to participate, he would be fortunate. For in typical Costa Rican fashion, even though many athletes told Diego that they would participate in his training runs, when it was actually time to run, they simply never showed up. They could never directly say, "No, I'm not interested" to Diego. Instead, they simply slept in on the days the runs were scheduled, and then they smiled and laughed with Diego when he asked them why they had not arrived as promised.

"Ah, Diego," they would say. "I am a soccer player, not a runner." Or they might say, "I am not a horse; only horses run that far." Then, they'd laugh again. For even though they liked this athletic American, most of them were not really willing to try something new. Still, Diego persevered.

Since Diego expected mostly young people to run the race, he decided to schedule it on a Sunday morning. He couldn't expect his runners to miss their Saturday morning classes, and an afternoon race in the hot sun would be too much for anyone. Diego worried a bit that Padre Roberto would object to the Sunday start, but he understood perfectly. "If you start having races every Sunday, I might have a problem," he said, "but why don't you go ahead and schedule this first one, and we'll see what happens."

So Diego began posting signs around town and also telling everyone he knew: "The first ever Golfito *Carrera* will be held on the last Sunday in July at 9:00 a.m. Participants should meet at the Post Office and be prepared to run three miles to the port and to the finish line right in front of the soccer stadium."

Putting up the signs was easy. Finding people to help Diego work the race was impossible, even more difficult than finding people to run the race. And Diego hadn't quite figured out where he should be. He wanted to be the official starter, yet he also wanted to be at the finish line to welcome and congratulate the winner. If he had a car and a driver, of course, that would be easy. Diego had neither a car nor a driver, and he was unwilling to ask Padre Roberto for help on a Sunday, the priest's most important day of the week. No, Diego was determined to work this out on his own.

For a few seconds, he actually thought about taking the bus. He felt he could start the race, hop on the bus, and arrive well ahead of the runners. What if, however, the bus were delayed for some reason, or, more likely, broke down during the trip. That would be just too embarrassing for Diego, so he couldn't take that chance. Finally, he decided he would simply borrow a bike from someone. Then, he could start the race, hop on the bike and serve as kind of a lead vehicle for the runners. He assumed, of course, that he could pedal faster than they could run. So that was his plan.

On the Saturday before the race, he borrowed a bike from one of his neighbors. The bike was an old, somewhat beat up, American Schwinn, bigger than any bike Diego had ever seen in the States. Its owner bragged that he bought if from an American family when they moved back home two years earlier. It looked to be two to four inches bigger than the 26-inch bike Diego himself had when he was a boy, and the original bright red had faded to a burnt orange. Though it had no gears, Diego liked it because the tires were huge and relatively new. He felt extremely confident that the bike would survive the sometimes bumpy, main road for his trip from his home to the Post Office for the start of the race and for the return trip from the Post Office to the port during the race itself.

And fortunately for Diego on the morning of the race, he didn't have to actually peddle himself to the starting point. For as he rode from his house to the port, he noticed than an empty banana train was slowly departing from the port to return to the plantations. And since Diego had hopped aboard these trains numerous times, he assumed he could do the same on this bright, Sunday morning. Granted, he had never carried a bike with him before, but he was confident and determined. After all, how hard would it be to set the bike into an open boxcar and then run alongside until he could hop in that same boxcar himself?

So he rode up to a flat, paved spot near the train tracks opposite the movie theater, and he waited for an open boxcar. As the first open car approached, Diego noticed that it was bright yellow in the midst of numerous red boxcars. Then, he also noticed a thin, smiling, man riding in the open boxcar, and when this man realized what Diego was trying to do, he reached out and offered to help Diego place the bike in the boxcar. "*Ola, Amigo*," the man said as he grabbed the bike from Diego and lifted it inside.

Though Diego didn't recognize this particular man, it never crossed Diego's mind that this man might be up to no good. For while most Golfiteños and Costa Ricans were somewhat unreliable, he had never found them to be criminal. This man, however, was a small-time criminal.

He took the bike easily from Diego with his right hand and held on to the moving boxcar with his left hand. But after he dropped the bike to the floor of the boxcar, he used his right hand to push Diego away when he tried to climb aboard.

"You son of a bitch," Diego swore for the first time during his tenure in Golfito. Realizing quickly that this man was not a Good Samaritan but a thief, Diego ran after the boxcar again. Three times, Diego tried to climb inside the moving boxcar, and each time, this thin man pushed him away. The task became more difficult each time, too, because the train was picking up speed. During the first two attempts, Diego had maintained his balance and kept running. On the third try, however, after he was pushed away again, Diego stumbled and fell. With bruised and bloodied knees, he recovered and righted himself, but by the time he did so, the boxcar with the bike was well beyond him, and the caboose was approaching.

"Just get on the train," Diego told himself, and he climbed aboard the side ladder on the far end of the boxcar just before the caboose. There, he stood, holding on, catching his breath, examining his wounds, and trying to quickly determine his next move.

If he remained on the ladder, he could easily ride to the other end of town in time to start the race. Though he didn't possess the bike at that moment, he was grateful to be on the train and still able to get to the starting line and figure out what to do from there. He felt just as he did that day in the bullring in Zapote, shaking, but unharmed, after his confrontation with the bull. On this new day, however, Diego was no longer the cowering boy who was content to be safe. He knew that if he stayed put, he had no chance of retrieving the bike which he needed to oversee the race as he had originally intended. He was feeling both angry and determined, so he decided he would not play it safe this time. He would go back into the ring; he would confront his enemy and try and recover the bike.

Climbing the ladder was easy. Once he got to the top of the boxcar, though, Diego's battle began. When he got to the final rung of the ladder, he climbed to the top of the boxcar and stood up. "Just relax," he told himself. "And stay focused." Diego had seen the locals walk on top of these trains many times, so he knew that physically, it wasn't that difficult. Actually doing it himself, however, was another matter.

As he stood atop the car, he looked straight down, focusing only at the walking surface available to him, and he gratefully realized it was much bigger than he had imagined. This flat area was a good two feet wide down the center before it tapered off towards the sides of the car. "Just walk slowly," he whispered, "and it will be just like walking on a narrow sidewalk."

Before he took his first step, though, he also looked ahead to see how far they had already progressed. Seeing the sawmill down the road a bit ahead of him, he felt confident that he still had enough time, so he readied himself and began walking. Gingerly, he took one step, then another, and then a third. Soon, he was walking at almost a normal pace, and he had almost reached the end of the first car.

Knowing he needed a little momentum to jump from one car to the next, just as he had seen the locals do, Diego accelerated to a slow jog and leaped across to the next car even before he had a chance to talk himself out of it. With his confidence building, he jogged the length of the second car and jumped again. Car after car, he proceeded until he finally found himself above the lone yellow car that contained both his nemesis and the bike.

"Now what?" He asked himself. If he climbed down the ladder at the front or rear of the boxcar, he'd be in no position to enter the car. His only chance to retrieve the bike was to crawl to the edge of the car above the opening, lower himself, and swing his body inside the boxcar. If the bike thief were right there at the opening, he'd probably try to push Diego away again, and Diego might take a more dangerous tumble. But if Diego could move quickly, he might be able to kick the thief away, and once inside the car, he could battle him for the bike.

"*Vamonos*," Diego coached himself again.

Though Diego couldn't see the thief from above, that thief had watched Diego climb onto the train and was still looking out for him. Utterly determined to succeed, Diego dropped to his knees on the top of the boxcar, grabbed ahold of the steel bar that ran across the length of each side of the boxcar, and swung his legs down into the boxcar's opening. As he lowered his legs, he kicked violently, and, fortunately, he caught the thief in the chest. When the thief fell to the floor of the car, Diego swung his body into the boxcar, ready for battle.

Fortunately, too, no battle ensured. The thief now feared this crazy American who was willing to risk his life for an old, battered bike. The thief stood up, grabbed the bike, placed it between him and Diego, like a shield, and said, "*Lo siento.* I am sorry. *Muy* sorry. Take the bike. I made a mistake. Beeeg mistake. I am so sorry."

Diego grabbed the bike while eyeing this man cautiously. Diego also looked outside the car to see the public *mercado* and realized that he needed to exit quickly. He looked first for a soft spot to toss the bike and then exit himself. Before two seconds passed, he saw exactly what he needed. Just beyond the hotel where he had stayed when he first arrived in Golfito, he saw a few small bushes with what looked like a small garden next to them. Diego tossed the bike into the bushes and jumped after it into the garden. The soft landing protected the bike and also allowed Diego to land on his feet and quickly roll forward with his momentum. He ducked his head under and allowed his back to absorb the blow just as he had done in Don Mario's classes four months earlier. "I must have taught that class for a reason," he said as he rolled to a stop, breathed deeply, and stood up to retrieve the bike.

Glancing at his watch, he noticed that he was about 25 minutes early, so he walked the bike over to the entrance to the hotel, set it outside the front door, paid a teenager a *peseta* to watch the bike for him, and went inside to wash his bruised knees before heading over to the Post Office for the inaugural Golfito *Carrera.*

Chapter 30

Expecting only five or six runners to actually show up, Diego was pleased to see almost a dozen, all males. Three or four of Diego's expected runners had brought friends, and a few never-seen-before faces were also anxiously ready to run. "*Hola! Buenas dias,*" Diego said to everyone while also introducing himself and thanking everyone for their willingness to run. Then, he pulled a small notebook from his back pocket and wrote down the names of all the runners, and since he didn't have numbered bibs for them, he also wrote down a brief description of what each runner was wearing.

Don Martin, the teacher from the grade school near the sawmill, wore his new running shoes with an old, white, buttoned-down dress shirt with the sleeves removed, and a boy Diego recognized from one of the restaurants near the port wore no shirt at all, only cut-off blue jeans and a pair of old dress shoes with no socks. Most of the other runners wore old tee-shirts of varying colors and team or company logos: Coca-Cola, LACSA, the country's airline, and Saprissa, the country's number-one soccer team. The footwear of the others ranged from cheap sneakers to construction boots, and Chili, who worked at the port, wore nothing at all on his feet.

Besides the teacher and the restaurant boy, most of the other participants were from the high school with one or two workers from the port and a few from the countryside plantations who had heard about the race and came to town for it. Trying to decide who might be the favorites from the group in front of him, Diego would have bet on Don Martin, since he had been training, or on Bernardo from the high school, who everyone knew was just naturally fast, or maybe one of the plantation workers who looked both big and strong. In fact, those unfamiliar faces from the plantations looked so big and so strong and so healthy that Diego began to worry that he might not be able to stay ahead of them on the bike.

In addition to the runners, a small crowd of friends and family members had gathered to witness the start of the race: parents of the runners, spouses or girlfriends, even a child or two. Also in the crowd of onlookers were a few drinkers who had not yet finished their Saturday-night revelry. "*Vaya con Dios*," one of them yelled to the runners, and another, who was probably close to 50, bragged that he could beat them all.

Once Diego finished recording all the participants' names, he briefly explained the directions: "I will say '*En sus marcas, listos, ya!*' Then, I will climb on my bike and ride alongside or slightly ahead of you to make sure there's no jostling. If you purposely impede another runner, you will be eliminated. The finish line is exactly three miles away, near the main entrance to the soccer field." Diego stopped speaking for a second to reach into his pockets and pull out three small medals that he had purchased earlier. "The first three finishers will receive medals for their performance." As Diego held up the prizes to the small crowd, the runners, who had been mostly silent and stretching, cheered along with the others.

"I'll take mine now," yelled the old, drunken observer, and everyone laughed.

"*Diego, perdoname por favor*" said one of the high-school runners timidly. "Can you start the race just after the bus leaves, so my parents can ride the bus to the finish and watch us run?"

Since that had been one of Diego's original ideas for himself, he quickly and easily said, "*Sí, por supuesto. No problema.*" Then, everyone looked back down the road to see that the next bus was already in sight. "Okay, any other questions?"

"Who stole my sneakers?" asked the same drunken man who had spoken earlier and who was, indeed, barefoot. "I can't run without my sneakers."

Since there were no other questions, Diego asked the onlookers to stand off to the side as he directed all the runners to the start. Most gave a quick hug or a kiss to their loved ones, and some began to loosen up by jumping or running in place as everyone waited for the bus to stop and take on passengers.

Then, with six or seven people still waiting to board the bus, one last participant came running from a building about three doors away. "*Espera!*" He screamed. "*Espera por mi!*" Diego recognized Alfredo and quickly jotted down his name and his shirt color, orange. Alfredo was one of the better soccer players in town and the only really serious soccer player who decided to run.

"This should be interesting," Diego thought as he pointed Alfredo toward the line of runners and quickly repeated the key directions for him.

Finally, when the bus was loaded and on its way, Diego waited one more minute to give the fans on the bus a bit of a head start.

"En sus marcas, listos, ya!"

Diego started his stopwatch, and as he expected, some of the runners blasted from the start as if they were running a sprint. Not wanting to fall too far behind the runners, Diego hustled to climb aboard his bike and chase after them, and at first, he struggled. Since the bike had no gears and since the road in this section of town was filled with bumps and potholes, Diego had to pump furiously and yet swerve occasionally to remain close. Within a few minutes, he was finally able to catch up to, and pass, one group of runners who slowly paced themselves, but the leaders – two plantation workers, two high-school kids, Don Martin, and Alfredo – still were far ahead of him and about to pass the bus when it made its first stop near the sawmill and grade school.

Since only two people exited the bus at that point and no one boarded, the bus was quickly moving again and pretty much keeping pace with the lead pack, which had finally begun to slow down. Diego pedaled himself into the picture at that point, too, and breathed a slight sigh of relief. "How embarrassing would that have been," he asked himself, "if some of the runners had arrived before me at the finish line?"

The next stretch of the race was the longest distance between bus stops: from the lumber yard and school to the strip of bars near the movie theater. Though Diego finally could have sped ahead of the runners and the bus, he remained just a bit behind the leaders, so he could better observe them and their progress.

The two high-school runners, Bernardo included, began to fade a bit as the strength of their elders demonstrated itself. Even one of the plantation workers dropped behind the first three, and those three began to take turns leading the way.

At first, Alfredo was purposefully trying to demonstrate his strength and his endurance. Yes, he wanted to win the race for the sake of winning, but he also wanted to show the other runners and the townspeople that soccer players in general were the best athletes and that he himself was even more than just a soccer player.

Don Martin, the teacher, had never really experienced any athletic success before, so he wanted to prove at least to himself that he could succeed physically. And since he was one of the few people in the race who had actually trained for it, he felt confident that he would breeze to the front and to the finish line when the others faded. In order to achieve his goal, though, he had to stay near the leaders, and the pace of Alfredo and the plantation worker was starting to make him nervous.

Meanwhile, the plantation worker seemed oblivious to everything and everyone around him. As someone who was used to rising before dawn, hiking out into the rows of banana trees with his machete, and cutting down and carrying to the truck huge bunches of bananas that each weighed between 50 and 80 pounds, this race was merely another task to be completed quickly and efficiently. In fact, he was only running because his co-worker, the one who had dropped off from the leaders' pace, had asked him to run to keep him company. So here he was, striding easily and confidently down the center of the main road, gazing periodically at the bay to his left and the mountains on his right.

As Diego pedaled nearby and observed the three of them, he tried to predict a winner and also tried to pick his favorite. He didn't really like Don Martin that much because he always teased Diego about being a rich American who had an easy life, as if Diego were on vacation in Golfito with nothing better to do. Diego knew, however, that if Don Martin won, it would be good for the work Diego was trying to accomplish because Don Martin would probably encourage his students to run more and to train more seriously.

Diego also saw the benefit of a victory by Alfredo, the soccer player. Too many young soccer players, in Diego's limited experience, played the game lackadaisically. When on the soccer field, they ran only when they actually controlled the ball or when the ball was near them. They rarely ran to get into position to receive the ball or to defend properly. Granted, the good players ran often to put themselves in position to play well, and they anticipated what the opposing players were trying to do in order to beat them to the crucial spots on the field. The average players, though, were always a step or two behind, and Diego felt their conditioning was part of the problem. After controlling the ball or defending the goal for a short time, they were winded and not at all ready to properly move on to the next play. So if Alfredo won, perhaps he could encourage his teammates and the younger players throughout town to use distance running as part of their training. Then, with better endurance, they might become stronger soccer players, and they, too, might spur an interest not only in distance running but also in all the other running events.

And what about a victory by plantation man? How would his victory help or hurt Diego's sports promotion? It had to hurt more than help, Diego reasoned. If plantation man could simply come into town on the day of the race, without even training or preparing in any way, and easily blow past everyone else to victory, it would simply prove to all Golfiteños something that many of them already believed: God gives certain people athletic abilities and denies these gifts to others. So if plantation man is a gifted runner, he will win no matter what else happens. Soccer man won't win a distance race because his gift is soccer, not endurance running. And teacher man, despite his training and perseverance, will not win because he doesn't have the natural talent to do so. According to a common Costa Rican belief, natural talent will always win out over hard work and determination. At least, that was Diego's take on the athletic situation, based on his six months in town. The American fairytale belief that the slow and steady tortoise can beat the quick and talented hare, a belief that was part of Diego's basic makeup, was not yet ingrained in the hearts and minds of the young athletes of Golfito and one that Diego felt was his destiny to pass on to them. Yes, they were willing to try sports like basketball, volleyball, baseball, and running, but if they did not succeed immediately, they gave up and moved on to another sport or activity. And the dilemma of talent versus hard work, the classic argument between nature and nurture, was the struggle that Diego himself was trying to resolve.

With all that in mind, Diego knew that he had to root for Don Martin. Despite Diego's established dislike for this somewhat arrogant teacher, his victory in the race would show the other participants and the townspeople at large that discipline and training are good things and that anyone can succeed if they dedicate themselves to their craft and are willing to invest the time and energy.

"Okay, I better get moving," Diego finally told himself in the midst of his philosophical reverie. Once the bus stopped near the movie theater and the bars, Diego knew the finish line was not far away, so he sped up to make sure he was at the finish line when the leaders arrived. Unfortunately for those on the bus, they would probably not arrive in time to witness the first runners cross the finish line. For outside the movie theater, a small crowd of seven or eight people waited to board the bus, and four or five riders had to get off before the others were allowed to board. In addition, one of the new riders had two large boxes to transport, boxes that were too large for the front door of the bus, so they had to be loaded through the back door. In fact, the bus driver himself wanted to tell this rider to wait for the next bus because the driver had also become interested in the outcome of the race and wanted to hurry ahead to the finish line. He knew he couldn't do that, however, so he put the bus in park, climbed out the front door, and opened up the exit door at the rear, so this passenger's boxes could be placed on board.

Diego arrived at the finish line when the runners were about a quarter of a mile away. From that distance, Diego could see that the three leaders were still pretty close to one another. The plantation worker, with his yellow Chiquita banana shirt, held a short lead and was flanked on his right by Don Martin in his white, sleeveless dress shirt and on his left by Alfredo in orange.

"C'mon, Don Martin," Diego mouthed silently. As the race promoter and its only official, Diego felt the need to remain externally neutral, especially in front of the crowd that had gathered near the stadium to witness the finish. Approximately 25 people waited near Diego, and another five or 10 stood on each side of the road, cheering on their favorites as the three leaders approached.

To Diego, the onlookers seemed to be pretty evenly divided between Don Martin and Alfredo, most likely because none of them had ever seen plantation man before.

"*Vamos! Vamos!*" yelled some of the fans without revealing their favorite.

"Apurarse! Apurarse!" screamed some of the others. Obviously, those who were specifically rooting for Don Martin or Alfredo included the runners' names in their exhortations: "*Ya, Ya, Martin,*" or "*Ven a mi, Alfredo! Ven a mi!*"

When the runners got closer, Diego could see that the leader, plantation man, was clearly struggling as were Alfredo and Don Martin, who were not far behind and in that order. Diego knew for a fact that Don Martin had run the entire course three times in training during the previous two weeks, and Diego wondered if plantation man and Alfredo had ever run that far in their lives. Both tried to will themselves to the finish, but they had no real kick left, and when Don Martin noticed them slowing down ahead of him, he found an extra jolt of energy that he himself never knew he had before. First, he shot by Alfredo with less than 20 yards to the finish, and, then, with all of the spectators jumping and screaming, he caught up to plantation man and barely, but convincingly, raced by him as Diego clicked off his stopwatch.

"Whoa, we almost had a dead heat," Diego said aloud though no one else at the finish could hear or understand him. The onlookers were all cheering, and most of them raced to catch up with Don Martin who had continued running past the nearby basketball court until he finally slowed down. When he stopped, the crowd surrounded him and rhythmically chanted his name – "Martin! Martin! Martin!" – until he caught his breath. Then, they lifted him on their shoulders and carried him back to the finish line.

Only then did they see that plantation man and Alfredo had both collapsed at Diego's feet, and Diego was trying to determine if they were okay. "Please be okay," he whispered. "No one can die here today. That would not be good." Both of the runners were obviously still breathing, sucking in huge breaths of air, but neither one was moving otherwise.

"Back up," said an older, heavy woman with authority. "Just give them some space. They need to breathe; that's all." And she shooed the people away from the two fallen runners. Diego had never seen this woman before, but everyone else seemed to recognize her and respect her.

"She used to work as a nurse in the hospital," the man next to Diego said. "So they'll be fine," and he walked off into the crowd. And sure enough, within two to three minutes, Alfredo sat up, and plantation man rose to his feet. And just as one of the fans had done for Don Martin, this same man brought drinks for plantation man and Alfredo. This Good Samaritan was a vendor who had set up nearby for the soccer game, and he was selling large coconuts which he had cut open with his machete, inserted a straw, and offered to these competitors.

Once Diego realized what the man was doing, he went over and offered to pay him for the three coconuts. And since they were so cheap – only two *pesetas* each – Diego gave the man 10 *Colonnes* and asked him to give one to each of the runners, most of whom were finally crossing the finish line or were about to cross. "I should have thought of that myself ahead of time," Diego realized a bit too late. "I gotta get better at planning these things. Too many things could have gone wrong here."

"Diego. Diego," a young boy shouted from afar, bringing the distracted American back to Golfito. "*Tiene los medallions por los victores*?"

"*Sí, sí*," Diego replied. "I have the medals right here, and again, he pulled them out of his pocket.

Everyone wanted to see the medals presented to the top three finishers, but Diego announced that they had to wait until the race was officially over, when all the participants had completed the course. When Diego explained this, everyone looked to the south to see if anyone were still running. Diego was also checking off the names on his sheet to see how many runners were still out on the course.

With Alfredo's late arrival, Diego had 13 runners on his list, and 10 of them had already crossed the finish line and were drinking from their coconuts. One more was barely visible in the distance, a high-school boy who was walking rather than running. The two other missing runners were the barefooted Chili, and Jorge, who Diego could not remember at all but who wore a green tee-shirt.

"Let's give the others a few minutes," Diego said, and the crowd, most of whom had never witnessed a race before, consented easily. Since it was a bright Sunday morning, and no one present had to go to work, they simply relaxed and talked about the day's soccer game which wouldn't start for another hour or so.

When the visible walker realized people were watching him, he began jogging and finished as quickly as he could to light applause. When Diego asked him about the other two runners, he said, "I think they're still out there."

"Are you sure they didn't quit and give up?"

"I don't think so," yet as soon as he said that, an old dilapidated pickup truck wheezed to a stop before them.

"There's Chili now," the runner said, and the crowd laughed because Chili had hitched a ride rather than complete the run. Chili laughed too and said, "Somebody get me a beer. This running thing is crazy."

With 12 of the 13 runners accounted for, Diego looked again to the south, saw no one, and said, "I'll take a quick ride to the bend in the road, and if I can't see Jorge from there, we'll have to assume he dropped out and went back home. And with that, Diego hopped on his bike again, hoping that Jorge would appear. "It would be nice if they all finished, one way or another" he reasoned.

When Diego reached the turn, he looked down the road and saw no one. Disappointed, he almost turned completely around and headed back, yet as he turned, he noticed Jorge sitting on the side of the road with his head in his hands, resting, waiting.

Before he rode out to greet this last competitor, Diego signaled to those at the finish line that he had found Jorge. Then Diego pedaled about 200 yards down the road and asked Jorge, "*Qué pasa?*"

"I don't think I can make it; I'm too tired. Can you give me a ride on the handlebars?"

Diego knew he could easily give this young man a ride on the handlebars, and he quickly recalled his own youth when he had often given rides to friends or when he himself had ridden on the handlebars of his friends' bikes. The memory was a fond one for Diego, and he almost said "*Sí*" quickly before he hesitated and considered another option.

"How about if I just walk alongside you, so you can actually finish this race?"

"*Por qué?*" He asked. "Why would I want to finish?"

"Because the people are waiting for all the runners, and the man who sells the coconuts has a big one waiting for you."

"*Realmente?*"

"Really. C'mon. Get up. I know you can do this."

Jorge looked at Diego for a good 10 seconds and said nothing. Diego, always the softie and always ready to break the silence, resisted this time. If he spoke, Diego knew he'd probably have Jorge on his handlebars, but if he waited silently, letting this tired, young man consider his options, and their consequences, he might have a finisher in his midst. He might have an almost perfect first race where all but one who started the race completed the race. "Just wait," Diego told himself. "Keep your mouth shut. Let him decide on his own. Let the idea of finishing, the idea of completing the task, become his own."

Ten seconds became 15, and 15 became 20. Jorge was no longer looking at Diego, though. His eyes had shifted to the remaining course ahead of him. Finally, he spoke.

"People are waiting for me?"

"*Sí.* All of the runners and others too."

"And I really get a coconut just for finishing the race?"

"*Sí también.*"

"*Bueno, vamanos*," he said as he stood up, and instead of merely walking to the finish line, Jorge began jogging slowly, so Diego had to hop on his bike and ride – rather than walk – alongside. With each step, too, Jorge became stronger. His time sitting on the side of the road had obviously refreshed him, and Diego's return for him had encouraged him as well. Then, once he made the final turn, he could see the small crowd up ahead, so he moved from a jog to a run, and when those waiting at the finish line, both runners and spectators, saw him and began to cheer him on, he raced forward at full speed, faster than he had ever run before. Jorge was running so fast that Diego needed to pedal even faster to maintain the pace. Rather than attempt to actually arrive before Jorge, though, Diego began coasting. He let Jorge have the finish line all to himself, and as he crossed, everyone nearby cheered, and they treated him just as they had treated Don Martin when he actually won the race approximately 20 minutes earlier.

Chapter 31

After six months of living with the Mora family, Diego made an important decision, one that he had been pondering all that time: he decided to move out. He decided he needed to be on his own, and he felt he needed to live at the other end of Golfito.

His time in the Company end of town with the Mora family had been wonderful They treated him well, like a family member, and during his time with them, his Spanish improved tremendously because he was using the language all the time. Losing that family connection and losing that opportunity to speak so much daily Spanish would be a sacrifice, but Diego felt he needed to try to help those less fortunate, and he could do that more effectively if he left the comfort and safety of the Company neighborhood and lived among those who lived a different life without the Company's direct support.

Diego had thought about moving to the other end of town every time he worked there, every time he checked his post office box down there, and every time he visited Christina, either at the clinic or at her small apartment. In fact, she encouraged him to move, and she even helped him find his place within the same neighborhood, basically around the corner and up the street from her apartment.

Diego's only real concern was Padre Roberto. When Diego arrived in Golfito, it was Padre Roberto who had encouraged Diego to live in the more affluent end of town because he viewed Peace Corps Volunteers as a type of American ambassador, and he wanted Diego, his Peace Corps Volunteer, to be in what he felt was a more positive situation and environment.

Diego, however, realized that the Peace Corps philosophy was a bit different. Yes, the Volunteers were ambassadors of sorts, but their main mission was not to live like ambassadors in a special embassy that was isolated and removed from the homes of typical Costa Ricans. Instead, the Peace Corps wanted its Volunteers to live among the common people to experience their lifestyle.

When Diego revealed his idea to Padre Roberto, he asked Diego a few questions: "Are you sure about this? Have you thought this through? How will you promote sports down there without any real facilities except for that small patch of grass near the school that serves as a poor soccer field?"

Diego had, indeed, analyzed the situation, and he felt confident that he could still promote sports with limited facilities, and he actually looked forward to the challenge and hoped that he might be able to develop some facilities down there.

"Will you still come to our end of town and work with our kids?" Padre Roberto continued.

"Absolutely. I'm not abandoning this end of town; I'm just changing where I live, so I can get to know better the people who live down there."

Padre Roberto was disappointed, he had to admit. He had grown fond of this young American and enjoyed having him close by and seeing him often. Once he put aside his own self interest, however, he realized Diego was probably doing the right thing. Padre Roberto also realized that perhaps he himself had become too comfortable in his end of Golfito after living there for 20-plus years. He knew he was too set in his own ways to move, so maybe the move would be better for both Diego and for that other community of Golfiteños.

"Okay," he finally said reluctantly. "But I still want to see you periodically. We'll have to get together for lunch or dinner once in a while."

"You're paying, of course," Diego said laughingly, and Padre Roberto laughed along with him. Then, Diego even offered to cook a meal for the two of them once he got settled in his new place.

"Oh, I don't know about that. I'm a man of faith, but," and he paused for dramatic effect, "that's a real leap of faith."

Diego's new, furnished apartment was not that much bigger than the one room he rented in the Mora's house. It was what they called in the States an "efficiency" apartment and a perfect square at that, approximately 15 feet by 15 feet. When Diego entered from the street, the kitchen was on his left, with an old stove, an old refrigerator, and an old table. The bathroom was in the back corner on the same side, and his bedroom was in the opposite back corner. The remaining front portion included a chair and an old couch that sat beneath the only window.

Fortunately, Diego didn't have many possessions or clothes; the only places to put his belongings were in the cabinets over and around the kitchen sink and a small closet between the bathroom and the bedroom space. Diego realized immediately that he'd like to purchase – or perhaps even build – a bookcase for himself and maybe a coffee table too. Though Diego didn't drink coffee, he knew most Golfiteños did, and he really wanted the coffee table as a place to keep his weekly *Time* magazine and any book he might be reading.

On the day Diego moved in, he realized, too, that he had ignored one key element of the place: ventilation. When he first viewed the apartment and agreed to rent it, he toured it in the early morning before the sun had a chance to warm it up. When he unpacked his belongings three weeks later in the late afternoon, however, he readily noticed the hot and stifling atmosphere. "I'll have to put up a screen door," he noted, "and

I'll have to buy a fan and a screen for that window. Only then did Diego truly realize and appreciate the beautiful situation he had with the Moras.

His room at the Moras was on the second floor, and the two windows in the room often allowed the nearby mountain breezes to cool that corner of the house. This new apartment, though, was tucked deep into a neighborhood where the breezes rarely reached. Not surprisingly, many of the neighbors sat outside on the front step or on a wooden box kept on the sidewalk. Initially, Diego assumed these people were just being social, and he assumed that he would be somewhat social too but just not as often. He envisioned himself relaxing alone in his new place, reading and escaping from people when they became too much for him. Soon, though, the beads of sweat rolling down his forehead as he tried to read and the stickiness he felt when he tried to recline inside quickly convinced him that he might be more comfortable, too, if he sat outside where the temperatures seemed a good ten degrees cooler no matter the time of day or the season.

At times, early in the morning usually, before anyone else was up and out, Diego could sit alone near his front door, but the sight of a friendly American attracted both the people who lived on or near that street and many of the passers-by.

"*Hola, Diego. Qué tal?*"

Those who knew him stopped often and sat down next to him with their questions or their stories. Those who did not actually know Diego quickly introduced themselves or just as easily struck up a conversation.

Though not always in the mood to talk, Diego was typically too polite to be rude or mean. He'd answer their questions and listen to their stories, and gradually, he acclimated himself to this new living situation. Within a short time, he realized it was very similar to Larry's front porch back home where he and Larry and their friends gathered daily both before and after playing baseball games, delivering newspapers, or preparing to go somewhere else. The tall American was not only settling in physically but also socially and emotionally.

Chapter 32

Despite his move, Diego still returned to the Santiago's house every Thursday evening to give them and Lilli their English lesson. They were excited to see him after his move, and they peppered him with questions about his new place. As Diego described it, he also promised that he would invite them all to his apartment some Sunday afternoon, and he said he would cook for them.

"*De verdad?*" Lilli asked in amazement.

"*Sí, sí.* I will. I promise."

And as Doña Santiago had promised previously, she had talked privately to Lilli to find out what was wrong.

"*Nada,*" Lilli answered the first time Doña Santiago brought up the subject. "Nothing at all. I think I must have gotten *la influenza,*" she lied. "It really made me sick. And really tired too. I was so sorry to miss English class and my school classes."

Doña Santiago had a feeling it wasn't a physical sickness at all. Rather than press the issue, though, she decided to wait to give Lilli some time and some freedom, so she could reveal the truth when she felt more comfortable

During subsequent Thursday English classes, Lilli gradually returned somewhat to her normal inquisitive and friendly self. Once again, she was speaking English more quickly and more fluently than the Santiagos when Diego walked them through practice exercises from his lesson book. During the conversations, though, Lilli was not as quick to respond. She appeared more guarded, as if she were afraid of being too honest, too open. Doña Santiago noticed, too, that Diego was right. Lilli no longer made eye contact with him or with Don Santiago. Instead, she always looked away or solely at Doña Santiago.

Since Lilli was no longer committed to babysit for the Wilson family, Doña Santiago asked Lilli to watch her two young children once in a while, so she and Don Santiago could have some time together. Though they didn't go out often and never for a long time, they did enjoy taking long walks together in the neighborhood and beyond, and they would sometimes ride the bus to the other end of town to eat in the Chinese restaurant located there.

When Doña Santiago asked Lilli to babysit on these occasions, she always asked Lilli to arrive 15 minutes before they planned to leave, so she could explain to Lilli any special instructions she might have for the children regarding their food, their activities, and their bed time. Doña Santiago also used this time to talk to Lilli about her family, about school, and about her relationships with her friends and her classmates. For the most part, Lilli shared freely with Doña Santiago. She told her about the underlying tension in her home because her grandfather still resented the fact that his daughter, Lilli's mom, had gotten pregnant so young and that her husband had abandoned her. Yes, Lilli's grandfather loved his daughter and Lilli, and he provided for them, but every once in a while when money got tight or when their small house felt too small, he lashed out at all three women who lived with him.

Lilli also told Doña Santiago about what she was learning in school and about her plans to study at the University in San Jose.

"Your grandfather will let you go to college in San Jose?" Doña Santiago asked in disbelief.

"No. Never. He probably won't let me go there just for college, but if I go there to work, I think he will permit it and especially if I go there and live with the Moras' daughter. Then, once I'm there, I can start taking courses and pay for them myself." Lilli and Doña Santiago giggled as they talked about Lilli's secret plan, and Doña Santiago shared with Lilli her own frustrated plans for education and travel.

"I had a chance once," she said to Lilli, "to leave Golfito right after high school." Then, she stopped and appeared to drift off, as if she forgot all about Lilli.

"What was it? Why didn't you go?" Lilli asked within seconds.

"It was a cleaning job on a boat."

"Do you mean one of the big banana boats – going to America?"

"No. This was a much smaller boat. A rich family from Argentina had sailed into the bay, and they spent almost a month in the harbor. Every day, an older woman came into the booth at the market where I worked. Like you, I was very friendly, and we talked often. She complained a bit about having to do so much work on the boat: shopping and cooking and cleaning for her husband and his brother and the brother's wife and for the six children in the two families.

"Jokingly, I told her I would gladly do the work for her if I could travel to Argentina with them. When I said that, she stopped her shopping, looked me straight in the eye, and asked: '*Seriousamente?*'

"Though I hadn't been serious when I first spoke about it, I said 'Yes' anyway. She asked again, and I said 'Yes' more enthusiastically. I was starting to get excited about the possibility, and so was she when she said, 'Let me ask my husband, and I'll come back tomorrow.'"

"And?" Lilli asked.

"And her husband said he would consider it, but he wanted to meet me and my family before he would agree. So three days later, on a Sunday afternoon, he and his wife came to my house and met my parents."

"Your parents were willing to let you go?"

"Not at first. My father especially thought it was a crazy idea, and my mother was nervous, but I convinced them to at least meet with this Argentinean family.

"Well, they came to my house, and the two men connected immediately, and the two women got along well too. We shared an afternoon dessert of fried *plantains* with them, and, then, they asked us if we wanted to see the boat.

"My dad said 'Yes' without a second thought, so we all walked down to the harbor, and they transported us in the small dinghy that they used daily to come to shore and brought us out to their big boat. And it was absolutely wonderful. We met his brother and sister-in-law and all the children. Then they invited us to stay for dinner, and we even decided that if I did go with them, I would sleep in the small section occupied by the three girls. I was ready to sail with them that day, but my papa said he had to think about it overnight. And since they weren't planning to leave until the following Friday, we actually had four full days to think it over."

"So your papa said 'No?'"

"Actually, he said 'Yes.' By the very next morning, he said I could go if that's what I really wanted."

"So your mama kept you back?"

"No. She was still nervous, but she agreed with my papa. They both felt confident that it was a good situation for me, and they let me make the final decision."

"And?"

"And I think that scared me more than anything."

"Why?"

"I didn't realize it at the time, but I never really expected my parents to say 'Yes,' so when they did, I think I panicked. I couldn't imagine my life without them, and the thought of being trapped on that boat with all those strangers scared me a bit too. So, when Friday came, I just couldn't go. I had actually packed a bag the night before just in case, but I was too nervous, much more nervous even than my mom. So I left my bag at home and walked down to the pier to tell them my decision. The *señora* was really disappointed, and the girls who came with her that day were sad too, but they all understood. I think they could all sense my anxiety. In fact, they said that they would come back for me in a year or two, but they never did. I never saw them again, and I never saw Argentina – or anywhere for that matter."

"I'm so sorry."

"*A mi también.* I think of that family often, and I wonder all the time what my life would be like today if I had gone with them."

After Doña Santiago had opened up to Lilli in that way, Lilli felt comfortable telling her a bit more about her situation and her feelings. And three weeks later, after babysitting again, when they were alone in Doña Santiago's living room, Lilli mentioned that ever since the morning that Tom had left, she felt different about everything.

"Did you like him?" Doña Santiago asked.

"*Sí, un poquito.* I thought he liked me too."

"But you knew all along that he would go home to America."

"Yes, I did . . . ."

Doña Santiago waited for Lilli to say more, but she did not, so Doña Santiago continued. "Did you think he would write to you?"

Lilli shook her head "No," and she began to shake.

Doña Santiago reached out to hug Lilli, and Lilli would not let go. "There, there, *mi hija.* It's okay. Everything is okay."

Lilli shook even more, and she finally spoke, quickly and almost silently. "No. No. It's not okay."

Doña Santiago pulled away from Lilli just a bit, so she could look the young girl in the eye. "What is it? You can tell me."

Choking back tears, Lilli spoke again: "He . . . he . . . he hurt me."

"What do you mean he 'hurt' you?"

Crying fully at that point, Lilli told Doña Santiago everything. Doña Santiago clenched her fists as she heard the story and began crying herself. "I can't believe it. *Yo no puedo creer,*" she repeated five or six times. "Oh, Lilli, I am so sorry. So, so sorry." Then the young mother held this neighborhood teenager as if she were her own, and they cried together.

They remained silent for a good 10 minutes: Lilli, having freed herself from her solitary burden and finally feeling somewhat safe and secure for the first time since the incident occurred, and Doña Santiago, silently trying to figure out what to say and what to do.

"We have to tell someone," she finally uttered.

"No. No. No. We can't," Lilli responded, and she started shaking all over again. "*Mi grandpapa* cannot know. No one can know. Only you can know. You're the only one. The only one."

"Okay. Okay," Doña Santiago comforted Lilli again. She said no more that evening about telling others. After Lilli went home, however, Doña Santiago considered the possibilities.

If she told her husband, he would go to the police immediately, and everyone in town would find out what had happened. That would be too much for this fragile, young girl.

If she told Padre Roberto, he would want Lilli's family to know the truth, and based on what Lilli had said about her grandfather, he might become violent. Who knew what he might do in his anger, especially since the boy would probably never return to Golfito. Yet someone would have to bear the grandfather's wrath.

Is there anyone at the high school, Doña Santiago wondered, who could help Lilli? Or maybe at the hospital? Someone who could definitely keep the information confidential? Doña Santiago didn't know the people at the high school or the hospital, so she was skeptical. She had lived in Golfito too long and had heard too many stories about too many people. Secrets were not secrets for long in this too small, too tight community.

Diego, she finally realized, would be someone she could tell. He was gentle and kind. He wouldn't rush to tell someone else. He knew Lilli well and cared for her. He would listen, and, then, the two of them could discuss it together without jumping into any dramatic confrontations that would only cause more problems for Lilli.

Before Doña Santiago could speak to Diego, though, she had to figure out a way to do so without initiating any other problems. She couldn't tell her husband why she had to talk to Diego, and she couldn't speak to Diego in secret because if their secret conversation were observed, that might become another piece of gossip that would then make its way through the community. "I must speak to Diego in public where people can see us but not overhear us," she decided.

So a few days later, when Diego arrived after supper to teach his Thursday English class, she greeted him at the door and escorted him to her garden: "Diego, come. I want to show you the new flowers I planted."

"*Por supuesto*," Diego answered, though he was a bit surprised because Doña Santiago had never before even mentioned her garden in all of their English conversational exercises.

"Aren't those yellow flowers really pretty?" She asked him as they walked away from the house to the extreme edge of the garden.

"Yes, they are."

Then, looking to make sure that no one was close enough to overhear her, Doña Santiago lowered her voice a bit and explained to Diego all that Lilli had told her.

"Oh, my God!" Diego said in a somewhat hushed tone. "Really? Is that why she's become so withdrawn?"

"*Sí.*"

"Does anyone else know?"

"Just you and I."

"What should we do?"

"I'm not sure. That's why I wanted to tell you. I thought we could talk it over without it becoming a huge, embarrassing situation for Lilli."

"You haven't even told your husband?"

"No. He would go straight to the police, and I think Padre Roberto would do the same if he knew what happened. I trust you, Diego. I hope you will not tell anyone until you and I figure out a way to help Lilli through this."

"So she hasn't been to a doctor or a nurse yet either?"

"I'm afraid someone would let the story out."

"Let me talk to Christina. I trust her to keep it a secret, and she can examine Lilli too. Does Lilli seem okay physically?"

"As far as I can tell, yes."

"Okay. We should go inside now."

"Yes, but let me first pick some flowers to bring in for the table." As Doña Santiago pulled a small bouquet together, Diego asked one more question."

"Does Lilli know that I know?"

"No. She does not."

"Okay, I'll talk to Christina and get back to you."

Chapter 33

That conversation prompted Diego to actually schedule the luncheon he had promised at his new apartment for the Santiago family and Lilli. He decided he would also invite Christina and perhaps then she could walk Doña Santiago and

Lilli over to the nearby clinic for an examination. And a week and a half later, on a Sunday afternoon, they all showed up at Diego's new place.

Diego had prepared what he described as an "American summer luncheon": hamburgers, a tossed salad, and a macaroni salad, with brownies and ice cream for dessert. Though he had to borrow a few chairs from the neighbors, all of his guests crowded around his small kitchen table and enjoyed their conversation – some parts in Spanish and some parts in English – and their laughter.

Since Diego and Doña Santiago and Christina had all pretty much scripted the day ahead of time, Doña Santiago delivered the key line to her husband after the meal but before dessert: "Samuel, Christina is going to show Lilli and me the clinic where she works, so why don't you stay here with Diego and the kids to help him clean up. Then, maybe you two can bring the kids to the small playground at the school, and we will all meet back here in about an hour for dessert."

Samuel, somewhat surprised by the freedom to just hang out with Diego and the kids without his wife and the other women, readily agreed: "*Sí, sí, mi amor*. That sounds great. We can handle this, right, Diego?" He said to his *amigo*.

"*No problema*," said the conspiring American. "*No problema*."

So the ladies left, and as soon as they did, Diego pulled out the brownies and the ice cream. "Let's just try a little bit of the dessert to make sure that it's okay," and the two men laughed even harder than the two little kids.

During the luncheon, Christina had asked Lilli and Doña Santiago quite a few questions about their lives and their future plans, and as they walked to the clinic, both Doña Santiago and Lilli asked Christina even more questions about her life in America and about how she knew she wanted to get into the medical field. Consequently, by the time they reached the clinic that afternoon, all three of the ladies felt comfortable together.

Though the clinic was modest by American standards, Lilli and Doña Santiago were impressed by the cleanliness of the clinic and by the display of medical supplies and furniture.

"What kind of medical problems do you treat here?" Doña Santiago asked Christina.

"Oh, most of the common injuries that occur like scrapes and bruises and broken bones, and we also have medicine for some of the typical problems like colds, and sore throats, headaches, those kinds of things." Then Christina, knowing well her part in the day's script, offered her piece of the dialogue: "We also have pregnancy services for the women, so we can let them know if they are pregnant, and, if so, we help them to take care of themselves and prepare for the baby."

Doña Santiago and Christina watched Lilli to see how she reacted to that piece of information, and, as they anticipated, Lilli froze and looked terrified. Four weeks had passed since Tom had attacked her, and once she had recovered somewhat from the reality of the attack, she had, indeed, begun to worry that she might be pregnant. She couldn't actually bring herself to tell Doña Santiago because she felt that if she verbalized her fear that it might somehow come true. On that day, though, and in that setting, Lilli realized that Doña Santiago was taking care of her – again.

"Does Christina know?" Lilli asked, embarrassed and starting to cry.

"She does," Doña Santiago answered, and both she and Christina put their arms around Lilli and led her to a chair near the examination table.

A small part of Lilli wanted to be mad at Doña Santiago for revealing the secret. A much bigger part of her, though, was grateful and relieved. Lilli wanted to put the whole terrible experience behind her, and if these two women could let her know that she was definitely not pregnant, she would feel so much better.

Lilli struggled to express all that was going on in her mind, and Doña Santiago and Christina were patient enough to let Lilli process her thoughts through her tears, and they encouraged her to sit down. After a few minutes and after both of the women had hugged Lilli and tried to comfort her, Doña Santiago finally spoke.

"Lilli, if you're willing and if you're ready, Christina can examine you today to make sure you're okay physically and to see if you're pregnant. If you want to wait and do it at some other time, we can do that too. But we both feel that you should be examined, and we know you don't want your family or anyone else to know what happened."

Again they waited while Lilli digested what Doña Santiago had said to her. Lilli's left hand covered her eyes, and she twirled her long, black hair with her right hand. Her body rocked just a bit as she rested in the chair. She breathed slowly and deeply. She was no longer crying or shaking. She looked up and asked, "Does Diego know too?"

"Yes, he does."

Lilli bit her lip just a bit and appeared about to cry again. "Is he ashamed of me?"

"No, he's not ashamed, and you should not be ashamed either. What happened to you is not your fault."

"But – "

"No 'buts.' You did nothing wrong. That boy had no right to treat you in that way. You were in his home. You were watching over his little sister, and he did a terrible thing to you."

"Maybe – "

"No 'maybes' either. It was wrong. Don't blame yourself. It's over. He's gone, and now you need to take care of yourself. So again, we can do this today, or we can do it next week or the following week, but we don't want to wait too long."

Doña Santiago then spoke to Christina: "Christina, about how long will it take you to examine Lilli?"

"Less than ten minutes."

"And will the examination hurt her?"

"No."

While Doña Santiago waited for Lilli to decide, Christina gave Lilli a bit more information.

"You may feel a little pressure when I examine you, but I promise to be gentle. I'll try to make it as easy and as quick as possible."

Lilli looked back and forth at Doña Santiago and Christina. Then, she looked directly at Doña Santiago. "Does Don Santiago know?"

"No, he does not."

"Will you tell him?"

"I'm not planning on it."

After a few more seconds, Lilli exhaled deeply and said, "Okay. Let's do it today. Right now."

With Lilli's permission, Doña Santiago escorted her into the examining room and helped her onto the table. Meanwhile, Christina prepared herself first, and then she explained to Lilli everything she was about to do and also why she needed to do it. Doña Santiago stood next to Lilli, holding her hand, and when Christina was silent, Doña Santiago whispered to Lilli, softly and gently, "Everything's going to be okay. Just stay calm. Relax. Everything's going to be okay."

As Christina had promised, the entire examination took less than 10 minutes and did not hurt. Even the "little pressure" that Christina had prepared Lilli for was less painful than Lilli had imagined it would be.

When Christina finished, she and Doña Santiago helped Lilli off the table and escorted her back into the front room.

There, they gave her a glass of water and sat down with her.

"Am I pregnant?" Lilli asked immediately.

"That we don't know," Christina replied. "We have to wait a while before the results are ready."

"How long?"

"About a week or so. We have to send the test to a lab in San Jose."

"What if I am pregnant?"

"We don't need to worry about that today. What we can focus on today is the good news."

"Good news?"

"Yes. Physically, you are fine. That boy did not cause any physical problems for you. You are a strong, healthy, 17-year-old girl. That's good news."

"*Gracias a Dios*," Doña Santiago exclaimed.

"Yes, thank God, indeed," Christina repeated.

"And we have some other good news today too," Doña Santiago added.

"More?" Asked Lilli.

"Yes."

"What is it?"

"We have brownies and ice cream waiting for us back at Diego's apartment."

Lilli made a funny face at first before she laughed, and the others joined in. "Okay, let's go."

"*Sí, vamanos.*"

Chapter 34

Once Diego had settled comfortably into his new apartment, he set out to meet his neighbors, and he tried to figure out the best way to do his job there, to promote sports.

He decided to begin by getting up early every day during the week to go to the small soccer field next to the school. There, he began his workout by stretching and exercising and by jogging around the perimeter of the field. He hoped that his presence there each morning would encourage some of the school children and maybe even some of the adults to join him. He purposely did not bring a ball with him because he knew if he brought a ball – any kind of ball – the locals would use it to play soccer. And while soccer was better than nothing, Diego wanted to move beyond soccer. He hoped to form a track team. He had decided upon track because he knew the sport was affordable, even for those who had nothing. All they needed was a desire to run or to jump. He could set up races of varying distances, sprints and longer. He could also set up relay races to allow the participants to focus on teamwork within the framework of this mostly individual sport. He could also show everyone how to do the long jump and the high jump.

At first, Diego was working out on his own. Those who were awake and nearby merely watched and wondered, "What is wrong with this crazy, young American? Why is he sprinting from one side of the field to the other, and why is he running slowly around the entire field?" Again, Diego's plan was to wait and let the observers come to him, but he couldn't hold out long enough. He was too much of a competitor himself to merely run on his own. He wanted a race. He needed a race. He coveted a race. So on the third day of his workouts, he jogged over near some of the older boys and boasted, "I bet I can beat all of you in a race."

When the three high-school boys heard Diego's challenge, they looked not at Diego but at each other, as if to say, "What do we do with this?"

Speechless, they waited for Diego to say more. He did not disappoint.

"Seriously, I bet I can run around that soccer field twice before any one of you can run around it once."

Diego himself knew this was impossible. These boys, after all, were about 15 or 16, and they appeared to be in good health and capable. If they ran a regular race, once around the field, Diego felt it might be close, but he'd probably win. After all, he was older, stronger, and in much better running shape than these three. Yet, even if one of them happened to be a natural runner, why would he take a chance on losing to this goofy *gringo* in front of his friends? So Diego had to up the ante, and, truth be told, he didn't really care if he won or lost. All he wanted was to get them to run. He would do whatever was necessary.

"All right, here's what I'll do. If you guys beat me, I'll buy you each two hot rolls from that bakery down the street."

"And if we don't beat you?" The shortest of the three boys asked.

"I'll only buy you each one hot roll."

"Really?"

"Really. I just want to race somebody. C'mon; give me a race."

The short one looked at the other two, asking them to join him. They both agreed quickly. Two free hot rolls, even one free hot roll, seemed like a good deal for a relatively short sprint around the small soccer field.

"Race! Race!" Some of the smaller boys nearby yelled once they knew that their elders had agreed to the challenge. And with that, a small crowd of people began to gather. Some got up out of their street-side chairs, and others exited their homes when they heard the commotion and discovered what was about to happen.

Diego led the three *amigos* to the corner of the field nearest to the front door of the school. Then, he explained that they would run in a counter-clockwise direction around the perimeter of the field just as if they were racing around the basepaths of a baseball field. He also explained that he would act as the starter. "I will say '*uno, dos, tres, vamonos*,' and off we go. Any questions?"

The boys had none. In fact, the boys were more silent than Diego had expected. The gathering crowd, though, was electric with excitement. They encouraged their boys with chants of "*Vamonos, Ticos*" and "*Vaya con Dios.*" Suddenly, what had been just a chance to get some hot rolls became a test of national pride: three young Golfiteños versus the older American. Diego noticed the change in the boys' demeanor as they waited to begin. He also noticed the contrast in their footwear.

While Diego was wearing his white, high-top Converse basketball sneakers from America, these boys had a much more diverse collection of shoes. The tallest of the three wore old, dress shoes that appeared to be a size too big, perhaps hand-me-downs from his father. The shortest of the three had sneakers, but they were the kind that people who owned boats wore; they slipped on and off like loafers and had no laces. And the third boy was wearing an old pair of black flip-flops, flip-flops that he discarded quickly and easily. Diego had seen many Golfiteños play soccer barefoot, so it didn't surprise him at all when this young man decided to run the race that way, and when the boy with the dress shoes saw that his friend would run barefoot, he decided to do the same.

But just before the race was about to begin, the shortest boy asked Diego to wait just a bit while he pulled his two friends together for a consultation. Diego couldn't hear what they were saying, but he assumed it was a short prayer because all three of them made the sign of the cross before they returned to the starting line. Finally, when they were all ready, Diego uttered the promised words: "*uno, dos, tres, vamonos.*"

Diego took off by running as fast as he could. Though he didn't seriously think he could run the perimeter twice before the boys ran it once, he wanted to give it his best effort and see how close he could come to actually beating them. Surprisingly, the boys stayed right with him. Diego hadn't expected this. He assumed they would simply jog behind him and not run hard until he had completed one lap. Then, they could sprint a bit if they needed to.

All three boys, however, were pretty close to Diego as they finished running the width of the field and made the first turn, and Diego began to doubt himself: "Did I really explain the directions properly to them?" He let that thought go quickly, though, because he couldn't do anything about it at that moment, and he wanted to pick up the pace as they ran the longer length of the field. Diego increased his stride, and he did manage to break away from the boys a little – but only a little. In fact, each time they turned, the boys appeared to catch up a bit because they were better than the long, angular Diego at turning without losing speed. And by the time they approached their finish line, one time around the complete field, all three of them were within 10 yards of Diego.

When Diego finished his first lap, he slowed down because he had obviously lost his bet; still, he was determined to complete his two laps as expected. The three boys, however, had a surprise for Diego. Instead of stopping after one lap, they ran even faster and flew by the jogging Diego to begin the second lap. The crowd realized what was happening even sooner than Diego, and they cheered on their boys when they passed Diego and opened up a substantial lead.

These boys would not be content by winning the two-for-one race that Diego had proposed. In their circle of prayer before the race, they had decided that they would try to beat Diego at the full distance, and they had a good shot at it.

The tallest boy was leading the way, and the two others were close behind. Diego's hesitation had cost him his lead, and he quickly realized he would really have to hustle to catch up. He was still well behind at the first turn. During the long stretch, though, he began to make up ground, and he passed the boy in the sailor's sneakers just before the second turn. All the runners maintained their spots on the third stretch, and as they made the final turn and headed down the length of the field for the finish, all four runners were breathing heavily, and most were losing speed; only the tall boy did not falter. Like many great runners before him, he found his extra burst, and just as Diego passed the second boy and threatened to move into first place, the tall boy pulled away from the others. His stride remained the same, but he planted his feet more quickly with each step, and he practically flew through the finish; he was moving so fast at the end that he crossed the street and ran down a full block before he could slow himself to a walk.

Though Diego managed to hold on to second place, the other barefoot boy wasn't far behind, and even the boy with the sneakers finished a respectable distance behind the first three. The spectators cheered for all of the boys and hugged them and patted them on the back. Two of the older men even picked up the victor and carried him to the bake shop where they knew Diego would have to buy the boys their prized rolls. Diego, though pretty tired himself, smiled all the way to the bake shop. He had found himself a real sprinter, and he felt he had found the nucleus for his running club.

"Congratulations, Gustavo," he said to the winner when he found out the boys' names, "and congratulations, too, Felix and Guillermo," who had finished third and fourth, respectively. As they ate their rolls, Diego discovered that all three of them were still in high school: Guillermo was a junior, and the others were a year younger.

"Would you like to run more, to practice, and maybe compete against other towns?" Diego asked.

"*Sí. Sí. Sí*," they all said, laughing and enjoying their new-found fame.

In the weeks following, Diego visited the schoolyard park twice a week, on Mondays and Thursdays before school, to work with the three young men and with the other boys who came periodically – sometimes five, sometimes eight or 10. Diego initially thought he would work out with them more often, but he worried that they might burn out quickly and lose interest. As a result, he used Monday as a training session when he led them through stretching exercises and long runs around town. Then, on Thursday, he hosted races of various lengths, and in a special notebook, he recorded all of the results and gave paper certificates to the top three runners. He wanted his young athletes to know that their accomplishments mattered, and he hoped that they would strive to break the local records and would cherish the modest certificates that Diego himself had created that very day.

Fortunately, the plan worked. Most of the runners began to attend regularly, and during one particular week, four young girls showed up and asked if they could run too. Naturally, Diego welcomed them and began a whole new notebook of records for them as well. Fortunately, too, for Diego, a few of the parents volunteered to help him by bringing water and fresh fruit for the participants and by beginning to help with the organization of the races and the paperwork. Diego was so pleased with what was happening that he looked forward to his next visit to San Jose to meet with all the other Sports Promoters, so he could tell them about his running club, and when he wrote to his family and friends back home, he proudly told everyone what he was up to.

Chapter 35

About 10 days after Lilli's pregnancy test, Christina received the results that showed that Lilli was, indeed, pregnant. Six weeks had passed since the incident occurred, and though Lilli was not yet showing any visible signs, those signs would appear soon enough.

After Christina told Diego, he passed the news along to Doña Santiago, and he asked her how they should go about telling Lilli and Lilli's family.

"*Oh, mi Dios*," said Doña Santiago when she heard the news. Like Diego and Christina before her, she knew a pregnancy was a possibility, but they all assumed that it would not happen. Lilli was too young, too innocent. They all knew, too, that the chance of a pregnancy during forced relations was generally about one percent. It couldn't happen. But somehow it did. Somehow, too, they all felt guilty for keeping the news of the initial attack from Lilli's family. Not only would they now have to tell her mother and her grandparents about the pregnancy, but they would also have to tell them about how it occurred.

Would it have been better or easier if they had told Lilli's family about the attack sooner? Would that knowledge have made receiving the news of the pregnancy more bearable? Could they have done anything? Would it have changed the outcome?

First, Diego and Christina debated these questions; then, Diego and Doña Santiago had a similar conversation.

"I have to tell my husband now," she said finally. "We can't keep this a secret from him. We may have to tell Padre Roberto too. We need help here." And Diego agreed, so they told Don Santiago that evening, and Diego went directly from the Santiago's house to tell Padre Roberto.

When Padre Roberto heard the news, he was surprised but not overwhelmed like the others. During his 20-plus years in Golfito, he had heard many terrible stories, and he had assisted those in need in the best way that he knew how. He asked Diego to join him in prayer immediately. And in his prayer, he thanked God for His presence in this situation, and he asked God for His assistance. The humble priest admitted that he was powerless to do anything without God, and he asked God to guide them all through this difficult circumstance.

As Padre Roberto prayed, Diego felt a peace come over him, one he had never felt before in his life and certainly nothing like what he had experienced just 10 minutes earlier when he and Doña Santiago revealed the secret to her husband. Neither Diego nor Padre Roberto knew what would happen in the days ahead, but both of them felt confident that God would help them all.

On the following Sunday, a bright, sunny morning, everyone in this new, small group gathered at church for Sunday Mass. Padre Roberto, of course, was up front celebrating the Mass. The Santiago family sat in their normal spot on the left, near the front, with Lilli, whose family had remained at home. Diego and Christina arrived 10 minutes late because they had taken the bus from their apartments, and the bus stalled and would not start again, so they had to walk the final half mile.

When the service was over, they all chatted with other parishioners for a short time before Padre Roberto motioned for them to join him up front, and he escorted them to the small area behind the sanctuary where he kept his vestments. Christina volunteered to take the Santiago children for a short walk while the other adults met with Lilli. Then, Padre Roberto spoke first.

"Lilli, why don't you and Doña Santiago sit here on this bench." As they did so, the other two men – Diego and Samuel – shifted nervously while trying to appear calm. Then, Padre Roberto nodded to Doña Santiago, and she spoke next.

"Lilli, do you know why we're here?"

"I think I do," she replied, surprising all the men but not Doña Santiago. "I'm pregnant, right?"

"Yes, you are. How did you know?"

"Everything feels different. I am not the same."

"Do you feel okay?"

"I am nauseous sometimes, but that's all."

"Have you told your family yet?"

"No."

"How do you want to tell them? Alone or with one of us?"

"I don't want to tell them." At this, she began weeping softly, but she continued. "I want to move away from here. I can't stay here."

Doña Santiago empathized with Lilli, and rather than contradict her, she prodded Lilli to see if she had any other options.

"Where would you go? Do you have any other family?"

Lilli cried even more, shook her head "No," and buried her face in her hands.

"There, there," Doña Santiago said. "We're going to help you, Lilli. We all love you and care for you, and we're going to help you through this."

Then, they all waited and allowed Lilli to express her sadness and her pain. Doña Santiago held on to her, and Diego and Samuel waited for Padre Roberto to speak again. Through their nervousness, they both felt confident he would know what to say and do next. Before he spoke, though, Padre Roberto also sat down next to Lilli. He gently lifted Lilli's chin toward him, so they could make eye contact. Then, he took her hands in his and spoke to her softly.

"Lilli, you don't remember this, of course, but I recall when your mother and father were pregnant with you. They were so young and nervous, and the families came to me first, and I told your mother at that point the same thing I'm going to tell you today. This child you are carrying is a gift from God. The circumstances under which you got pregnant are not ideal, not what you wanted or expected. But even though your birth and the future birth of this child were not planned by your parents or by you, both you and this child in your womb are part of God's plan. God knows you and your child, and He will not abandon you. He will watch over you, take care of you, and provide for you. God has also asked all of us to walk alongside you through this difficult time, and we will do that with you."

Just as Diego had felt a peace come over him three days earlier when Padre Roberto had prayed for Lilli, Lilli immediately felt that same peace come over her. Her God in heaven would oversee her situation; all she had to do was persevere. And she would persevere with Padre Roberto and Don and Doña Santiago and with Christina and Diego. And once her mother and her grandparents knew the truth about everything, they would be there for her too. Everything would be okay, including her baby.

"Maybe we should go tell my family now," Lilli said.

Padre Roberto agreed and asked, "Who do you want with you?"

"Would you come with me, Padre?"

"*Sí. Absolumente.*"

"And Doña Santiago, would you come too?"

"*Sí por supuesto.*"

Then, Lilli looked at Diego and Don Santiago and spoke as if apologizing to them. "I think any more people would be too many for our little home."

Both Diego and Samuel nodded. They understood. "I'll take the kids home," Samuel added, "and feed them lunch."

So Lilli, Padre Roberto, and Doña Santiago walked up to Lilli's house. When they arrived, Lilli's grandfather was reading

La Nacion, the San Jose newspaper, in the living room, and his wife and daughter were in the kitchen, cleaning up the dishes from lunch. One place setting, Lilli's, remained, and her food was hidden under a pan cover to keep it warm and fresh.

"Oh, Lilli, you were later than expected so – "

Lilli's mother stopped speaking when she realized Lilli was not alone. And when she realized that Padre Roberto and Doña Santiago were with Lilli, she remained silent and became frightened. She remembered immediately her own moment of fear 17 years earlier.

Her mother, however, Lilli's grandmother, remained oblivious to the reality that was about to hit her, and she welcomed the guests into her home.

"Please come in. It's a beautiful day, isn't it?" Then, she spoke to her husband. "Don Pedro, come here. We have guests."

Lilli's grandfather was also surprised but not apprehensive. The two people with his granddaughter, Padre Roberto and Doña Santiago, were two of the friendliest people in town, and he assumed they were there for a good reason, perhaps to announce a new project at church or to ask for help in some kind of upcoming festival.

"Yes, please come in and sit down." Then, Lilli's grandfather began pulling out the chairs from the table, so they could do so.

Lilli sat down near her plate of food but remained silent as Padre Roberto and Doña Santiago greeted everyone and commented on the weather and purposely stood on both sides of Lilli.

"Padre Roberto, may I get you a drink, a lemonade, perhaps, or a cup of coffee?" Lilli's grandmother asked.

"No, thank you," he answered, and he encouraged everyone to sit down. Lilli's grandfather sat in his chair at the head of the table with his wife opposite him. Padre Roberto and Doña Santiago pulled the nearby chairs to the table and sat next to Lilli who sat opposite her mother.

Padre Roberto sat between Lilli and her grandfather, and when everyone was settled and silent, he nodded to Lilli. With her hands clasped in front of her and with her fingers intertwined, she looked directly across at her mother first, then to her right and to her left before she spoke: "Mother, grandmother, grandfather – I'm going to have a baby."

No one moved; no one said a word. Lilli's mother looked at her daughter and felt torn. She wanted to embrace her immediately, but she knew her own father would be disappointed, perhaps even angry, so she sat frozen – her worst fear confirmed.

Padre Roberto and Doña Santiago both realized immediately that they had made a mistake. They should have told Lilli's mom first, alone, so she could comfort her daughter in her duress, and together, they could tell Lilli's grandparents later. In their haste, they failed to see the bigger family dynamic.

Fortunately, Lilli's grandmother understood that dynamic perfectly, and despite the approaching storm she expected from her husband, she rallied to the side of her only granddaughter, a now trembling, frightened, young girl with tears on her cheeks. Doña Santiago stood, so Lilli's grandmother could sit and embrace the 17-year-old and the baby inside her. And encouraged by her mother's courage, Lilli's mother also stood and joined the embrace, four generations of this family wrapped together as one.

At that point, Lilli's grandfather erupted. "That's it. Out. Everyone out. Padre Roberto. Doña Santiago. I'm sorry, but you must leave now. This is my family, my problem. I will handle it."

Doña Santiago was shocked. Padre Roberto was not. He had known Lilli's grandfather for a long time, and he had expected some kind of outburst, though the intensity and the immediacy were heightened. So rather than making it worse by trying to stay, he escorted Doña Santiago out the door with him, and he offered their help at any time, if needed.

After they left, Don Pedro insisted on knowing everything.

"Who is the boy who did this to you? When were you together? We must meet his family."

He assumed, of course, that Lilli had a boyfriend. He would insist on a quick marriage, and Lilli would go live with the boy's family. He would not be embarrassed again.

When Lilli revealed the details of her pregnancy, his anger only intensified. In his outburst, he screamed a word not often heard in the mostly Catholic homes of Costa Rican families: *aborto.*

The three women were shocked and speechless. He could not be serious. Disappointed? Yes. Angry? Yes. Frustrated? Of course. But abortion? No. That could not be.

"Let's go upstairs," Lilli's grandmother said to her daughter and granddaughter. She knew better than to argue with her husband when he reacted in this way. If he were left alone, he might calm down. He might reconsider. Then, as a family, not just Don Pedro alone, they could decide what to do.

Determined to act immediately, Lilli's grandfather left the house and visited the same man he had consulted 17 years earlier. Lilli's father walked immediately to the thin strip of bars near the movie theater. Though not a regular drinker, when living with three women became too much for him, he did periodically enjoy escaping to the bars. He wouldn't overindulge. Rather, he would simply sit at the bar, gradually sip a beer or two, talk to whomever was present, and enjoy the masculine presence of those who visited regularly or of the visitors who were in port.

On this particular Sunday afternoon, the bar wasn't even half full. Don Pedro recognized most of the regulars, and he noticed a table full of light-haired Europeans who he assumed were part of the banana boat being loaded in port. As he drank his first beer, he talked to no one and simply pondered his current situation. He was almost 60 years old and feeling it. Though his office job at the hospital wasn't that strenuous, he had begun to feel the normal aches of aging, especially in his back. He wanted to retire soon, and like some people he had known, he wanted to move to San Jose. There, he and his wife could buy a small house, live near the bus line, and enjoy a simple life away from the stifling heat of Golfito, the town of his birth and a town he had come to detest. He wanted something new and different, and San Jose, nestled on a plateau in the Cordillera Mountain Range, called to him as convincingly as Florida called to the senior citizens who had grown up in the cold northeastern United States.

If his granddaughter were allowed to have this baby, he felt he could never retire or move. He would be looking at another 15 to 20 years of child support, and he worried that he might have another female in his home. And even if Lilli's baby were a boy, he feared even more that the son of an American father would look too much like an American and remind him – and his neighbors – of the embarrassment that Lilli had brought to his family.

Don Pedro was in the midst of this mild depression when Don Eduardo walked in. Since Eduardo was the bar's owner, Don Pedro had seen him there many times before. And though they were not close friends by any measure, Don Pedro knew Eduardo because everyone in Golfito knew Eduardo. Eduardo was the one man in town who knew how to get things and how to get things done, legally or otherwise – mostly otherwise. In fact, Eduardo had approached Don Pedro with the offer of an abortion 17 years earlier, and Eduardo had also provided other connections for Don Pedro a few times through the years.

Once, for example, Don Pedro had wanted to give his wife a nice ring for their anniversary, but he didn't have enough money. So, he discreetly asked Eduardo if he knew anyone who sold "discounted" jewelry. Naturally, Eduardo knew everyone in town who sold stolen goods, and Don Pedro paid half the value of the ring's worth.

A few years later, one of Don Pedro's American supervisors had asked him if he knew anyone who sold cocaine. Don Pedro saw a small opportunity for himself in that situation and told his supervisor that he did, indeed, know someone, but that he would require a finder's fee for himself. This American, who was both rich and desperate, paid that fee freely and willingly when Don Pedro introduced him to Eduardo. In fact, three months later when that American was caught and arrested and sent back to the States, Don Pedro worried that he would be implicated, though that never happened.

Don Pedro recalled some of these experiences while he waited for Eduardo to settle in. Typically, on these visits to his bar, Eduardo greeted most of the customers and checked in with his employees before sitting at his special corner table where he often conducted his "business" deals. Since that particular Sunday afternoon was rather slow, he actually sat alone for 10 to 15 minutes drinking a beer and eating banana chips before Don Pedro approached him with his own beer in one hand and a fresh bottle for Eduardo in the other.

"Don Eduardo," Don Pedro said with some hesitancy. "May I offer you a drink and sit with you for a bit?"

The big man shook his head "yes" and shook Don Pedro's hand, as well, when he offered the beer.

"*Como esta?*" Don Eduardo asked.

"*Muy bien,*" answered Don Pedro, though he was anything but "very well."

"*Gracias para la cerveza,*" Eduardo added as he polished off his own beer and began to drink the one Don Pedro had brought him.

Don Pedro nodded his head and said quietly, "*Yo tengo una problema.*"

"Tell me all about your problem, and I will try to help you."

Chapter 36

Within ten minutes, a tentative plan had been made. Eduardo knew a man who lived on the side of the bay opposite the port, and this man could perform the procedure. He was from England, Eduardo said, and people in Golfito actually referred to him as "Doctor Tom" because he cultivated various plants and herbs that could be used medicinally in addition to other plants that were used for recreational purposes. Even Diego, who had lived in Golfito for less than a year, had heard Doctor Tom's story.

Doctor Tom had come to Golfito from England 12 years earlier after he had been strongly encouraged by the authorities there to leave his homeland or face serious consequences. One of Tom's many worldwide contacts had told Tom about this isolated town with ideal working conditions: a vast, fertile, growing area with a nearby port and airport. Doctor

Tom used his previous earnings to buy 20 acres of land and to build a home there. He also bought a small motorboat to ferry him and his products across the bay when needed.

The local police pretty much ignored Doctor Tom because he lived far enough away from the town itself and because so few people ever complained about his activities. Many of Tom's customers, after all, were those sailors and workers who visited the port only periodically when their ships were in town or the nearby American workers who could afford to purchase Tom's somewhat expensive medicines.

The tentative plan called for Don Pedro to bring Lilli to the port on the assigned day, and the two of them would be driven to Tom's place in a small motorboat, one even smaller than the one Tom owned.

"Can't we just walk there by taking the path around the inlet?" Don Pedro asked. "I'd rather we didn't have to walk through the port where everyone can see us."

Don Eduardo consented. "*Sí*, you can walk over there – it will take about an hour – but you don't want to walk back because your granddaughter may not feel well at that point. So . . . ." Don Pedro waited as Don Eduardo pondered the situation. "So, here's what we'll do after the procedure is completed. I'll have my guy with the boat bring you home."

"Okay," Don Pedro agreed. Before he left the bar, Don Pedro also agreed to Eduardo's price, and they arranged to meet again to set up all the final details.

Lilli's mother and grandmother knew Don Pedro had a plan because he came home somewhat calm and composed. He wasn't drunk either, as sometimes happened when he visited the strip of nearby *cantinas*, and he was no longer angry.

When Don Pedro's wife asked him where he had been and what he had done, he refused to give her any details. Like a young, petulant school boy, he answered only that he had been "out" and that he had done "nothing."

Naturally, the women worried for Lilli's safety and the safety of the baby, so they agreed that one of them would be with Lilli at all times. Lilli's grandmother would walk to school with Lilli in the morning, and Lilli's mother would adjust her work schedule, so she could walk Lilli home. Lilli, of course, would not want to be babied in this way, but she would consent, especially when they told her that Don Pedro might try to arrange an abortion.

"*Aborto?*"

Just the sound of the word frightened Lilli; yet, it also intrigued her. Her life would be so much easier if this pregnancy went away. She could be an innocent, young girl again. She could follow through on her plans to move to San Jose and study at the University. She could meet a handsome, young man who was also serious about his education, one who wanted to be a doctor, perhaps, or a lawyer, not a laborer who loaded and unloaded boxcars and not someone who worked for the Company that controlled so much of life in Golfito.

Lilli's long-range thoughts and dreams disappeared, though, whenever she found herself kneeling over the toilet in the early morning darkness or when she could feel activity inside her womb. That movement wasn't the baby exactly – the baby was still too small for that – but just the way her body reacted at certain moments during the day. During these latter moments, when Lilli imagined this child coming to life inside of her, she knew she would never consent to an abortion, no matter what her grandfather said.

Lilli also daydreamed often about the child. She imagined a dark-haired and light-skinned child like herself with a big smile and bright, beautiful teeth. Lilli had always been a bit self-conscious about her own teeth because they were a bit too big for her small mouth. As a result, she often covered her mouth when she smiled. Her own child, however, she imagined as perfect in every way.

"Maria," Lilli would call her, named after Mary, the mother of Christ. Maria would be alert and happy at all times. She would giggle when Lilli tickled her, and she would reach out and hug Lilli often. Lilli would sing to Maria, and Maria would softly repeat the key words. When Maria was older and could walk on her own, the two of them would explore the paths and gardens nearby, just as Lilli had done with her own mother.

From her experience as a babysitter, Lilli knew, of course, that even her baby would fuss and cry and be miserable at times, but Lilli didn't see any of that in her daydreams. She saw only the wonderful moments and magical experiences that a mother and child should experience together.

In her innocence, Lilli also failed to see how coldhearted her grandfather could be. She had always viewed him as simply an old man who wasn't motivated to do much. Yes, he went to work every day to provide for his family, but at the end of the day, all he wanted to do was eat a warm meal immediately and then settle into his wooden rocking chair where he would slowly drink one beer, read the paper, and think about retiring and moving to San Jose.

So on that Thursday afternoon a week later when her grandfather showed up at school just before the last class of the day, Lilli, though surprised and though she had been warned by her mother and grandmother, trusted him and believed what he said.

"Your mother fainted at work and maybe broke her arm," he told Lilli and the school authorities. "She's in the hospital now for tests, and she would like to see you."

"Oh, my God! Is she okay?"

"Let's go."

Chapter 37

Lilli gave her books to her friend Eugenia and asked her to hold them for her. Then, she walked quickly with her grandfather from the school toward the nearby hospital. Before they reached the hospital, however, Lilli's grandfather slowed down when they arrived at an opening in the brush alongside the main road. A muscular young man, who was only slightly older than Lilli, a man she had never seen before, emerged from the brush, and Lilli's grandfather explained what was about to happen.

"Lilli," he said sternly, as the young man walked behind her and put his hands on her arms just below the shoulders. "You are not going to have this baby."

Lilli began crying in fear immediately.

Her grandfather continued. "The three of us are going to take a walk. You will not fight or argue or attempt to run. At the end of our walk, you will have a minor medical procedure. When it's finished, you will no longer be pregnant."

"But, but – "

"No. You will not speak. You will do as I tell you. I am your grandfather. Now, let's go. Walk alongside me."

The other man let go of Lilli's shoulders and pushed her from behind, not strongly enough to knock her over but firmly enough, so she would begin moving. Though feeling as if she were in a trance, one she did not at all comprehend, Lilli began walking. She moved so slowly, though, that her grandfather grabbed her right arm and dragged her a bit to make her match his speed. When she resisted, the other man grabbed her left hand and began to do the same.

"We will drag you there if we have to," her grandfather said sternly. "If you cooperate, you can walk on your own, but if you don't cooperate . . . ."

His words trailed off. Obviously, he couldn't speak the words he was thinking, and Lilli began to imagine what might happen to her as well as to her baby if she didn't do as he said.

As they walked, Eugenia sat in her history class and began looking through the notebooks Lilli had asked her to hold. The first one she opened was a history notebook with all the same notes Eugenia had in her own notebook. The second notebook, though, was Lilli's journal where she still recorded her daily thoughts and observations. As the girl read, she began to learn a bit about Lilli's family, and one line, written only two days earlier, frightened her into action: "My mother and my grandmother say that I should not be alone with Grandpa."

Immediately, Eugenia asked her teacher's permission to go to the bathroom, and when permitted to do so, she left the school and sprinted to the nearby restaurant where Lilli's mother worked. When Lilli's mom realized what might be happening, she told her boss she had to use the phone to make an emergency call.

"Padre Roberto," she screamed into the phone when he picked up at the rectory. "I think father has taken Lilli from school."

"Okay," he answered quickly. "I'll try to get out there before anything happens." They both knew where Don Pedro would take Lilli, so Padre Roberto hopped in his four-wheel Jeep and headed out. He didn't want to go alone, though, so he drove quickly to the grade school where Diego was teaching basketball that day and where the janitor, Juan Pablo, was sweeping.

"Get in. Both of you." he ordered. "Lilli's in danger." Stunned for a second, both Diego and Juan Pablo hesitated. "Now! We have to go now."

Juan Pablo threw down his broom, and Diego told the boys to keep playing. Diego then hopped in the front seat, and Juan Pablo climbed in back. Padre Roberto drove faster than he had ever driven before in his life. As he did so, he quickly explained to Diego and Juan Pablo what was going on. "This won't be dangerous because Doctor Tom won't fight us, but we have to get there before he begins."

Though the path to Doctor Tom's house was mainly a walking path, it was big enough for the Jeep to squeeze through. The drive took them almost 10 minutes, and as they reached the clearing that opened up to Doctor Tom's house, they could all see three figures approaching the house.

"*Gracias a Dios*," Padre Roberto exclaimed when he saw them, knowing that they had arrived just in time.

Diego and Juan Pablo jumped out quickly and put themselves between Lilli's grandfather and the young man. Surprised by what had happened, and so quickly, the young man looked to Don Pedro to see what he wanted him to do. At the same time, Padre Roberto exited the Jeep, and Doctor Tom appeared at the rear door of his home, startled by the noise of the Jeep.

"Padre Roberto, this is none of your business," Don Pedro shouted. "This is my family, my business."

Diego and Juan Pablo were already escorting Lilli to the Jeep.

"What's going on out here?" Doctor Tom asked when he got closer to all of the others.

"I think you know what's going on," Padre Roberto replied, "and if you try to touch that young girl, you will have a major problem on your hands."

Not wanting to jeopardize his own life or his livelihood, Doctor Tom backed off immediately.

"We had a deal," Don Pedro exclaimed. "You have my money."

"Sorry, Old Man. You better talk to Don Eduardo. I'm out," and he walked back to his house, leaving the others to resolve their differences.

"That girl will not live in my house. She is no longer family to me."

"Don Pedro," Padre Roberto began. "Please understand – "

"Don't you tell me what to do with my family."

"But – "

"You've never had a wife or a child. You know nothing."

Diego left Lilli in the Jeep with Juan Pablo and returned to Padre Roberto.

"*Vamonos*," Padre Roberto said when he realized that Lilli's grandfather was not to be reasoned with. Meanwhile, the young man who had fulfilled his task and had prevented Lilli from running away from her grandfather also decided to abandon Don Pedro. The young man walked to the beach where he would wait for Eduardo's motorboat to bring him back to town. When the Jeep drove off, Don Pedro was left completely alone, cursing aloud and feeling totally overwhelmed by what had just happened to him.

In the Jeep, Lilli was crying in the back seat where Diego tried to comfort her. "Let's bring her to the clinic," he said to Padre Roberto, "to make sure she is okay."

"Not yet. We first need to bring her home, so her mother and her grandmother can see that she is safe. There, she can gather her things, and she will have to move. You heard her grandfather."

Lilli began crying even more.

"Where will she live?" Juan Pablo asked.

"I don't know," Padre Roberto answered. "I don't know."

Everyone pondered that question as they drove back to town. Obviously, Lilli could not live alone, but her only other family members – her mother and her grandmother – lived in the house she now had to leave.

Would the families of any of Lilli's friends consider allowing Lilli to live with them? Perhaps, but most of those families lived nearby, and that would be too difficult for everyone.

When the group reached Lilli's house, they explained the situation, and both elder females began packing Lilli's possessions immediately. They wanted to protect her by moving her out before her grandfather returned. So even though Lilli's next destination was not yet decided upon, everyone agreed that she was not safe at home.

Lilli's possessions were mostly clothes, school books, and magazines. Diego and Juan Pablo carried two large banana boxes to the Jeep and set them in the small storage area behind the back seat. Juan Pablo, knowing that Lilli's mother would want to go to the clinic with her daughter, offered to walk back to the school, so Padre Roberto and Diego could drive Lilli and her mother to see Christina at the clinic.

During the entire reunion with her family and during the packing of her possessions, Lilli had remained in the back seat of the Jeep, directly behind the driver's seat. She had stopped crying and looked up periodically when others tried to comfort her, but mostly, she kept her head down with her hands over her eyes. Like her grandfather, she, too, was overwhelmed by what had just happened to her.

As they drove to the clinic, Diego had asked aloud, "Do you think we should ask Christina if Lilli can live with her – at least temporarily?"

"That's actually a good idea." Padre Roberto replied. And Lilli's mom, who had never met Christina but had heard about her from Lilli, reacted positively as well, and asked, "Do you think she would allow that?"

"I do," said Diego. "Lilli, what do you think of that idea?"

Sniffling just a bit, Lilli consented by softly and silently shaking her head "Yes."

Chapter 38

When they arrived at the clinic, Christina was talking to two older women, but that conversation was more social than medical, so Diego interrupted them and pulled Christina aside.

"I hate to put you on the spot like this, but Lilli needs a place to stay; can you put her up for tonight?"

"She can stay for as long as she wants," Christina answered. "In fact, we can borrow a cot from the clinic. Where is she now?"

Diego pointed to the nearby Jeep, and Christina responded by giving him the key to her apartment. "Why don't you bring her there now, and I will come by in about twenty minutes."

"Okay, that sounds good. I can bring her stuff over there, but can you also see her now and make sure that she's okay? She had a rough afternoon."

"Absolutely. Bring her in."

By then, the two older women who had been talking to Christina realized that she had someone who actually needed care at that moment, so they said their good-byes and ambled off.

Diego and Lilli's mom escorted Lilli from the Jeep to the clinic, and Padre Roberto entered as well to thank Christina for her generosity. After Diego brought Christina up to date on what had happened, he and Padre Roberto left Christina and Lilli's mom to care for Lilli, and they brought Lilli's possessions to Christina's apartment.

Christina spent almost an hour with Lilli, talking to her first about what had happened that afternoon and then examining her to make sure that the stress of the day's events and the exertion of the forced walk out to Doctor Tom's house had not harmed her or the baby in any way. Lilli's mom remained with Lilli throughout the examination, so she witnessed firsthand the gentle touch and the patience of the kind American nurse. By the time they finished, Lilli's mom felt confident leaving her daughter with Christina, and she began to worry not about Lilli but about her own situation at home with her father.

"Do you think he will force you to leave as well?" Christina asked Lilli's mom as they prepared to leave the clinic.

"No. Probably not. My rent money helps him to pay his bills, and I think he knows that I do most of the housework now, especially the cooking and the cleaning. My mother is not as strong now or as capable as she used to be. He may not be happy with me, but I don't think he will kick me out."

When the three women exited the examination room, they found Diego waiting for them, and all three women – Lilli included – assured him that Lilli was okay. Padre Roberto had returned home, but before he left, he and Diego had purchased some food, so Diego and the three women walked to Christina's apartment for dinner. Diego carried the borrowed cot from the clinic and squeezed it into the bedroom, and within 10 minutes after eating, Lilli went to Christina's bed and fell asleep immediately.

As Lilli slept, Diego, Christina, and Lilli's mom ate rice and beans and discussed everything that had happened and tried to plan for the days and weeks ahead. They decided that Lilli would not go to school for the next two days, Friday and Saturday, and during the upcoming weekend, they would try to determine what to do next.

Before leaving and returning by bus to her home, Lilli's mom said she would contact the school about Lilli's future absences. Diego offered to go home with her, but she reassured him that it would not be necessary. Diego knew Lilli would be safe with Christina, so before he walked Lilli's mom to the bus stop and returned to his own apartment, he told Christina he would check in on them the following morning.

At about 8:00 a.m., Diego arrived with fresh bread he had purchased from the nearby bakery and with oranges he had purchased from a street vendor. When he entered, Lilli and Christina were both awake and sipping coffee at Christina's small kitchen table. Though Lilli generally loved school, she was pleasantly relieved to know that no one would expect her to attend for a few days.

"You were right," Lilli said to Christina when Diego showed up with the food. "How did you know he would bring food for breakfast?"

"He's done that a few times for me since I've been here."

"I can make orange juice if you'd like," Lilli offered, desperately wanting to help those who had helped her.

So while she cut the oranges and began squeezing them and while Diego cut the bread, Christina spoke to Diego: "I already told Lilli that she didn't have to go to school for a few days. I also told her that she could just stay here and read or study, or if she wanted, she could spend part of the day at the clinic."

"Like an assistant?" Diego asked.

"Like an assistant," Christina repeated.

"Did you decide what you want to do?" Diego asked Lilli.

"Yes. I would like to stay here this morning, if that's okay, and do my schoolwork and go to the clinic with Christina this afternoon."

Diego and Christina agreed that Lilli would be safe there as long as she kept the door locked until Christina returned for her at lunch time. Lilli secretly looked forward to her time alone because she had so rarely been left completely alone in her own home.

Lilli spent that Friday as planned, and her mother visited her that evening to talk to her about her schooling. Lilli's mom had visited the school and explained the situation to Lilli's teachers, and they agreed that since Lilli was such a good student, she could continue her studies without actually attending classes each day. However, they did request that Lilli visit the school one day per week, so she could turn in her work, take tests, and meet with her teachers as needed. To spare Lilli the difficulty of having to appear in front of her peers, they said

Lilli could arrive during the late morning and take care of whatever needed to be done and then leave before classes let out in the afternoon.

Lilli was pleased with the arrangement because she feared the taunting of her classmates, and she also hoped she could continue to live with Christina for as long as possible. And when that subject came up for discussion, Christina affirmatively repeated what she had said earlier: "She can stay for as long as she wants."

"You must allow me to pay you for her rent then and give you some money for her food," Lilli's mother insisted.

"I'm sure we can work that out."

So by Saturday, Lilli felt totally at home in Christina's apartment, and Christina felt comfortable with Lilli there because Christina had already grown to love the sweet, young, pregnant *Tica.* Christina felt, too, like she was back in college again, with a roommate, someone with whom she could share her day's adventures.

Within a week, Diego replaced the cot with a single bed, and Lilli would spend the remaining months of her pregnancy sharing the bedroom and the apartment with Christina. Lilli easily kept up with her schoolwork, and she discovered that her weekly visits on Wednesdays were not as difficult as she had anticipated. Her teachers were all supportive and encouraging, and when she did bump into classmates – both male and female – they were kind and considerate as well. Having been a daily part of that school environment previously, Lilli knew that many students were probably talking negatively about her and her situation, but in her brief meetings with them, they did not scorn her or criticize her; they merely asked her how she felt, admired the growth in her womb, and wished her well.

Medically, Lilli's situation was also stable. Unlike many pregnant women, the first months or so of her pregnancy had been only mildly uncomfortable, as she hid her pregnancy from her family until she was forced to tell them the truth. The next few months, however, were a bit more difficult. She was nauseous each morning, and she usually threw up. Fortunately, she did not have to go to school, nor was she alone. Christina was always nearby to assist her if needed and to talk her through the most difficult mornings.

"This is your baby telling you that she's growing just a bit every day," Christina told her. "This is your baby saying 'Mama, I can't wait to see you. Please take good care of me. My fingers are growing, and I can't wait to wrap them around your fingers when we meet. And my arms are growing too, so I can reach out to you and hug you. And my legs are getting longer, so I can walk with you when I get older.'"

Christina had never given so much thought to the birth process before, but when she saw the tears in Lilli's eyes and the pain on her face each morning as Lilli experienced her daily sickness, Christina felt she had to do something to encourage Lilli and help her through. Lilli, of course, loved Christina even more for her gentle care and encouragement, and she thought about naming the baby after this young American Peace Corps Volunteer.

Chapter 39

As Lilli gradually established a comfortable routine for herself, Diego began his work with the high-school basketball team. When he posted signs at the school for tryouts, only nine boys showed up. As a result, Diego had to step in and play alongside them, so they could have a normal scrimmage with five players to a side. Diego didn't mind at all because he loved playing, and he also felt that he could be even more effective as an instructor by playing. For instead of yelling or trying to teach from the sideline, he was in the midst of the action. By example, he could demonstrate how to give up on an open shot from 15 feet away and pass to a teammate who had an even better shot from 10 feet away or less. Similarly, by his hustle and his determination, he could actually show his players what it meant to play aggressive defense and to properly box out to secure a rebound.

After a few practices, though, when one or two players failed to show up for various reasons, Diego realized he definitely needed more players. He would have to recruit.

"Why aren't more guys trying out for the team?" Diego asked the teachers at the high school.

"Their parents won't let them," they all replied. "Many parents here place so much emphasis on education that they don't want their children to be distracted by other activities."

As a teacher himself, Diego understood perfectly the parents' point of view, but he also understood the educational value of sports and teamwork. So, next, he began talking to certain athletes he thought might be interested, and he asked them if they would be willing to play if their parents consented. Most said "Yes" immediately, so Diego visited their homes and spoke to their parents.

One by one, Diego convinced the parents to allow their children to play. Assuming that the fathers would be easier to convince than the mothers, Diego approached them first. He found out from the boys where their fathers worked, and he waited for them and walked home with them. Two of the three fathers agreed easily, and even the third, the one Diego had heard would be the most resistant, agreed before he reached his home. All three of the men respected Diego for talking to them first and also for his willingness to visit the entire family later on.

Diego had been in Costa Rica long enough to know that the culture was extremely *macho*, and even if some husbands and fathers were not as strong as the stereotype, they didn't want anyone outside the home to know that.

Part two of Diego's plan was to win over the mothers as well, so the fathers could make the final positive decision without having to upset or distress anyone. So when Diego arrived at each home, he brought fresh flowers for the mothers and a bottle of wine for the parents to enjoy together. Then, rather than ask the question immediately, Diego patiently met with the entire family, listened to their stories, and sometimes remained to enjoy a meal with them. By the time the subject of basketball came up, Diego had already invested three or four hours, and the mothers usually responded by speaking to their husbands with a comment something like the following: "It sounds like a good idea; what do you think?"

Within two weeks, Diego had increased his roster from nine to 12, and the team was practicing three days a week after school. At that point, of course, Diego had to give up his role as player-coach and focus solely on the teaching aspects of the game. Fortunately, by then, Diego's original nine players had learned and accepted the hustling style of play that Diego wanted, and the three newcomers bought into it fully. By then, too, the team members were actually tired of playing against themselves and were ready for some different competition. Thus, Diego set up their first game against a team of men who had graduated from high school within the previous two to three years but who were also still interested in playing. These were the same men who visited the outdoor court near the port every evening, and the first game between the two teams was a great workout for everyone and a great entertainment for the local townspeople.

The game was scheduled for a Wednesday night at 7:00, and people began talking about it from the moment it was scheduled almost a week earlier. All the high-school kids were excited because these types of activities, so common in the United States and even in the bigger cities in Costa Rica, were so rare in the small town of Golfito. The townspeople were excited, too, because the rainy season had finally come to an end, and the people were looking forward to coming out again in the evening for walks or other activities. This mid-week game was a perfect social activity for everyone.

Since Golfito didn't have an electric scoreboard or a clock, Diego had to improvise, and he also had to find someone to referee the game and to keep score. Padre Roberto agreed to be the timer and scorekeeper, and Don Eduardo, the same Don Eduardo who had arranged for the abortion, agreed to referee. Though the two men were at opposite ends of the Golfito spectrum in terms of good and evil, both were equally respected in the world of basketball. Padre Roberto had actually played college basketball at his small seminary outside Philadelphia, and

Don Eduardo had all kinds of informal yet international experience during his years as a sailor and as a businessman.

When the game tipped off at 7:10 on that Wednesday night, the court was surrounded by fans and onlookers. The real fans and those connected to the players had arrived early with their own chairs, and they surrounded the court on both sides with a few more along the baselines. The high-school students stood and filled in behind the seated fans, and those who were simply passing by during their evening walk watched from beyond the baselines or from a distance on the small hill that sloped upward away from the sideline opposite the adjacent soccer field and stadium. Some of the younger fans, those who were in elementary school, even climbed the few nearby trees and sat on the branches or squeezed in among the adults.

When the first quarter began, the high-school kids were full of energy and raced off to a 12-point lead with aggressive full-court pressure and quick, easy baskets off turnovers and fast breaks. They were jumping and congratulating one another as if they had just won the national championship. While Diego was more than pleased with their efforts, he had witnessed enough basketball in his short life to know that few games ended that quickly or that easily, especially when a man's pride was at stake.

The older players called a few time-outs to regroup and refocus and also to slow down the frenetic, early pace. Those older men, most of whom worked all day, either in the port or in the fields, knew that they couldn't run with the youngsters, so they felt they had to be more aggressive and more calculated. Thus, the game gradually switched from a free and wild horse race in the early going to more of a physical and deliberate chess match. The older guys couldn't catch up immediately, but by the end of the second quarter, they had reduced the lead to five points, and they had also reduced the boys' early enthusiasm.

The men, though not playing dirty, were holding a bit on the defensive end and pushing a lot underneath as they battled for rebounds. This assertive play slowed down the speed of the boys and also drained some of their energy. Though the young men became frustrated and complained to their coach and to the referee, Don Eduardo didn't call many fouls because he knew the game demanded a certain amount of physical contact, and even Padre Roberto and Diego acknowledged that things were not out of control. "Just calm down, and push back a bit without committing a foul," Diego said during the halftime break. "Don't get frustrated; get tough. Show them your strength and your endurance. We have to play four quarters, not just two."

Padre Roberto visited both benches during the break to remind them of the score, and he thoroughly enjoyed what he was seeing. Like a ritualistic passage into manhood, the older men were testing the younger men, and the boys were responding with passion and fervor. The town was alive.

The third quarter resembled the end of the first half. The older men gradually reduced the deficit and even took the lead by three points. Then, the game became even more exciting because the older men could not increase their margin, and the lead alternated between the two sides. When the fourth quarter began, the score was tied.

At that point, Diego and many of the fans were torn. As the coach of the high-school boys, he naturally wanted them to succeed, but because he knew so many of the opponents, he also enjoyed watching them do well. In some ways, too, the game was a bit of a civil war because two sets of brothers competed against each other, and a set of cousins also fought for bragging rights within the town and within the family. The majority of the fans seemed evenly divided too. They cheered every basket, and because there was so much scoring compared to a soccer game, the crowd demonstrated a passion that in some ways exceeded the passion of the town's Sunday morning soccer games. No one would verbally express that sacrilegious thought, of course, not even Diego, but a neutral observer might ponder the idea.

The game remained close until the final minute. With no official clock available, the teams had to rely on Padre Roberto with his wristwatch to periodically call out the remaining time. "One minute," he announced loudly and clearly as the old guys brought the ball up the court for what they hoped would be the last possession and the final winning basket. The young men had just scored to take a one-point lead, so they hustled back on defense and instead of playing their normal man-to-man defense, Diego shouted to them to switch into a zone. Diego hoped that a switch in defense at that point would surprise the older men and cause confusion and perhaps a turnover. The move worked – but only temporarily.

The older men were stunned for a few seconds, but when they recognized the zone, they quickly passed the ball to their best shooter. Since he was more open than he had been during the entire game, he confidently shot the ball rather than wait for the time to run down. When his shot swished through the hoop, Diego called a time-out to set up what he now hoped would be the final possession.

"Forty seconds," Padre Roberto called out, and as the teams returned to the court, the fans of the older men began shouting "De-fense. De-fense," just as some of them had seen the Americans fans do on television.

Diego instructed his players to pass the ball on the perimeter until Padre Roberto called out "ten seconds." Then, Diego wanted one of his two guards, which ever one had the ball at that point, to drive to the basket and try for a layup. If he were open, he should shoot, and everyone else should rush in for the rebound in case he missed. But if he were not open, he was supposed to pass the ball to the corner where a teammate would hopefully have an open shot.

The play worked perfectly. Diego's number-one guard drove the ball to the right side of the hoop, and when three defensive players converged on him, he easily and quickly passed it to the corner where a confident teammate lofted a high, arching shot toward the rim. Everyone in the crowd inhaled and waited – and waited. The other offensive players, as instructed, pushed toward the rim just in case the ball bounced out. But it did not. The shot hit the far side of the rim, bounced high in the air, and then bounced against the other side of the rim before it settled into the net.

The young men went crazy, and half of the crowd cheered. The victorious players hugged each other and danced in celebration and yelled "Goooooooaaaaallllllll," just as the soccer players typically celebrated their scoring moments.

The older men, though, were not as impulsive. A few of them realized immediately that Padre Roberto had not yet blown the whistle for the end of the game. Their center grabbed the ball as it fell through the net, took it out of bounds as required, and passed it quickly to a teammate who was rushing toward midcourt. When the pass arrived, the receiver, knowing little time remained, instantly fired up a desperate heave. And as he let go of the ball, Padre Roberto blew his whistle, and again, everyone inhaled and waited.

"It's good if it goes," Padre Roberto shouted, and the shot, like its predecessor, hung in the air for a second or two before it caromed off the wooden backboard.

"Too strong," Diego thought when he saw the impact. "We win."

Amazingly, though, after the ball hit the backboard, the ball bounced back and hit the front of the rim, and then it spun around the circumference of the rim before it hung just on the front edge for just a fraction of a second – and dropped in.

Again, half of the crowd erupted. The older men began to dance at various spots on the court, and the young players, who had been dancing themselves just seconds earlier, fell to the ground in disbelief.

Diego, though disappointed, immediately went to his distraught players and encouraged them to get up. "You just played in one of the most exciting games I've ever seen," he said. "Now, let's go and congratulate the winners – and see if they'll play us again next week."

And so a weekly routine was established. Every Wednesday night during the dry season, the two teams gathered for a friendly competition. Though not all the players could make it every single week, the precedent had been set. If a young man were still in high school, he was eligible to play with the high-school team, but if he had graduated from high school or stopped attending classes there, he had to play with the older men. The games were usually close, but it took the young men four weeks before they could overcome their elders. Once that happened, the big crowds dwindled a bit, yet the games continued. And even on nights when Padre Roberto or Don Eduardo could not keep score or referee, others volunteered to help. And the popularity of the Wednesday-night games caused a ripple effect at the grade schools where Diego instructed the younger boys.

Previously, the grade-school boys groaned and complained whenever Diego made them go through drills for passing, shooting, or rebounding; all they really wanted to do was play games. As these young boys watched the games on Wednesday nights, however, they began to understand and appreciate the need to practice basic skills and to recognize the need for teamwork. When possible, Diego began to bring two of the high-school players with him to the grade schools. He had previously spoken to Don Mario about using the high-school boys as coaches or mentors to the younger boys. Don Mario realized it was a good idea, so the players who had a physical education class as their last class in the afternoon were excused from that class and allowed to meet Diego at the grade school where they helped him spread the gospel of basketball.

Diego gave these older boys lots of responsibility. He assigned each of them half of the young boys and half of the court. Then, he allowed them one hour to practice whatever basic skills they felt were most important for their teams. Then, during the second hour, the two teams squared off while Diego refereed and kept score. Naturally, the high-school boys used many of the same drills Diego had used with them, but they also devised their own drills or tweaked the ones that Diego used.

In addition, each of the high-school boys brought his own personality and skills to the task, and the grade-school boys, for the most part, respected their elders and looked up to them. Benardo, for example, was the shortest player on the high-school team, but he was a quick and efficient point guard who always encouraged the boys to pass the ball to the open shooter. He also had a quick wit and an outgoing personality, so he loved to tease the young players as they ran through their dribbling and passing drills.

At the other extreme was Fausto. He was one of the taller players on the high-school team, and his strengths were his defense and his rebounding. As a result, he pushed his players to always maintain proper defensive position and to box out the opponent before attempting to secure a rebound. He taught mostly by example, and he was somewhat stern compared to Benardo's outgoing and playful personality.

Since Diego always mixed up the teams, so the players would be exposed to different coaching styles each week, the camaraderie that developed between the young and the old was enjoyable for both parties. On the streets and during the games on Wednesdays, the middle-school boys would call out to the high-school boys when they saw them and cheer them on during the weekly competitions. Similarly, the high-school boys would look out for the younger boys in the neighborhoods and give them special attention before and after the games on Wednesday nights.

Chapter 40

Meanwhile, Lilli was gradually adjusting to her new life as a somewhat independent, pregnant, young woman. As the baby grew inside her womb, Lilli began to ignore and later forget the memories of how her child was created, and she began to focus, instead, on the baby that she would soon deliver into the world. During her weekly trips to school to turn in her assignments, Lilli would not only meet with her own teachers, but she also began to seek out other teachers who could help her understand what was going on in her body and how her baby was developing. These teachers had loved Lilli before she became pregnant because Lilli had always been such an ideal student. They loved her even more afterwards because of the way she had gradually come to embrace her pregnancy and educate herself about it. In fact, once these teachers recognized that Lilli thoroughly understood the workings of her body and easily grasped all the terminology, a couple of them suggested to Lilli that she might consider a career in the medical field. At that time and in that country, a medical career for a woman generally meant becoming a nurse, but Lilli's science teacher, Señora Morales, stepped over the line in Lilli's case and told her she could one day become a doctor.

"Seriously, Lilli, think about it," Señora Morales said. "You are an intelligent and mature, young woman. You have always had tremendous potential."

"But with a baby, how can I – " Lilli's words faded because she was unable to look that far ahead.

"Yes," Señora Morales continued, "your life right now seems so focused on today and on the day you will deliver this baby that you can't see beyond the next three months. But just because you become a mother doesn't mean your education has to end. In fact, you'll need even more of an education as a mother because you will have to care for both yourself and your baby."

A few afternoons a week, Lilli would also visit the clinic to see Christina and to offer what assistance she could. Lilli so desperately appreciated what Christina was doing for her that she wanted to repay this kindness with kindness of her own. So without being asked, Lilli would clean the clinic as much as she could, and she would look for other tasks that needed to be done while Christina was busy helping the patients who came to see her.

Some days, that meant Lilli spent time watching children who accompanied their parents to the clinic. On other days, Lilli unpacked medical shipments when they arrived and stocked the shelves. And every once in a while, Christina would ask Lilli to go into the examining room with her if she needed an extra set of hands. One day, for instance, Christina had to administer a shot to a young child, but the mother was not strong enough to hold the child down, so Lilli helped. At other times, Lilli would act as an assisting nurse during minor surgeries when Christina had to stitch up a patient's injury. Lilli even assisted at the births of three babies, two at the clinic and one at a woman's home. Lilli was fascinated by Christina's ability to calmly minister to the patient and also handle the medical situation.

"Maybe Señora Morales is right," Lilli thought. "Maybe I can work in the medical field. Maybe I could be a doctor someday."

After these experiences and these thoughts, Lilli and Christina would have long conversations about medicine and about how Lilli might pursue her career while still taking care of her baby. The formal studies and certification were far off, of course, but Christina emphasized to Lilli that her medical education was occurring every time she stepped into that clinic, and she told Lilli, too, how taking care of her own child would be part of that education as well.

"You could be a pediatrician some day," she told Lilli. "I have no doubt that God has amazing plans for you and for your life."

As Lilli's due date approached, her mother and her grandmother visited her more often. Lilli's grandfather was still angry, of course, and he still forbade them from seeing Lilli, but they disobeyed him discreetly. Initially, they visited Lilli weekly, and they did so separately. One would cover for the other, and they visited while he was at work or busy elsewhere. They often brought food for Lilli and Christina, and they also brought gifts for the baby. Within a few weeks of their secret visits, Lilli's grandfather realized what was going on. He did not, however, let on that he knew. He wanted, as much as possible, to retain the appearance of being in control, yet he had also experienced a certain softening in his heart for his granddaughter. He finally had to admit to himself that he missed her gentle, sweet presence in his home. And as he discreetly asked others around town about the American boy who had fathered his future great-grandchild, the reports on that boy were not good. Lilli's grandfather heard about the boy drinking and spending time in the bars near the port. He also watched the boy's friends, and he gradually realized that Lilli probably was an innocent victim of the boy's lust. As a result, Lilli's grandfather shifted his anger from Lilli to the boy, and though he wanted to change what had happened within his family, he wasn't sure how to do so. Thus, he passively and stubbornly lived his life in isolation, and he tolerated his wife and his daughter's visits to see Lilli. Though he was not yet willing to give up his masculine appearance of authority and control, he was willing to let his wife and his daughter "secretly" take care of his granddaughter and her child.

Lilli's grandmother was the first to see the change in her husband's attitude, and she shared that change with her daughter. Then, together, they decided not to address the change with him; they knew he needed to maintain his pride. So once they realized that he would no longer object to their visits to Lilli's new home, they began to visit her together. In reality, he wanted to join them, but he was stuck in the quicksand of his foolishness and his macho exterior. He wasn't yet willing to admit to his family that he had acted foolishly when he first heard of Lilli's pregnancy, and he wasn't yet willing to give up the public appearance of being the strong and determined master of his family. In his heart, he knew he had to apologize to his family, and he knew he had to forget about his supposed image in the community, yet with each day that passed, it became harder for him to change or to admit to his foolishness.

Initially, when Christina heard Lilli's mother and grandmother talk about their family situation, she offered to go out, so they could talk privately with Lilli.

"No, no, no," they said. "You are also a part of our family now. You have been so kind, so generous. If we are bothering you, we will take Lilli out to be with her, but you must not leave your home on our account."

Not surprisingly, Christina urged them to stay, and gradually, she began to actually feel as if she were, indeed, a part of Lilli's family. In many ways, she felt as if she were Lilli's big sister, almost as if she had returned home after being away at college. During these family visits, the four women began to think about names for the child, and they began to consider where Lilli and the child would live.

"If it's a boy, I think you should name him 'Diego,'" Lilli's mother offered. "And if it's a girl, I think you should name her 'Christina.'"

"Really?" Lilli responded. "I assumed you would want the child to be named after a famous Costa Rican like 'Jose Figueres,' the first president," she explained for Christina's benefit, "or 'Chavela Vargas,' the famous singer."

"Those two individuals are great examples of Costa Rican people, but we don't know them personally; Diego and Christina are great examples of people in general, and they are living right here in our midst."

Once they finished talking about Lilli and the baby, Lilli's mother and grandmother began to ask Christina about her family and her background and, like two schoolgirls, whether she liked Diego.

Christina laughed at the Diego question and distracted them from it by talking about her family. She told them about her small, Irish hometown outside Boston. She was the middle child with both an older sister and a younger sister. Her father worked as a car salesman, and her mother worked as a nurse. Her mom mostly had stayed home when her girls were young, but she also worked part-time one or two evenings a week when her husband was home, so they could use the extra money she earned to buy nicer clothes for the girls or to finance piano lessons or educational trips that they might not be able to afford otherwise.

"Did your mom encourage you to become a nurse?" Lilli's mother asked.

"Yes and no," Christina answered. "She told me nursing was a great job, but that I should only do it if I absolutely loved it. She told me I shouldn't do it for the money or for the fact that I could always find work because if I didn't really love helping people, the actual work was too hard."

"Too hard physically or too hard emotionally?" Lilli's grandmother asked.

"Both. Mom always came home tired from all the walking and the carrying and the moving and the lifting, but she sometimes came home even more exhausted because one of her patients was really suffering or, worse yet, had died. My mom always gets really close to her patients and to their families, so when a patient doesn't get better or doesn't survive, she cries right along with the family."

Christina actually got a bit choked up at this point in the story. Lilli's grandmother pulled a tissue out from her blouse and handed it to her.

"*Gracias*," Christina spoke softly.

"What kind of patients does your mother work with?" Lilli's mom asked.

"She usually works with children in the pediatric ward but sometimes also in intensive care. She loves helping children and their families. When those children are really sick, though, that's when the job is the most rewarding and the most difficult.

I could always tell that my mom just loved her work, and I think I got caught up in her enthusiasm and excitement."

"So what made you join the Peace Corps?"

"Honestly, I joined mostly for the chance to travel. Yes, I love nursing too, but I can do that anywhere. I used to see commercials or shows on television about really poor and really sick children in Africa, and I felt like I had to do something, somewhere."

"Did you have a chance to go to Africa?"

"Yes, I did actually. When the Peace Corps told me I had been accepted, they said I could go to work almost immediately in Costa Rica, or I could wait six months and go to a program in Mozambique. Since I was just about to graduate from college, I didn't want to wait. Even though I had always envisioned myself in Africa, I also had a good feeling about Costa Rica, so I said 'Yes,' and here I am."

"And we are so grateful," Lilli's grandmother added. Up to that point, Lilli had been mostly silent. She had previously asked Christina pretty much all of the same questions at various times, so she was content to listen as her mother and grandmother discovered more and more about her new friend, her new, big sister.

"And what about Diego?" Lilli's mom asked again, bringing Christina back to the question she had deflected earlier.

"Oh, we both love Diego, don't we, Lilli?" Christina answered, and everyone in the room laughed. "But we know he has a girlfriend back home. He doesn't say a lot about her, but he has a college prom picture of the two of them on his wall. So until that picture comes down, or until he tells me otherwise, I won't get too close to Diego."

So in the final months and weeks leading up to Lilli's delivery, Lilli and Christina and Diego were really like siblings, caring for one another as if they had been orphaned. Diego visited Christina and Lilli almost every day, either late in the afternoon at the clinic or later in the evening at their apartment. Sometimes, too, perhaps once a week or so, Diego invited them to his place for a meal, so that Christina wouldn't feel as if she were totally responsible for Lilli's care. Diego also gave Christina some money each month to help with expenses, and each week, too, he brought over some food: bread, fruit, rice, beans, meat, and sweets, especially sweets.

Lilli's mother and grandmother continued to visit at least once a week, usually on Sunday afternoons after church. Thus, despite all the tension and the nervousness and the drama that Lilli felt during the first few months of her pregnancy, she had settled into an almost ideal situation, and the baby inside her womb developed fully and naturally.

Then, three weeks before Lilli was due, her mother informed Lilli – and all of their friends – that she had been looking for a place of her own; she was finally planning to move away from her own parents, and she hoped that Lilli and the baby would live with her.

"Really, Mama?" Lilli asked. "Really?"

Lilli hadn't told Christina or Diego or anyone that this was exactly what she had been praying for. Though Lilli loved living with Christina and seeing Diego often, she felt that everything would change drastically once the baby arrived, and Lilli wanted to be with her own mother as she learned how to be a mother herself.

When Lilli's mother, Rosa, first considered the idea of leaving her parents, she felt torn, but her own mother, Lilli's grandmother, actually encouraged her to move.

"We should have encouraged you to move sooner, but your father and I were selfish," Lilli's grandmother admitted to Rosa. "We wanted you and Lilli to be with us. We appreciated your help, and we loved watching Lilli grow up. Your father, however, as you know, can be a stubborn and bitter man. I'm not sure I'll ever understand why, and I don't think he will ever change. And I don't want you and Lilli and now this new gift from God to be caught up in his problems forever."

"But, Mama, who will cook and clean for you?" Rosa asked.

Rosa's mama laughed and answered, "The same woman who cooked and cleaned for me even before you were born."

"But, Mama . . . ."

"I will be okay, my child. We will be okay. Have you done a lot of work for us? Of course you have. But are we incapable? Are we invalids? Not yet. No, not yet."

"Does Papa know?"

"He knows."

"And?"

"He's not happy. He will just have to get used to it. We'll manage. And you'll manage too. We'll all learn a new way. And you and Lilli and the baby will learn a much better way to live."

The two women hugged, and Lilli's mom explained her search for a place to live. Since she herself did not work for the banana Company, she and Lilli and the baby could not live in Company housing, so they had to find a place at the other end of town. Lilli's mother had actually considered a job within the Company to acquire Company housing, but she decided that a fresh start would be a stronger move forward. Soon, she committed to a small home on the main road just outside the downtown area of the public side of Golfito, less than a 10-minute walk from Christina's place. The house was owned by a man who had moved to San Jose, and, fortunately for Rosa and her family, he opted to rent the home rather than try to sell it.

Rosa moved into her new home a week before Lilli was due, and she moved most of Lilli's belongings into the home as well. Christina and Lilli's family agreed that Lilli should stay with Christina until the baby arrived, so that Lilli would be close to Christina and/or the clinic just in case any complications occurred.

Chapter 41

In her first year in Golfito, Christina had already delivered over 30 babies, sometimes by herself and sometimes accompanied by a family member who assisted her, usually the mother or an aunt of the girl giving birth. Since Lilli's family might not be nearby when the time came for Lilli to deliver and since transportation could be an issue as well, Christina suggested to Diego that he might be a good person to assist her during the baby's delivery.

"But – but . . . ." Diego stammered when Christina first mentioned the idea.

"Diego, relax. It's not a big deal," Christina countered even before he could offer an actual excuse. "I know you're not the baby's actual father, but Lilli could use a good coach in there with her, someone who knows her and cares about her. And that's what you do. You're a coach."

As soon as Christina said the word "coach," Diego realized he had to be there for Lilli if at all possible.

"Okay, you're right. I'll be there."

Lilli, too, was a bit apprehensive when Christina first mentioned the idea.

"A man at the birth of a baby?" Lilli asked. "I've never heard of that before. It's always the women who are present."

"Yes, that's true, and if your mother and grandmother are available, they will be there with you, but if not, I think it would be good for you and for your baby to have a father figure nearby. Most fathers in America do it now."

"But Diego's not the father?"

"No, he's not. But guess what? When that baby comes out, no other man will love that baby as much as Diego will. You know he loves you, and you know he will love your baby. So don't you want him to be there when that baby is born?"

"Yes, but . . . ."

"No 'buts.' Just say 'thank you' when it's all over, and he's holding your baby in his arms."

On the following Tuesday, at around 5:30 a.m., Lilli awoke in a sweat and knew immediately that her time had come. Though the apartment was still quiet, and the sun was just coming up, Lilli called out to Christina, and Christina awoke quickly and ran to Lilli.

Both of them had prepared for this moment well in advance. Christina had insisted previously that Lilli sleep in the bedroom. There, Lilli had propped herself up, but she was afraid to actually stand; even though she knew better, a part of her feared the baby would fall out immediately.

"Will we stay here or go to the clinic?" Lilli asked.

Christina asked Lilli a few questions in return, examined her quickly, and decided that walking to the clinic would not be necessary – or practical.

"Your baby is coming soon, and everything looks okay, so we can stay here."

Lilli's breathing was faster than normal, and Lilli was feeling movements inside her. "Should I be pushing or anything?" She asked.

"Not yet. I'll let you know."

"I'm afraid," Lilli admitted. "What if the baby won't come out?"

Christina chuckled inside and was tempted to make a wise remark. Lilli was so afraid and sincere, though, that Christina stayed in caretaker mode and reassured the frightened, young girl.

"Your baby is as anxious to see you as you are to see her. So try to relax. Try to slow down your breathing just like we practiced. Breathe with me."

As Christina moved closer, she glanced out the window and noticed the bakery boys moving down the street with their goods. Then, she took Lilli's hands in hers and accentuated her own breathing pattern, so Lilli could consciously imitate hers. Together, they slowed down, and Christina could feel some of Lilli's anxiety drain away.

When Lilli appeared a bit less nervous, Christina gave her instructions. She squeezed Lilli's hands and said, "Now, I'm not leaving you alone. I'm just going to the front door for a second, and I'm going to have one of the bakery boys run and get Diego. You keep breathing, and I'll be right back."

Christina opened the front door, and though the street was mostly empty at that early hour, she saw again the two bakery boys delivering fresh bread to both sides of the street. The boy across the street was handing rolls to his customer, and the other was waiting for a customer two doors down. Christina called out to him, and though he hesitated at first, Christina's repeated cries to him made him realize she wanted something other than bread.

"Leave your basket with me, and go get Diego, please," she implored him when the boy arrived. "Tell Diego the baby is about to be born."

The boy sprinted away immediately. Everyone in the neighborhood knew, of course, that Lilli was due any day, and everyone knew where Diego lived. When the boy arrived at Diego's place and banged loudly on the door, he woke not only the tall American but also those who lived nearby.

"*Diego! Diego! El bambino es aqui. El bambino es aqui. Venga. Venga. Venga.*"

Diego was awakened by the banging at his front door. Then, when he heard the young boy yelling about what was going on, Diego sprinted into action. Like a fireman in an emergency, he quickly put his feet into the sandals at the foot of his bed, grabbed a tee-shirt from a nearby chair, and rushed out the front door.

"*Gracias. Gracias,*" Diego said to the bakery boy, and together, they ran back to Christina's place. There, Diego hurriedly took the few coins he found in the pocket of his shorts and gave them to the bakery boy, who retrieved his basket of baked goods, gave some rolls to Christina, and disappeared.

When Diego saw Christina and Lilli, however, he was stunned. They appeared so relaxed that he wondered why he had rushed so. "Is everything okay? Has the baby been born already?"

Christina again resisted the urge to make a wise comment and began to coach the coach. "Thank you for coming so quickly, Diego. Why don't you sit right over here next to Lilli and talk to her while I get everything ready."

"*Hola, Diego,*" Lilli said in the midst of her breathing pattern. "*Gracias para venir.*"

"Are you kidding? I am so excited to be here!"

Christina could see that Diego was a bit too excited, so she kiddingly told Lilli to help Diego control his breathing, and the three of them laughed heartily. Then, once Diego calmed down, Christina explained that they still probably had two or three hours to wait, so they all settled in for the morning. Lilli tried to close her eyes to rest, but she couldn't do so. Despite her exterior calm, her mind was racing, and the labor pains, though not yet overwhelming, did have her concerned.

Diego calmed down by eating some of the fresh rolls from the bakery boy and by reading nursery rhymes to Lilli, first in English and then in Spanish. At Christina's urging, Lilli had been reading this same book of rhymes to the baby in her womb for over four months, and she had asked Diego to read for her on this day.

Meanwhile, Christina had set out all of her doctorly tools, medicines, and bandages. Though she was not expecting a difficult delivery, she wanted to be prepared for everything. And during the next few hours, Christina periodically sent Diego on short errands: first, to Lilli's mother's new place to let her know what was happening and, then, to the clinic to use the phone to call the neighbor of Lilli's grandmother who had a phone and would deliver the news to Lilli's family; next, to the store to buy some fruit and some juice, so they would all have plenty to eat and drink if the delivery were longer than expected; and, finally, to the nearby school to apologize to the principal and to let him know that Christina would be unable to speak, as previously scheduled, to the fifth graders about healthy eating habits.

During one of those errands, Diego also stopped at his own place to change and quickly freshen up and to retrieve the special gift he had made for the baby. When he returned to Christina's apartment, he carried with him a large, cardboard box, one big enough to hold a washing machine or a dryer. He carried it so easily, though, that whatever he had put inside was much lighter than its original content. At the apartment, he gently set the box inside the front door. Both Lilli and Christina were somewhat surprised to see such a huge box in the small apartment, but neither said a word to Diego. Christina had an idea all along that Diego was preparing something special for the baby, but she didn't ask what it was, deciding, instead, to wait for him to reveal it. Meanwhile, Lilli was so caught up in her own birthing pains that she didn't give any real thought to what was inside.

By approximately 9:30, everyone and everything was set; even Lilli's mother and grandmother had arrived to witness the birth. Lilli, though near exhaustion from all the pushing and the accompanying emotions, persevered, and with encouragement from everyone, she drew the strength she needed to push out a light-skinned but dark-haired baby girl.

The child cried immediately, and Christina quickly but efficiently cleaned her, wrapped her in a blanket, and placed her on Lilli's chest. Everyone was crying.

Christina attended to Lilli's physical needs while Lilli's mother, on one side of the bed, and grandmother, on the other, hugged both Lilli and the baby, a four-generation expression of love.

Diego, somewhat tired at this point himself, wiped at his tears and watched as the four females embraced. Though he had seen newborn babies before, he had never seen one so soon after its birth, and he marveled at how small and how perfect she appeared. Feeling a father's pride and a man's need to embrace someone, he watched Christina and waited for her to complete her work. Once she appeared finished, he went to her, and they, too, embraced, a congratulatory hug and a prayer of thanksgiving.

By then, Lilli's mother and grandmother had retreated somewhat, so Christina and Diego joined Lilli and the baby to welcome this gift of life to the world.

Ironically, while everyone else was thoroughly drained by the experience, Lilli came to life. Her exhaustion and weariness disappeared, and for a short time, she became again the excited and enthusiastic girl everyone remembered from before the whole experience began.

"We did it!" she exclaimed to all the loved ones surrounding her. "We did it!"

"No, you did it," Christina responded. Then, she laughed and added, "And you worried that you wouldn't be able to push her out. You were awesome!"

"And look at this beautiful baby," Lilli said.

"Have you made a final decision on her name?" Lilli's mother asked.

"I think I have."

Everyone looked at Lilli expectantly – and waited – and waited.

Lilli had a big smile on her face, and she laughed as she teased them by making them wait even longer.

"Tell us, my child. Tell us now," her grandmother piped in.

"I've decided to call her 'Maria.'"

"Maria?" Her grandmother asked. "Where did that name come from?" No one in their family had that name, and Lilli had never mentioned it before.

"The mother of Jesus," Lilli replied. "And I want my baby's full name to be 'Maria Christina.' "

At that point, Christina, who had been mostly quiet and efficient during the delivery beamed, looked at Lilli, and softly said, "Wow! Are you sure?"

"You have been so kind to me, Christina, and I want my daughter to remember you always, even after your time here is complete, and you return to America."

"That's a beautiful name," Diego chimed in. "It's so poetic, so musical. In fact, I think I feel a song coming on."

"No, no," Christina cried, for she knew what was about to happen, and she and Lilli laughed because they often teased Diego about his singing. Lilli's family appeared perplexed until Diego began his solo of the song "Maria" from the musical *West Side Story.*

When he finished, everyone cheered and applauded. Diego took a deep bow, and even the new baby cried out in appreciation.

"Okay, now, why don't we all give this new mother some space and some time to rest," said Christina.

"Wait," Diego interrupted. "I have one more thing to say." Everyone looked at the big guy, and he continued. "Lilli, I have something that I made for your baby."

"Really?"

"Really. Here, let me show you." At that point, Diego walked over to the box, opened it, and gingerly lifted out what appeared to be a big, wooden bread box.

Christina realized immediately what Diego had built, but Lilli needed a few seconds to recognize the box's purpose, and she made the connection only when Diego set it gently on the floor next to her.

"*Dios mio*," she said softly, and tears appeared at the corners of her eyes. "You made a bed for my baby."

"Yes, I did. I know the baby will probably sleep with you a lot, especially at first, but I wanted her to have a bed of her own, too, so you can both get the sleep you will need."

"It's so beautiful, Diego. Thank you."

While Lilli was too tired to inspect it closely, Christina admired the grain of the wood and touched its smooth surface. As she did so, the bed moved to one side, and she realized the base was curved, so that it served as a rocker, too, so when Lilli was ready to put the baby in it, she could gently rock Maria Christina to sleep. "How did you manage to build this?" Christina asked, as if she didn't believe Diego were capable of such craftsmanship.

"One of the older basketball players who works at the wood shop helped me to design it and then showed me how to use the tools to actually cut the wood and put it together."

"It really is beautiful, Diego," Christina added. "And this little mattress, where on Earth did you find this?" The mattress was about three feet long and two feet wide and fit perfectly inside the hand-crafted cradle.

"You've seen that older woman who has the small sewing shop at the top of the street?"

"Yes."

"Well, I told her what I was making, and I asked her if she could make a mattress to fit inside."

"Wow, it's really soft," Christina commented. "Maria Christina will sleep well on this."

"And that woman wouldn't let me pay either," Diego added. "She said this was her gift for Lilli and the baby."

By then, Lilli was becoming drowsy, so Christina took the baby from her and encouraged her to close her eyes and sleep. Next, she escorted the others out of the bedroom, and she allowed the grandmother and the great-grandmother to hold the baby while Lilli slept.

Chapter 42

The next few days were extremely busy for Lilli as she learned to care for her baby and as she greeted all the people who came to visit her and to see Maria. The people who lived nearby, those who had seen Lilli's growth and watched her walk pregnant through the neighborhood, stopped by with small gifts and with fresh food. Some of Lilli's classmates from the high school visited too; they were both curious and amazed that one of their own had actually given birth to a child. Also, a few of the families who lived near where Lilli grew up traveled to see her and to welcome her to the world of parenthood. While visiting, Lilli's old neighbors all told stories of their own pregnancies and deliveries, and they compared the size and weight of this new born angel to their own children, some of whom were now parents themselves.

One person who did not visit, however, was Lilli's grandfather, Don Pedro. He was working, of course, the morning of the baby's delivery and was unwilling to ask for time off to be present for the birth of his first great-grandchild. In the days that followed, though, he still could not bring himself to see Maria. Yes, he had softened somewhat during the months of Lilli's pregnancy as he listened to his wife and his daughter talk about the impending birth. He had even begun to dream about the child, evidence in his own mind that he was thinking often about this new member of the family. He did not, however, share those dreams with his family or with anyone else. And though he really was curious to see the child, he was also afraid. He was afraid that this little girl would possess facial features of her American father, features that would only reignite the hatred he felt for the boy who had barged into his family and stolen a valuable treasure. And since Don Pedro knew he could never recover that particular treasure, he was not yet ready to see the new treasure that God had given them in return. Fortunately for this old, stubborn, macho Costa Rican, Lilli herself had overcome her own hatred for what had happened, and despite her mother's and her grandmother's worries and concerns, Lilli was determined to bring Maria Christina to visit her great-grandfather.

So on the second Sunday following the delivery, when Maria was only 10 days old, Lilli, her mother, Diego, and Christina climbed into a battered, old taxi with the baby and rode to St. Michael's Church in the American Zone and attended Mass together. Though the baby's formal baptism would take place the following week, Padre Roberto sprinkled a few drops of holy water on the baby's forehead during the service, and when the service finished, many of the people in attendance gathered around the new mother and child. There, they hugged Lilli and took turns cradling young Maria in their arms.

Later, when the crowd had dwindled, Lilli and her mother led Diego and Christina to their former house where Maria Christina would meet her great-grandfather. Lilli's grandmother knew they were coming, yet she did not tell Don Pedro. She feared that he might become angry and leave the house before they arrived or that he might lock the doors and prevent their entrance.

Thus, unprepared for their arrival and feeling totally relaxed in his own home, Don Pedro did not even look up from his newspaper when the front door opened. He had watched his wife go out into the garden just ten minutes earlier and simply assumed she had returned with fresh vegetables or with flowers for the vase on the dining-room table.

"Good morning, Grandpa," Lilli said softly as she walked up behind him and placed little Maria in his lap. "I would like you to meet Maria Christina."

Startled and speechless, Don Pedro dropped his newspaper, reflexively embraced his great-granddaughter, and cried immediately and uncontrollably.

"Lilli, my Lilli," he said as he wept and as he returned her embrace while still holding the baby. By then, Lilli had knelt down beside him.

"I love you, Grandpa. And this little angel will grow to love you too."

Still somewhat at a loss, Don Pedro eventually spoke through his tears: "No. No. I don't deserve it. I have acted so foolishly. I am so sorry. Please forgive me. Please say you will forgive me."

"Of course, I forgive you. You are my *abuelo*, my only *abuelo*."

When his eyes were finally free of tears, Don Pedro looked deeply into the dark, dark eyes of Maria Christina. Though a few people from the church had noticed small signs of the baby's American father in Maria's face – like the high cheekbones and the small wrinkle above her nose – they had said nothing, and Don Pedro noticed nothing. For only those who knew the boy well or who had looked at him closely would notice and remember these minor facial characteristics. No, Don Pedro noticed only the deep similarity Maria Christina possessed to her own mother and grandmother: dark eyes, dark hair, and light skin, characteristics that many beautiful Costa Rican females possessed.

"Did you know that my great-grandmother on my father's side was also named Maria?" Don Pedro asked Lilli.

"No. Really? I don't think you ever told me that before."

In fact, Don Pedro had rarely spoken of his own family during Lilli's youth, for they had lived far out on the nearby peninsula, and when Don Pedro left their small village to work for the Company, he had returned to visit only infrequently and never after his marriage to Lilli's grandmother. Though he was not really a religious man, he did appreciate the Bible verses about leaving one's mother and father and devoting oneself to his new bride and family. As a result, he took those particular verses literally and never returned home again. Only the baby's arrival and her name, Maria, had resurrected his family memories.

"But tell me, Lilli," he said, "about her middle name: Christina."

"Oh, *Papito*, you must have forgotten. We have told you about Christina, the kind American nurse who has allowed me to live with her all these months. In fact, she is right outside – with Diego. Let me go get them."

Don Pedro had, in fact, remembered the nurse's name. Though he had never actually met Christina, the three women in his family had, indeed, spoken of her often. He had asked only because he didn't know what else to say at that moment. Holding the beautiful baby in his arms had overwhelmed him in some ways, and he was relieved that Lilli had gone to retrieve the others. Then, he could retreat again into the background. Since he had previously ostracized his own granddaughter and only great-grandchild, he couldn't now realistically play the role of the proud family patriarch, and he needed some time and space to figure out how he could work his way back into his family's heart.

When all the others gathered around the baby and Don Pedro, he did disappear again somewhat into the shadows. Lilli's mother and grandmother began setting the table and setting out the food for the meal they had planned all along without, of course, telling Don Pedro. As they worked, Lilli showed Christina the home where she had grown up, and Diego was left to sit with Don Pedro who was now holding a sleeping baby.

Diego, trying to ease the tension, began asking Don Pedro about his work for the Company and about his life. And though Don Pedro really didn't want to talk much at that moment, the sincere and inquisitive American had a gentle way of asking questions, and Don Pedro gradually opened up and told his stories, stories that he had repressed about Lilli's father and about how he had deserted Lilli and her mom. "I was so angry then," Don Pedro admitted, "and I think that's why I reacted so poorly when all of this happened to Lilli." He paused for a few seconds, teared up again, and finally acknowledged, softly, "I am so ashamed."

Diego remained silent but reached out and squeezed his hand. Then, the two of them waited without speaking for a minute or two as the women made the final preparations for lunch and called them to the table.

During the latter stages of the meal, Don Pedro began to talk about Lilli's living situation. Now that the baby was born, he knew that Christina's small apartment would be too small for the two young women and the baby.

"Maybe you and your mom and the baby could move back in here," Don Pedro suggested, though he had never previously mentioned the idea to his wife or seriously entertained it during his quiet times alone. Though the idea seemed reasonable to Diego and Christina, the others were all shocked and surprised by the offer, pleasantly surprised, but surprised nonetheless.

Don Pedro looked at Lilli for an answer, but she remained quiet and looked at her mother who addressed Don Pedro, her father, boldly and confidently, just as she had weeks earlier when she moved out on her own.

"Father, I told you this a while back; Lilli and Maria Christina are going to live with me in my small house at the other end of town. It is not far from where our good friends Christina and Diego live, and they have volunteered to help us as much as they can."

"But you are so far away from your job."

"That's true, but I will simply take the bus to and from work each day."

Don Pedro looked to his wife as if to ask if she knew anything about this. She remained silent but did nod her head "Yes."

"Father," Rosa continued, "having my own place is something I should have done a long time ago, and while Lilli and I appreciate your offer to let us live here, we must take care of ourselves."

"But when will we see the baby?"

"You may visit as often as you like; you are always welcome. And I am sure we will come to visit you as well."

Don Pedro remained silent as he digested this new information. For a short time, the others were silent as well until Maria, who had been sleeping on the couch for most of the meal, began to stir and cry out for food and attention.

Already an alert and attentive mother, Lilli stood and went to her baby. She picked Maria up, soothed her with her soft words and caresses, and prepared to feed her.

Chapter 43

Within the week, Lilli and her mother and Maria had all settled into their new home on the main road. During the first few weeks in the home, Lilli's mother focused on Lilli's recovery and Maria Christina's growth. At first, Lilli was too exhausted to do any schoolwork. Her entire day was spent holding the baby, feeding the baby, burping the baby, and resting or sleeping when the baby rested or slept. Lilli's mother pampered the two of them as she had never pampered Lilli. For when Lilli was born, Rosa was so young and inexperienced that she did only what she was told to do by her mother and her father. As traditional parents, they had warned her about holding the baby too much. They told her to let the baby cry for a bit before responding, and they didn't encourage singing or reading to the baby at all. "Just put her down and finish your work," they said often even when the work – sweeping, dusting, washing dishes – was insignificant or could easily be postponed.

With this grandchild and without interference from her own parents, Rosa allowed and encouraged Lilli to give Maria Christina all her love and all her time. Rosa took care of all the chores when she was home, and before she went to work, she prepared all the food that would be needed for the day, so all Lilli had to do was retrieve the food from the refrigerator and warm it on the stove. Rosa even arranged for the older woman who lived next door to check on Lilli periodically, and this woman gave Lilli a large, old bell and encouraged her to ring it loudly if Lilli ever needed anything.

Around lunch time each day, either Diego or Christina would visit and, if needed, help out too. If Lilli were heating her rice and beans on the stove, Christina would hold Maria Christina and walk her or sit down with her in the rocking chair that Lilli's mother had purchased specifically for holding and feeding the baby. If Lilli and Maria Christina were resting when Diego arrived, he pulled out their food and began preparing it for them. Typically, too, Christina and Diego would arrive with fresh fruit or some sweets to add to the lunch.

In the evening, this new family – Lilli, her mother, her baby, and her Peace Corps friends – would gather together for dinner at least once a week and sometimes more. Typically, Lilli would feed the baby first, and then one of the others would walk her and burp her. Once Maria Christina settled in comfortably, she would rest either in someone's arms at the table or in the cradle that Diego had built. And as the baby rested, the other four would share the stories of their days. So, even though Lilli often felt confined and limited to this small house on the edge of town, she shared in the adventures and experiences of the other three.

Christina, without giving away any names or identities, spoke about the medical emergencies or triumphs of her week. Some weeks brought the sadness of death while others included the joy of a new life. Many stories involved minor cases like broken bones at work or various cuts that required stitches. And others were enduring stories of slow but gradual healing. And when cases arrived that were well beyond Christina's abilities or that required special equipment or treatments, she encouraged the patient's family to taxi the patient to the hospital at the other end of town for treatment or, if needed, to fly the patient to San Jose. In some extreme cases, too, especially when finances were an issue, she had to tell the family to prepare for a disabled life at home or for a premature death. These cases disturbed Christina the most because she knew that more money and equipment and trained personnel could save some of these people or at least dramatically ease their situations, but these poor Costa Rican families typically didn't know any better, and they stoicly and matter-of-factly adjusted and coped or simply said their good-bye's and moved on.

Diego's stories were usually more upbeat and positive because he was chronicling the athletic adventures of his young charges. Each week, for instance, at least one athlete at one of the schools did something that had never been accomplished or recorded before: a new record in a race or a new number of consecutive made free throws. For in each school where Diego worked, he found a place and secured the principal's permission to hang a four-by-eight foot piece of plywood where he painted the names and the accomplishments of the record breakers. The left side of the board usually held the names and best times of the boys who ran the hundred-yard dash, and the mile, and other accomplishments, and the right side of the board held similar information for the girls. To fit as many names on the board as possible, Diego broke the records down by grade. Diego knew, of course, from his own experience how such public acknowledgment would motivate his athletes to practice and achieve. For while he was never good enough himself to see his own name on the record board at his high school, he did get to see his name in the paper once in a while, and he remembered vividly the day he broke the record for the best score on a new pinball machine at a nearby amusement park. Since Golfito had neither a local newspaper nor an amusement park, he knew his Board of Champions would serve the same purpose for his pupils.

Lilli's mom sometimes felt that her experiences at the restaurant were nowhere near as interesting as Christina's medical stories or Diego's athletic narratives, so when asked, she would usually say, "Oh, nothing interesting happened this week," or, "My job is so boring; you don't want to hear about it." The others refused to let her off so easily, though, and they pressed her with questions like "What about the people from the ships in port? Who was the most colorful or most interesting person you have seen this week?" Or they encouraged her with statements like, "You must at least have seen some new products in the store when you shopped." After a while, knowing these questions or statements were coming, Rosa began to pay more attention to her restaurant's customers and the products at the *mercado*. Then, when coaxed, she would begin to describe the new breakfast cereals that the American families would buy for their children, cereals with raisins or marshmallows mixed in. Or she might describe in vivid detail the Europeans who entered the restaurant speaking a language she had never heard, like Swedish or Norweigan, but who were also able to switch quickly and efficiently to Spanish or English or French to talk to her or to other customers in the store. This ability to easily speak so many languages impressed her so much more than their colorful outfits or their outrageous hairstyles.

Meanwhile, Lilli soaked in all their stories and experiences, and she, of course, told them stories about Maria Christina's small changes or firsts: "I think she recognized me today, really recognized me as her mom for the first time," or, "She almost rolled over on her back today when I set her on a blanket on the floor." In addition, Lilli continued to read her news magazine and keep up with her homework, so she also shared her new knowledge or asked questions about things that puzzled or perplexed her or pertained directly to her: "Why is this whole Watergate thing so important?" she asked her American friends, or "Mom, do you agree with the experts that breastfeeding is the best nourishment for the baby, and how long did you breastfeed me when I was little?"

As the baby grew, these four individuals grew as well, and their relationships grew even stronger. Lilli and her mom became so much closer because Rosa, finally freed from the influence and the negativity of her own father, felt so much more comfortable with her daughter and shared so much more with her. She finally told Lilli about her father and described how sweet and kind he was, not the selfish and irresponsible man that Lilli's grandfather described. "Your father was too young, too immature, really," Rosa said. "And he was overwhelmed by what happened to us. I was overwhelmed, too, and I wish I could have been stronger for him, for us, for all of us. His leaving was my fault, too, because I relied too much on my parents when I should have relied more on him."

"Do you still think about him?" Lilli asked.

"Just about every day."

They were both silent as they considered that answer. Then, Rosa continued. "Especially now. He's a grandfather, and he doesn't even know it. He has a beautiful eighteen-year-old daughter that he doesn't know either. He would be so proud of you for the young woman that you have become."

"You think he'd be proud of me in this situation?"

"Lilli, your situation – young and single and a mother – may not look good to most people, but your situation is unique. You didn't seek out your pregnancy. You didn't make it happen. But when it occurred, you didn't run away. Some girls your age would have sought what your grandfather sought. You are different. You did what was right for your baby. You're doing what is right for you every day. Your father, if he knew you, would admire what you're doing for Maria Christina."

"Mama," Lilli asked hesitantly.

"Yes, my child."

"Do you think Papa will come and visit us some day?"

Rosa stopped folding the blouse she held in her hands and looked directly at her daughter and the baby in her arms. She pondered the question and hesitated before answering. "Lilli, my child." She paused again. "I have to be totally honest with you now. As much as I want to believe that your father will return to Golfito some day, I don't think he will."

"But then maybe – "

"Lilli, I don't think he can."

"Because?"

"I really believe something bad happened to him. All these years I've been telling you that he's going to come see you some day, but I don't believe it any more. He's too good of a man to ignore you all these years, and it would be so easy for him to hop on a bus or a plane to come here from San Jose. I just feel like he's gone forever."

"But maybe he moved to another country and . . . ."

"Maybe. And I hope you're right, but he was never that adventurous. Leaving Golfito, that's easy. Leaving Costa Rica, that's too ambitious for him. I'm sorry, Lilli. I've held out hope all these years myself, for you, but I don't know if I can do it again for this baby."

"My father is dead?" Lilli couldn't actually speak these words aloud. Still, she thought about what her mother had said to her. "What could have happened to him?" Lilli wondered. "How could he have died? And if he did, why didn't anyone ever tell us?"

Chapter 44

The Wednesday-night basketball games were still a popular event in town, but the high-school boys were beginning to dominate. After all, they practiced regularly, they were young and in great shape, and they were open to Diego's instruction. The men, by contrast, never actually practiced as a team, they never had the same players from one week to the next, and they often argued about who would coach them from week to week. So after the boys clearly outplayed the men on one particular Wednesday, a few of the boys approached Diego with another idea.

"Could we play games against other schools," one of the boys asked, "like they do in San Jose?"

"I guess we could," Diego replied tentatively, "but who would we play? And how would we get there?"

"There's another high school in Villa Neily," one boy responded. "That's not that far away. We could probably ride the train out there."

"And there's another school across the border in David," another boy added, referring to the city that was just across the border in Panama."

"Do the trains go down there too?" Diego asked.

"Yes. The Company owns plantations down there too, and their bananas come to Golfito to be exported."

Though initially overwhelmed by the idea of traveling to road games, Diego was also extremely excited. He didn't know if it could happen or how it could happen, but he knew the challenge and the experience would be good for everyone.

During the next few weeks, he mentioned the idea to Don Mario, the physical education teacher at the high school, and to others in the community. Some people immediately brushed off the idea because it appeared too complicated or too expensive, but others, like Diego, became excited at the prospect, and they began offering suggestions or assistance:

"I think Eduardo would pay for uniforms. He loves that kind of stuff."

"I know a guy who works in the train office; I'll ask him if he thinks the kids could ride the trains for free to and from the game."

"We used to do that a lot," one older man said, "when there were a lot more Americans here. They loved that stuff too."

While Diego appreciated all the positive comments, he knew that he would have to do most of the actual work. The Costa Ricans had a unique word for talk without action, and Diego felt much of what he was hearing fell into the category of "Mickey Mantling."

Mickey Mantle, as Diego well knew, was the New York Yankee Hall-of-Fame centerfielder from 1951 to 1968. He was a powerful hitter, a fast runner, and a great fielder; in other words, unlike the average player, he could actually do it all. So when Costa Ricans heard average people claiming that they, too, could do it all, they were said to be "Mickey Mantling" because what they claimed they could do was, like The Mick himself, too good to be true.

Fortunately for Diego, after some failures and frustrations, a few key people actually did what they promised they would do. Eduardo did agree to buy team jerseys for the kids, and a Company official in the train office said he would add a passenger car for them, so the team could ride the trains to and from the games as long as they traveled when the trains were scheduled to run anyway. As a result, that meant the team would generally have to stay overnight at its destination and return the next day, so overnight accommodations would also be required.

Once Diego heard that detail, he assumed the project would fall apart; surprisingly, though, the high-school principal came through with an idea. When he heard what was being planned, he suggested that the teams agree to two games, and the host team would house and feed the visitors. Then he added that they should have a three-team tournament with teams from Golfito, Villa Neily, and David as participants, and each team would play the other teams twice. The Golfito team would travel once to both Villa Neily and David, and it would also host each team once, and the other schools would do the same.

Golfito's first game was scheduled on a Sunday morning in David, Panama, so the team members attended their normal Saturday-morning classes and ate lunch before boarding their train. Everyone was excited. Most of the boys had never even been on a train before, and a few of the fathers had volunteered to travel with the team as chaperones. On their way out of town, everyone stood near the windows and waved to their fellow Golfiteños, and once the train had left the town and entered the countryside, they settled in for the almost two-hour ride.

During a good portion of the trip, the boys looked out over the vast acres of banana plantations and were overwhelmed. Sure, they knew that bananas were the main crop in that section of the country, and, yes, they had seen the trains come into town regularly to load the ships in port, and they all definitely ate bananas daily, but to finally see the trees and the fields go on and on and on for miles and miles amazed them all.

And when the fields ended or were interrupted in some way, what the boys saw amazed them even more. Periodically, in the midst of what seemed to them like a huge jungle of banana trees, they viewed small homesteads or settlements unconnected to the banana Company. The view stunned them.

The small homes where these people lived were nothing more than cardboard shacks constructed from old banana cartons. How they stood or supported the corrugated sheet metal that served as a roof was not evident, and it appeared as if the next rainstorm would wash them away.

Outside these feeble structures, small children, mostly naked, played with one another and waved to the passing train. The adults sat on old tree stumps and merely watched. Some smoked; others drank. Nearby, hanging from a tree, they saw an animal, a bull or a cow, recently slaughtered and ready to be cooked over an open fire.

When Diego's team saw these poor, isolated families, they spoke in low tones or ceased talking altogether.

"Wow! How do they survive out here in the middle of nowhere?" one of the boys finally asked. No one, not even an adult chaperone, had an answer.

When they arrived at the Panamanian border, the train stopped briefly, so the border guards, who were used to seeing only cargo trains pass through, could verify that the one passenger car contained only basketball players and chaperones. Their inspection took only minutes, and most of that time involved the guards teasing the young players about playing basketball instead of soccer and promising them that they would be defeated by their Panamanian opponents.

And they were.

Most of the Costa Rican boys were so excited about their first road game, and for some of them their first trip outside Golfito, that they didn't sleep well the night before the game. They had eaten a team supper offered at the local high school, they visited the small business section of David, and then they individually went to stay with their host families. And while the Panamanian boys and even the Costa Rican chaperones slept peacefully, the young *Ticos* thought about all they had witnessed and experienced that day and also nervously anticipated the game that awaited them.

As a result, the team played well at first and actually led by three points at halftime. The 11:00 a.m. start, however, meant that they played the second half during the hottest part of the day, and the sleep-deprived boys wilted in the direct sun overhead. Though Diego tried to compensate by playing everyone, the stamina and the well rested and fresh legs of the Panamanians prevailed, and they won by 11.

On the ride home, Diego sat with each of his players for a few minutes to discuss how that player had performed. Yes, they were all disappointed by the loss, but Diego tried to end each short conversation on a positive note. He emphasized not only the weak area of the boy's game but also the boy's strength. A boy named Che, for example, was the most energetic player on the team. He could run all day and out jump everyone, even those who were three or four inches taller. Che's problem was that he was either too fast or too strong, and he couldn't quite control all his energy. Diego gently reminded him to slow down at times and play under control, so he wouldn't commit so many fouls. Diego also encouraged Che to study the flow of the game more carefully, so he could outrun his opponent on offense when the opportunity presented itself and also position himself properly for rebounds rather than bang into everyone. "You are going to be one of our best players, Che. Keep practicing, and keep learning."

Chapter 45

After Lilli and her baby moved in with her mother, they settled into a comfortable new life. Like everything on the bay side of the road, the house was beyond the railroad tracks and set back from the road and tracks by about 50 yards; from the rear windows of the house, they could actually look out over the bay. When Diego saw the place for the first time, he wondered if he, too, should move to that area of town. For he realized quickly that the people at that end of town, those literally on the outskirts, were extremely poor, and some of the children who lived there didn't even bother to attend school because they didn't have the proper clothing or because they often worked with their parents to raise money or to grow their own food.

Lilli's new home was also at the extreme end of the bus route. When the bus reached that point, it actually turned into the dirt road that led to her house, so the bus driver could turn the vehicle around and make the return trip to the port and beyond. So when Rosa boarded the bus in the morning to go to work, she traveled almost the entire length of Golfito to reach her job in the small restaurant near the main entrance to the port. After reaching the restaurant, the bus traveled through the American Zone to the airport before it turned around again and started all over.

In the early morning, at around 6:00, when Rosa boarded the first bus of the day, the trip to work took about a half hour, but when she returned home in the late afternoon, the return trip took at least 20 minutes longer because there were so many more stops and passengers at that hour of the day.

During her time on the bus, Rosa, who had previously walked from her parents' home to and from work each day, found herself browsing through Lilli's old news magazines which Lilli kept piled up in the corner of her bedroom. Though Rosa did not understand written English very well, she enjoyed looking at the pictures and discussing what she had seen with Lilli when they sat down for supper each night.

For the first five or six weeks of Maria's life, Lilli did not go to school. Instead, her classmate Eugenia took the bus out to visit Lilli and Maria once a week and to bring Lilli her new assignments and, of course, to take Lilli's homework from the previous week to her instructors. Lilli and Eugenia were good friends prior to Lilli becoming pregnant, so once Eugenia realized that Lilli might need some help, she volunteered immediately.

"This is so kind of you," Lilli said to Eugenia when she arrived that first week.

"Oh, I am happy to do it," Eugenia replied. "I get to see both you and your beautiful new baby, Maria."

In many ways, Eugenia was a lot like Lilli: quiet, reserved, sweet, and serious about school. And, like Lilli, she didn't quite fit in with the rest of their classmates. When Lilli and Eugenia were actually in school together, they rather quietly shared their conversational time, but when they met in the privacy of Lilli's new home, they were so much more lighthearted and exuberant, especially when Maria Christina was awake and entertaining them with her movements and facial expressions.

Eugenia usually stayed for about an hour, and she willingly offered to do anything Lilli needed: housework, baby care, food preparation, anything. What Lilli most wanted, though, was simple, ordinary conversation with a peer, a fellow classmate. Lilli peppered Eugenia with questions about school, and Eugenia asked Lilli questions about the baby and taking care of her. In this new environment, Lilli and Eugenia learned so much more about each other's lives and aspirations.

Outside of Eugenia's weekly visits, Lilli spent most of her days alone at home with Maria Christina while Rosa worked. When the baby was sleeping, Lilli would catch up on her own sleep and also take care of the house and do her schoolwork. Though she wasn't sure how – or when – she would ever make it to San Jose and the University, Lilli held on to that dream.

"Just get your high-school diploma first," she told herself, "and God will help with that next step."

While Lilli had always been a firm Christian believer, the arrival of Maria Christina had only intensified her faith. Lilli now felt a new sense of responsibility, one she had never experienced before. When she looked into Maria Christina's eyes and rocked her to sleep, Lilli talked softly to the baby: "I'm your mama, Maria, and I love you. I love you so much that I will always take care of you and be here for you."

After Lilli moved out of Christina's apartment and into the house with her mother, Christina noticed a significant change in her own life; she discovered that she missed Lilli's presence. So at least once a week, she visited Lilli after work. Usually, Christina arrived before Lilli's mom had returned from work herself, so the two young ladies had some time to themselves with Maria Christina. Christina typically offered to stay with the baby if Lilli needed a break or needed to run an errand. Some days, Lilli did, indeed, need a break, so she might go for a short walk or simply take a nap, but usually she stayed there because she missed Christina just as much as Christina missed her. They talked quite a bit about what was going on in their lives, but mostly, they talked about the future.

Lilli wanted to know what Christina was going to do once her two years in Golfito were up, and Lilli also wanted help figuring out her own future, especially now that she had a baby.

"I'll probably go back to Boston and get a job near where my parents live, at least for a little while. I never imagined I'd miss my family as much as I do, and I think maybe I might go back to school too."

"Really?"

"Really."

"For what?"

"I think I'd like to be a doctor."

"Wow! You can really do that in America?"

"You can do that in Costa Rica."

"No, I don't think so."

Christina laughed. "Golfito is a small town, Lilli, and Costa Rica is a small country, so you may not see or hear what is going on in the world, but great things are happening. More and more girls are going to medical school in America, and if it happens there, it will happen here some day too. You are fortunate. Even though you may not be able to see beyond this small town today, your country is a democracy, and your country has more teachers than soldiers; isn't that what they tell everyone who visits? So you will have an opportunity. You are not trapped in a country that does not allow freedom or that does not value women."

Lilli nodded and agreed. "I know."

"Of course you know. You read that news magazine every week. How could I forget that? So trust me, you will have a chance to be a nurse or a doctor or a teacher. You can be whatever you want to be."

"But not right away."

"No, not right away. Not right away."

Chapter 46

While Christina and Lilli were having this conversation, Diego was in San Jose for his semi-annual meeting with his supervisor and his fellow Sports Promoters. They gathered at the Peace Corps offices for one day of meetings and one day of fun. During the meetings, they shared with one another their accomplishments and their frustrations, and they traded their ideas and their personal stories. The gathering wasn't extremely productive in terms of actually accomplishing anything, but it did allow each Volunteer to re-energize and re-focus. For as Diego well knew, working alone in a small, faraway town could make one feel pretty lonely and isolated. On many days, Diego himself had been tempted to sleep in and pretend to be sick, and on many nights, he had been tempted to drink too much and visit places where he should not have been. So as he listened to similar stories and similar temptations from his co-workers, he knew he was fortunate to have Lilli and Christina in his life. They gave him a sort of stability that the other Volunteers in his group did not have. So, as they partied on the following day on a short trip to a lake in the countryside, Diego did not drink as much as the others, nor did he give in to the pleasures that the local women offered to the young Americans. Instead, Diego and two other like-minded Volunteers separated themselves a bit and tried to encourage one another to remain strong and idealistic. And when Diego returned to the Peace Corps offices the following day, he took care of one bureaucratic detail that he had been considering for months.

When Diego and the other Volunteers in his group had met in Miami, Florida, over a year and a half earlier to complete their paperwork and travel together to Costa Rica, one of the forms they had to fill out involved insurance. In addition to providing full medical and dental coverage while serving as a Volunteer, the United States' government provided each Volunteer with a life insurance policy that covered the Volunteer's time in service. When they filled out the form for the insurance, the Volunteers submitted the names of the people who would receive the insurance money if the Volunteer died while serving his country. At the time, Diego simply put his parents' names on the form and forgot about it. At age 22 and single, of course, he assumed he was both invincible and immortal, so death was as far from his mind as Pluto. During Lilli's pregnancy and subsequent delivery, however, Diego began to think more and more about what would happen to Lilli and Maria Christina when he returned to America or if something happened to him while he was still in Costa Rica. For while he was not Lilli's husband and not the baby's father, he had begun to think of himself as a sort of provider for them; while Christina hosted Lilli during her pregnancy, Diego had helped to pay for Lilli's food and other expenses. And because he knew how difficult it was for Lilli's mother to provide for her daughter and granddaughter on her meager wages, Diego continued to provide food for them and to help financially in other ways. His Peace Corps salary wasn't a lot, but he still had enough for himself and for Lilli.

When Diego asked to change the beneficiary on his insurance forms, the Peace Corps administrator asked him to explain what had happened and why he needed to make the change.

"I don't really 'need' to make the change," Diego explained. "I want to. I'm sure my parents don't need the insurance money, and I've met someone in Golfito who could really use the money if anything were to happen to me."

"Are you sick or anything? Are you in danger?"

"No. No. No. Nothing's wrong. I just know a young girl who could use some help; that's all."

At that revelation, the administrator really began to pepper Diego with questions. As a lifetime, foreign-service bureaucrat, this older gentleman had experienced numerous similar situations, both in Costa Rica and in other countries. These situations usually involved young, innocent American Volunteers and natives in the areas where the Volunteers were serving.

"Can you tell me more about this young lady?"

"Well, she's eighteen now, and she just had a baby, and she lives with her mother in a small house on the edge of town."

"Are you the father of the child?"

"No, I'm not."

"So how do you know this girl?"

"When I first began serving in Golfito, I lived with a family, and Lilli lived nearby. In fact, I used to give weekly English lessons to a married couple there, and Lilli joined us for these classes"

"So, she was your student?"

"Yes."

"And the father of the baby is?"

Diego hesitated a bit at that question because he wasn't sure how much to reveal. "The father of the baby is actually an American boy who lived in Golfito for a while but who has since returned to America to attend college." Diego paused again.

"Is there more I should know?" The bureaucrat asked.

Slowly, Diego explained. "This boy and his family don't even know Lilli became pregnant, and they don't know anything about the baby, so it's pretty unlikely Lilli will ever have any kind of support from him."

As the administrator digested all this information, he recalled some of those other situations he had encountered previously. In some situations, local girls who were early in their pregnancies gave themselves to male Volunteers and then claimed the male Volunteer was the father of the baby. Often, these unsuspecting and righteous Volunteers married the girls only to find out later that they had been duped when the baby arrived too early for the Volunteer to have been the father or when the baby showed no physical signs of American heritage. In other cases, some native girls simply wanted a ticket to America, so they offered to work as a servant for the Volunteer. Later, they might move in with the Volunteer or have sex with him, so he would also marry her and bring her home to America when he left the country.

From what this administrator heard from Diego, it didn't sound like Diego was in one of those situations, yet the administrator persisted in his questioning.

"Jim, does this girl know you are assigning your insurance proceeds over to her?"

"No."

"Are you planning any other activities with her?"

"What do you mean?"

"Do you plan on dating her or employing her as a housekeeper, for example, or anything like that?"

"No. She's just a sweet girl in a difficult situation, and I would like to help her in any way I can."

"You realize, of course, that you would have to die as a Peace Corps Volunteer for her to ever receive any insurance money?"

"I know how life insurance works."

"Of course you do. It's just that some Volunteers think that the life insurance covers their whole lives and not just the term of their service."

"I understand."

"So then, yes, you can definitely make this girl the beneficiary of your life insurance policy, but I am curious about one more thing."

"What's that?"

The administrator flipped through Diego's folder and said, "According to your records, you will leave Costa Rica in December of this year."

"Right."

"So do you expect to do anything for this girl before you leave?"

"I will probably give her any money I have at that point, which I know won't be much."

"I wasn't really thinking in financial terms."

"What are you thinking?"

"Jim, over the years, some Volunteers have married local girls and brought them home to America. I know you said you weren't planning on dating this girl, but some Volunteers will marry a Costa Rican girl, just so the girl can leave Costa Rica and have a better life in America."

"Quite honestly, I have thought about trying to bring Lilli and her baby and even Lilli's mother to the States because I think they would do well there and have a better life there. I don't, however, plan on marrying Lilli just to make that happen. I was thinking more about being a sponsor for her. Is that the right word?"

"Yes, it is, and you can definitely do that. Have you talked to her already about this idea?"

"No. It's just an idea at this point."

"Well, if you want to talk more about it as you get closer to December, just let me know."

"Okay, I will. Thank you."

When Diego returned to Golfito, he pondered the administrator's words about helping Lilli and her baby and her mother move to America. Rather than ask them directly, though, if they were interested in moving, he decided it would be better if he just let it come out naturally. So every once in a while, when he and Christina were sitting around the table after supper at Lilli's house, Diego would casually shift the conversation from the present to the future to see what Lilli and her mother were planning for their lives when the baby was a little older and when Lilli had earned her high-school diploma.

Diego would usually begin his search by talking about something he had to do to move onto the next stage of his life. One night, for instance, he shared the story of Bob, another Sports Promoter in his group, who was actually leaving four months early because he had already lined up a teaching job at his old high school in the States. Since most American teaching positions began in either late August or early September, Bob had asked if he could leave early because that particular job would not be available if he returned in December, and he would probably have to wait another eight or nine months before he could find another comparable offer.

Since the Peace Corps had employed thousands of teachers through the years in various countries, the administrators and decision makers were very familiar with that employment dilemma. In Bob's case, since he wasn't leaving behind any students who were depending directly on him for required coursework, he would be allowed to leave early, and because Bob knew Diego also wanted to teach when he got home, he encouraged Diego to also explore the early-departure option.

"You might leave us early?" Lilli asked with a bit of sadness in her voice.

"No, I'm not planning on it. But I did give it some thought before I decided that I would like to complete my two full years here."

"But won't it be difficult for you to find a teaching job when you return?" Christina asked.

"Yes, it probably will be, but I'm not in a real hurry to start teaching full-time. I think I might like to travel a little or even try some other jobs for a short time before I settle into my teaching career."

"Really?" Lilli asked. "What kind of jobs?"

"I think it might be fun to work a construction job for a while. I know a guy back home who builds houses, and he's always looking for guys to help out."

"But isn't that hard work?" Lilli's mom asked, ever protective of Diego and ever a mother. "And you don't have any training or experience, do you?"

"You're right; I don't have any experience in that field, but if that guy hires me, I would start out as a common laborer doing whatever needs to be done: carrying materials and tools, loading and unloading trucks, anything and everything, and cleaning up at the end of the day. Then, if I'm reliable and working hard enough, he or one of his supervisors will start to show me how to do siding and roofing and eventually framing. I think it would be so cool to learn all those skills. Then, who knows, during my summer vacations as a teacher, I could possibly build my own house or do work for others if I wanted to."

As Diego talked about such things, Lilli would also begin to talk about her career in either the education field or the medical field, and she wavered between wanting to stay in San Jose after she finished school or moving back to Golfito or to another small town in the countryside where there might be more of a need for teachers or medical professionals.

Even Lilli's mother chimed in at times: "If I move to San Jose to be with you and to help you take care of Maria Christina, do you think I could also go to school and take a course or two?"

"Oh, Mama, that would be so wonderful. What do you think you would want to study?"

"I don't even know. I just know I'm tired of cooking and serving food and making change for people. I think I can do more. I know I can do more."

When talking about the future failed to arouse any interest in moving to America, Diego sometimes talked about all the places he wanted to visit when he returned to the States: "I definitely want to see California. They say the ocean there is spectacular, and they have Redwood trees there that are thousands of years old and hundreds of feet high."

Lilli and her mom, though, didn't seem that interested in going to America. They talked more often about other destinations where they could speak their own language: the countries of Central and South America and even Spain in Europe. Consequently, Diego put on hold his idea of helping them go to the States. "Maybe Costa Rica is enough for them," he reasoned. "Not everyone has to go to America."

Chapter 47

Meanwhile, besides doing whatever he could to promote exercise and sports among his new neighbors, Diego was also trying to finance and build a basketball/volleyball court for that end of town, one similar to the court that existed in the Company end. He spoke to businessmen in the area, men who ran the small shops that provided food and necessities for those who lived there. He also spoke to Juan Baptista who ran the big store on the main street and owned many of the small apartments nearby, including those where Diego lived and where Christina lived.

"Yes, I think that's a great idea," they would all tell Diego, and, "Yes, I would be willing to donate some money or some goods to help finance that project. However," they all added, "you must get permission from the local politicians to make this happen."

Diego knew that was true, so he had approached the local elected officials as well. He spoke to them when he saw them on the street and he approached them when they attended public events.

"Let's have a meeting about that soon," they might say without actually scheduling one, or they might suggest that Diego attend the monthly meeting of the neighborhood athletic club.

"What neighborhood athletic club?" Diego would ask, and the politician would give Diego the name of someone who was supposedly in charge. Then, Diego would spend the next week trying to find that individual only to be told that, yes, he was on that committee, but that another individual was actually in charge. Naturally, then, Diego would have to find the next man, and, unfortunately, he would refer Diego to still another.

Gradually, though reluctantly, Diego figured out that no one really wanted to do anything to help him; still, he persevered. Each disappointment set him back a bit, and he neglected his goal for a few days. Later, though, that disappointment, like a small cut or scab, would disappear, and Diego would begin his quest all over again.

"Ah, Diego," these men would say when they saw him again. "How's the project coming?" Patiently, they listened to Diego's imperfect Spanish, and politely, they agreed with every point he made and every plan he suggested. Nothing happened, though, until one man, a middle-aged barber who loved sports and who owned one of the few televisions in town, admitted finally that his committee would meet the following Thursday at 7:00 p.m., in the meeting hall next to the Post Office.

Excited by the prospect of actually talking to adults in the community about the basketball/volleyball court, Diego prepared his plans diligently. First, he outlined the problem as he saw it. The youth in that section of town had so few organized or structured activities that they often drifted into activities that were not good for them: smoking, drinking, using drugs. Even some of the kids who came from stable homes and who took their education seriously were so bored by the lack of activities in Golfito that they often found themselves doing dangerous things, like climbing to the tops of the moving banana trains or performing foolish stunts just for laughs or excitement.

The solution, as Diego saw it, was a public place where these young people could gather and play ball, a place that would be far superior to the restless boredom that these teens experienced otherwise. "How difficult could it be," Diego asked himself, "to set aside a small piece of land for the court itself with perhaps a small playground and picnic tables nearby? And how expensive would it be to set up the basketball hoops and the volleyball poles?" Though Diego didn't actually know how much such a project would cost or what needed to occur to secure a piece of land for the project, he felt confident that the locals who had lived there forever could supply the answers and put the plan into action.

He was wrong.

When that Thursday evening arrived, Diego showed up 15 minutes early at the appointed location, and he waited. And he waited. And he waited. No one showed up. Not one person. Yes, Costa Ricans were notoriously late for all their engagements and appointments, but on that night, at that time, no one showed up.

Not surprisingly, the good-hearted *gringo* assumed he must have gotten his days mixed up, so he visited the barber the next day to find out if he had, indeed, missed the meeting.

"Oh, no, Diego. We canceled the meeting because Arturo couldn't make it. He didn't tell you?"

"No, he didn't." Diego waited for the barber to respond; the barber silently kept sweeping the floor. "So when will the meeting occur? Next week, maybe?"

"No, next month, probably. Just like always." The barber was unable to see the irony in his own statement, and Diego wanted to scream.

"Be still," he told himself. "This is their country. This is their project – or should be. Wait patiently. Persevere. Persist." Too polite to leave immediately, in the midst of his anger, Diego dawdled for a few minutes and made small talk about the weather. Then, he exited and ran home – literally. He ran to burn off his energy and frustration. When he arrived at his apartment within minutes, he kept running. He couldn't stop. He ran a good 20 minutes away from town and toward the plantations before he turned and ran back. By then, he was a sweaty mess, and he collapsed on the small patch of grass across the street from his place. Breathing heavily, he looked up at the blue sky and said to himself, "I have to go see – and hold – Maria."

Chapter 48

While Diego tried to visit Lilli and her baby at least every other day, he had somehow gone days without seeing them, and he realized at that moment what a joy it was to see new life. He loved looking into Maria's dark eyes. He loved holding her and burping her after she drank her milk. And he especially loved that warm feeling that overcame him when she fell asleep in his arms. When that occurred, he closed his own eyes and relaxed, totally. It was the most peaceful moment he had ever experienced: a young, beating heart resting next to his own, totally innocent and totally helpless, dependent on him in that moment for safety and protection.

Diego was so enamored with Maria and the experience of holding her in his arms while she was sleeping that he had already written a short poem about it:

Sleeping in My Arms

From the mountains to the valleys,
From the cities to the farms,
Nothing is more peaceful
Than you sleeping in my arms.

Silence all the cannons;
Turn off all alarms;
Nothing is more soothing
Than you sleeping in my arms.

I'd give up all possessions,
All money, luck, and charms
To experience this moment
With you sleeping in my arms.

In that moment, Diego could forget completely the fact that he missed his own family and friends back in the States or that he felt as if his work there in Golfito were a waste because no one really cared or really wanted to work with him to develop a recreational facility for the children.

"I have to go hold Maria," he said again, and he pushed himself off the ground, so he could shower and get moving.

When Diego arrived at Lilli's place, he brought with him fresh bread, milk, bananas, and oranges. Lilli's mother was already at work, and he found Lilli sitting in the rocking chair. The baby was resting peacefully, but Lilli looked exhausted.

"*Buenas dias*," Diego said when he knocked on the screen door and entered. "*Como esta mi pequeña angel?*"

"Your little angel was up all night, fidgeting and fussing; she just couldn't settle in."

"She looks okay now."

"*Sí.* I just fed her again, and she seems at rest finally."

"So you didn't sleep?"

"No."

"Okay, get up. Go to bed. Get some rest. I'll hold her. I'll take care of her."

"But . . . ."

"Don't worry. I don't have to go anywhere. I don't have to be anywhere this morning. You get some sleep."

"Ah, Diego," Lilli replied with both exhaustion and joy, and she gingerly stood and handed the sleeping baby over to the tall, young American who sat in the rocker immediately and tried to find a comfortable position for Maria. "*Gracias, Diego. Muchas gracias,*" Lilli said as she prepared to finally get some rest in her own bed. "You're sure about this?" She asked, desperately wanting to sleep but also, like a good mother, wanting to make sure everything was okay.

"*Sí, sí,*" Diego responded. "*Vaya. Vaya con Dios.* Sleep. Sleep."

Convinced, Lilli turned to go. Before taking even two steps, though, she turned back, walked up alongside Diego in the rocker, and kissed him gently on the cheek. "*Gracias,*" she whispered. "*Gracias, mi amor.*" Then, she entered her bedroom and fell asleep immediately.

"Wow!" Diego thought. "That's never happened before."

Diego knew, of course, that Lilli was attracted to him. From the day he first met her, she had always been smiling and friendly, and as they got to know one another, their relationship had deepened. In addition, during the previous year, they had become even closer. Neither one of them ever spoke of what was happening, but they both felt it. Neither one of them had ever actually said that particular word before regarding their relationship: *amor.*

"*Amor?*" Diego thought? Could he be in love with this 18-year-old beauty? Of course he could, he had to admit. In some ways, he had loved her since that very first day he met her. He had marveled at her beautiful smile and at her infectious enthusiasm for life. He began to love her even more when they spoke periodically in the neighborhood and when she began to study English with him and the Santiago family. When he thought about her then, though, his love for her was like that of a big brother for his younger sister. After all, five years separated them, and he had a girlfriend back home, a girl he planned to marry one day.

After Lilli was attacked and became pregnant, however, Diego's relationship with Lilli intensified; it reached a different level altogether – and a new dimension. Like Lilli's grandfather, Diego experienced anger toward the boy who had hurt her, but unlike her grandfather, Diego never blamed Lilli for what had happened, and Diego's brotherly affection for her gradually turned into something different, something deeper, something he couldn't quite grasp as he experienced it.

Yet, just as the life inside of Lilli was growing, the life of Diego's relationship with Bridget was deteriorating. Her letters became shorter and arrived less frequently. Later, the letters were replaced by Hallmark cards; yes, they contained beautiful sentiments, but Bridget had not written them. Like a factory supervisor, she had merely signed off on them. And gradually, they, too, arrived less often and then not at all.

During that time, Diego wanted to believe that Bridget was simply too busy, too caught up in the hectic pace of college life in America. He wanted to believe that though she didn't write, she at least thought of him periodically and said a short prayer for him at night. After all, she had not yet sent him the dreaded "Dear John" letter, the one that would officially end everything. As a result, Diego held out hope. He wanted to believe. He wanted desperately to believe in their love, in their "*amor.*"

As Diego thought about his life and the women in it, the little girl in his lap slept so soundly that Diego did not want to move. So he closed his eyes and thought again of Lilli. "Ah, Diego," she had said so gratefully when he had offered to watch Maria Christina. Those were the same words that the older men in town had said to Diego when he approached them for help, yet their sentiments were so different. They treated Diego like a young boy who had to be tolerated and patronized. Yes, he was helping the young people in town stay out of trouble, so they endured his requests for help, but they were unwilling to commit real energy or resources to him.

Lilli's "Ah, Diego" was so much different, and she so enjoyed being with him. Despite their language difference, they communicated in a combination of English and Spanish that made both of them smile and laugh.

"What *ees* your word for '*anteojos?*'" Lilli might ask, and she would bring together her thumbs and forefingers and wrap them around her eyes like glasses.

"We call them 'glasses,'" he'd respond with a big smile, and then he would ask, "How do you say the word 'hug?'" And he would wrap his long arms around her.

Not surprisingly, during Lilli's pregnancy, she grew to love Diego even more. His constant presence in her life made it easy for her to pretend, like the schoolgirl that she was, that Diego was actually the father of her child and not the selfish American boy who had tricked her and used her for his pleasure.

In her reverie, Lilli imagined Diego not going home when his two-year commitment to the Peace Corps ended. She imagined him becoming an English teacher at the high school or an office worker of some sort at the banana Company. Surely, Diego could easily find a permanent job in Golfito. Then, he would seriously begin to court her according to Costa Rican customs, and eventually, he would propose to her. Padre Roberto would marry them in Saint Michael's Church, and the building would be packed with all the people who had come to know and love both of them.

Thoroughly enjoying the fantasy, Lilli would smile until she noticed all the empty pews at the front of the groom's side. "Where is Diego's family?" She would ask herself. "Surely, his parents and his sisters would come to the ceremony. And what about his best man? Who would that be?"

These questions sent Lilli off in all sorts of imaginary directions. In one scenario, she didn't meet any of these people until they arrived for the wedding, but in her most practical and realistic fantasy, she saw herself traveling to the United States with Diego and Maria Christina, so his family and friends could all meet her and the baby beforehand. Then afterwards, she and

Diego and the baby would return to Golfito, and a few months later, his immediate family and closest friends would visit Golfito for the wedding.

But what if Diego wants to live in America? Though many Costa Rican women sought out American men just so they could marry and move to the promised land, Lilli had never viewed Diego as simply a ticket out of Golfito. Rather, she imagined him as her husband, her true love no matter where they lived. Could she leave her mom behind to go live in America? Would she herself feel comfortable there without knowing anyone? Would her English be strong enough? How would she adjust to new foods, to American culture, and to the new way of living?

Lilli loved playing with these questions and ideas, and she often fell asleep with her imaginary visions in her mind. Then, too, in her sleep, she would often dream about these same scenarios, and when she awoke, she was often startled to be back in Golfito, alone in her own bed or sitting in the rocker with her sleeping baby. In those waking moments, Lilli sighed and convinced herself to return to her reality. She knew, after all, that her fantasies were just that because Diego had a girlfriend, a serious girlfriend, back home. He would leave Golfito when his time was up, and he would become merely a memory, one she would add to the photo album in her mind.

Chapter 49

As Maria Christina grew and began crawling, Don Pedro and his wife began to visit their child, grandchild, and great-grandchild more often. The anger and the frustration and the helplessness that Don Pedro had felt when he first heard about what had happened to Lilli gradually dissipated. Each time he saw the baby and each time he held her, he thought less and less about how she had been conceived and more and more about how she would grow up. His paternal instincts surfaced again just as they had done when Lilli's mother, Rosa, was born and, later, when Lilli was born. Though he was now a great-grandfather, he was still only 58 years old. Except for some soreness in his legs and except for the extra weight that was a result of his daily beer, he was still in pretty good shape, and he was determined to stay that way. He was still the only male in the family, and in the *macho* Costa Rican culture, he once again felt an obligation to demonstrate a strong, masculine presence in the lives of his daughter, his granddaughter, and his great-granddaughter.

In the midst of that situation, Don Pedro wondered somewhat about Diego. Initially, he liked the friendly, young man, especially when he heard that he was providing free English lessons to Lilli. When Diego had interfered in the plan to abort the baby, however, Don Pedro resented him vehemently. At that point, Diego represented all that was bad about Americans. Yes, they sometimes did good things, but they often went too far as if they – and only they – knew what was best for everyone. Fortunately for everyone, Don Pedro's resentment for Diego had gradually disappeared as well. When Don Pedro watched Diego interact with Lilli and Maria Christina, he could see that Diego loved them both, and when Diego was in Don Pedro's presence, he showed the proper respect for Don Pedro's age and for his position in Lilli's life. Don Pedro knew, too, that Diego could have lorded over him the fact that Don Pedro had almost committed a tragic, tragic mistake. Diego did not, however, even let on that he knew about the plan much less that he was only 10 minutes and 50 feet away from the mistake when it almost occurred.

As December approached, Lilli and Christina jointly realized that they wanted to host a party. Christina raised the idea first. She said, "We definitely need to have a party before Christmas."

"I agree," Lilli responded. "And I think we should have it outside at our house because we have more room, and I want to invite lots of people."

"Really?"

"Why are you so surprised?"

"I didn't know . . . You usually don't want a lot of people. When I gave you that baby shower back in March, you didn't want me to invite many people."

"But this party's not for me."

"Yes, it is; you're graduating from high school in December."

"But this is going to be a going-away party for Diego."

"Oh my God," they said in two different languages, and then they laughed in the same language.

"You thought . . . ?" Christina asked.

"And you thought . . . ?" Lilli responded.

"*Es perfecto,*" they responded again in their respective tongues, and they hugged happily.

"We'll tell Diego that it's a graduation party for you," Christina began.

"But we'll tell everyone else that it's really a farewell party for Diego," Lilli finished. And so the planning began.

Try as they might, Christina and Lilli couldn't keep the idea of Diego's party a secret. In fact, most people just assumed there would be a party; they just needed to know when and where. Ironically, one of the grade-school teachers was actually talking to Diego about the party at the same time Christina and Lilli were first considering it.

"When do you leave, Diego?" This teacher asked as the two of them watched the fifth-grade girls practice their layups.

"I don't have the exact date yet but probably during the second half of December."

"So when will the party be?"

"What?"

"C'mon, Diego. There has to be a party. We may never see you again, so we're definitely going to have a party for you."

"I don't know anything about it."

"Neither do I, but I do know there will be a party."

And in a small town like Golfito, where news traveled quickly, secrets traveled even more quickly.

Within days after Christina and Lilli had set a tentative date, everyone in Golfito – even those who did not personally know Diego – knew that his friends and his co-workers were planning a *fiesta.* Some tried to say it was going to be a *sorpresa,* but most assumed an actual surprise party was impossible and treated it that way.

Diego himself found out about the actual day and time of the party when he overheard some of the school children who lived near Lilli. They were talking about their mothers making special dishes and desserts to bring to "*la fiesta para Diego.*"

Remembering that the same thing happened in the States before he left for Costa Rica in the first place, Diego knew he could easily play along, so he simply pretended that he didn't know, and he wondered if anyone, anywhere, had ever successfully pulled off a real surprise party for the intended recipient.

"Mission Impossible," Diego thought as he pondered the situation and compared it to the old television show he had watched when he was younger.

The party was scheduled for Saturday, December 19, the last Saturday before Christmas and three days before Diego was scheduled to fly out of Golfito and later fly home to America. Christina and Lilli told everyone to arrive around 2:00 p.m., and they told Diego the same thing. Since Diego was supposed to believe that he was attending a graduation party for Lilli, they didn't need any special arrangements. They would simply pretend that everyone showed up for Lilli, but when it was time to present Lilli with a cake and gifts, she would turn the party into a celebration for Diego.

"You realize, of course," Christina said to Lilli, "that some people are going to bring gifts for you too."

"Oh, no," Lilli protested. "This is Diego's party."

"When it happens, just smile and say 'Thank you,'" Christina advised. "And besides, you deserve a celebration too for all you've been through and accomplished."

"But – "

"No 'buts'; just smile and say 'Thank you,' especially to Diego. If I know him, he'll probably bring you the best gift of all."

"Really?" Lilli responded, more like the innocent girl she was than the mature adult she aspired to be. "Like what?"

"I don't know. I just know Diego loves you and will do something wonderful for you."

"He loves me?"

"Of course he loves you. It's so obvious."

"You mean he 'likes' me a lot?"

"No, he 'loves' you."

"Like a big brother, you mean?"

"Well, yes, he does look out for you like a big brother, but I think it's more than that."

"Tell me more," Lilli responded, and she and Christina began another one of their Diego conversations.

Chapter 50

Fortunately for everyone, the day of the party was perfect: sunny and warm but with enough of a breeze off the bay that the heat was bearable.

Diego arrived an hour early at 1:00 p.m., to help set up tables and chairs that he borrowed from one of the schools and transported the day before with Padre Roberto's Jeep. When the preliminary work was done, Diego washed up and changed from his sweaty tee-shirt into a fresh, clean, short-sleeve dress shirt more appropriate for the special occasion.

During the first hour or so, most of the people arrived: neighbors, friends, teachers, athletes, people from all over town who had come to know Diego. Gradually, they put their offerings in place: drinks and bite-sized foods outside for immediate consumption and dinner dishes and desserts inside for later. Some of the high-school students also began kicking around a soccer ball.

During that first hour, just about everyone greeted Diego personally. Some asked him questions about his departure and his future. Some began reminiscing about his first days in Golfito or when they themselves first met him. And still others either asked if they could visit him in America or simply said that they would do so.

The ever gracious Diego politely told everyone, "*Mi casa es su casa*," even though he didn't actually have a "*casa*" of his own. He knew, of course, that just about everyone he ever met in Golfito had said they planned to visit America someday, but he also knew that very few of them would ever actually follow through. And quite honestly, for the few who did make it to the States, Diego didn't expect any of them to ever find their way to Amsterdam in upstate New York.

By 3:30, Christina and Lilli decided to officially welcome everyone and turn the graduation ceremony into a farewell party. They had previously asked Padre Roberto to serve as the master of ceremonies, so when they asked the neighbors to turn down the party's music, Padre Roberto stood at the rear gate of his Jeep and called for everyone's attention.

"*Silencio, por favor*," he shouted, and then he put two fingers into his mouth and whistled for added emphasis, and the whistle, more than his words, caught everyone's attention. Gradually even the most boisterous partiers settled down and waited for him to continue.

"As you all know, we are here today to celebrate Lilli's high-school graduation, so let's first of all give her a big round of applause and bring her up here."

"*Gracias, gracias*," she said softly. "Thank you so much for coming today." Before she continued, she waited for the applause to die down, and she made sure to find Diego in the crowd; she didn't need much time. He had positioned himself to Lilli's right near the old baby carriage that sat near the entrance to the house. When she made eye contact with him, she began speaking again.

"As you all know, Padre Roberto just lied," and everyone laughed, especially Padre Roberto whose face turned a bright red. "We are not here today to celebrate my graduation; we are here to say 'good-bye' and 'thank you' to . . . ."

At that point, Lilli got choked up and struggled to speak. Christina, who was standing nearby and holding Maria Christina, moved next to Lilli and put one arm around her and whispered, "You can do this."

Lilli composed herself and repeated what she had said: "We are here to say 'good-bye' and 'thank you' to our good friend Diego."

Diego, who had begun to tear up when Lilli struggled, quickly rubbed the tears from his eyes and tried to act surprised.

"C'mon, Diego. Nobody's surprised, not even you," said one of Lilli's neighbors who often played basketball with Diego.

Diego laughed as Lilli called him forward, and the crowd began to chant, "Diego. Diego. Diego. Diego."

When Diego made his way up to Lilli, those he passed on the way shook his hand and slapped him on the back. Then, both Lilli and Christina hugged him separately, and they all posed for Padre Roberto who used Diego's small camera to record the moment.

"*Discurso. Discurso,*" some in the crowd yelled, but Lilli wasn't quite finished herself, so she put up both hands and motioned to Diego and to the crowd to wait.

"Before we say 'good-bye' to Diego, we have a few, small gifts to present to him, so he can remember us when he gets home. First, we have a big card here," and she pulled out a poster-sized, homemade card filled with signatures and farewell greetings. "I think most of you have already signed it, but if not, we still have a little bit of room for signatures on the back.

"Next, we have this special item that Diego can hang in his home in America," and she pulled out a large, bright yellow, triangular soccer banner that said "Golfito" in bold, black letters.

When she handed it to Diego, he smiled and held it high above his head, and the crowd cheered and chanted: "Golfito. Golfito. Golfito."

"Finally, we also have one more gift that Diego needs to bring back home with him to America. This is something that we've been trying to give to him for almost two years, but he's still not receiving it well." At that moment, Lilli reached into a big, banana box and retrieved a brand new soccer ball. Again, everyone laughed, especially Diego. For as often as he played soccer with the locals, both children and adults, he still hadn't quite mastered the skills of the game. For when playing, Diego often still touched the ball with his hands, he still didn't feel comfortable with the overhead inbounds pass, and he still struggled with headers.

"Alright," Diego said to those who were laughing at his soccer abilities as he stood between Lilli and Christina and spun the ball on his left index finger. "If you continue to practice basketball and baseball and volleyball after I leave, I promise to practice my soccer skills when I get home."

Everyone laughed and cheered, and when they settled down, Diego continued: "But if I make the American National team and if we beat Costa Rica in the World Cup in 1978 in Argentina, it will be your fault."

Everyone laughed even harder this time, and some of the young men near Diego teased him as if he were dreaming or drunk to make such a ridiculous statement.

Finally, Diego knew it was time to make a few serious remarks to sincerely thank the people of Golfito for their generosity to him during his two-year stay in their community. Fortunately, because he knew in advance about the *fiesta sorpresa*, he had prepared a few thoughts, and at that moment, he was ready to express them.

"First of all, I want to thank all of you for being so kind to me and so patient and so generous. I don't know how well you remember my first days here, but I remember them vividly. I was so nervous, and my Spanish was so poor at that time, but you all put up with me and helped me so much. I will never forget you for that.

"Then, as I got to know so many of you, you invited me into your homes, you invited me to your family gatherings and your celebrations, and you made me feel like a part of your family. That means so much to me because I've been so far away from my own family for so long now.

"And finally, I want to say how enjoyable it has been to work with so many of you during these last two years. Yes, you take your soccer a little too seriously, but you also let the big *gringo* play once in a while. In addition, you let me teach you and your children some new games, and that has always been fun. So as I get ready to leave, I hope you'll continue to play and have even more fun. That's the picture I want to take with me when I leave: all of you enjoying life and also enjoying one another. *Pura vida!*"

When Diego finished, those at the party started a new chant: "Diego. Golfito. Diego. Golfito. Diego. Golfito," and as they chanted, about five or six of the bigger high-school boys picked Diego up and set him on their shoulders and carried him in a circle around the front yard. Diego was a bit nervous because he was so much bigger than those who carried him. Fortunately, after one lap around the yard, they gently let him down and the party continued for another few hours.

First, the main dishes came out, and later, the desserts were served. By the time everyone had finished eating, the sun was beginning to disappear, and darkness was settling in. Unfortunately, that darkness may have also contributed heavily to the event that occurred next.

Chapter 51

Most of the people at the party stayed near the yard in the front of the house. At various times during the party, however, small groups of boys or men would walk toward the train tracks and the road. There, they crossed over into a big, open field for a spontaneous soccer game. The field itself had no markings or goal posts, but when it came time to play their national game, the *Ticos* improvised easily and efficiently.

They would toss two shirts or two extra balls at each end of the field, and these would serve as goals and end lines. Then, they would figure out the sidelines; in this case, the road served as one sideline, and the line of small trees on the opposite side served as the other. Within minutes, they chose up sides, and the game began. Sometimes, they divided up the talent equally and played shirts versus skins, but more often, they would set up teams based on age or family or where they lived. On this day, most of the games involved the young versus the old. The students loved playing against their teachers, and later, in another game, the new teachers enjoyed playing against the older, more experienced veterans.

The games appeared to occur randomly, but usually they occurred whenever there was a short gap in the day's activities. The first game started shortly after most people arrived and had eaten a few snacks. The next game began after the main meal and before the dessert. And the final game commenced after the dessert and after Padre Roberto had departed but before everyone else was ready to head home.

The last game was a bit unique because the males finally allowed the females to participate. The earlier games were all pretty serious, and most of the girls understood that they would be overmatched. As the day progressed, though, some of the younger girls began to talk about playing as well. These were mainly the girls who had learned to play volleyball and basketball from Diego. By that time, most of the males had played quite a bit, so when Diego, ever the ambassador, asked them if it were okay to include females, everyone agreed it was alright. And in the spirit of the theme of old versus young, they decided to match the young boys and older females against the young girls and the older males. This unique makeup of the teams attracted many participants, and even Lilli and Christina, who rarely played sports, decided to join in. And many of those who didn't want to play were intrigued enough by the division of teams that they crossed the tracks and the road from the party to the field to stand on the edge and watch.

Meanwhile, back at the house, Lilli's mom and her friends and co-workers were beginning to clean up the leftovers and wash the dishes and put them all away. In the midst of all that activity, a young, neighbor girl of about 11 held Maria Christina on the small, front porch. This girl was one of the many people who had held or watched over the baby throughout the day. Maria Christina was not yet standing or walking, but she was crawling quite a bit, and she was always smiling brightly. People were naturally attracted to her and wanted to hold her and look into her bright eyes. The girl who had been watching Maria Christina at that point, however, had been watching the baby for over 30 minutes and was beginning to get antsy. She, too, wanted to be near the soccer action. So rather than continue to sit and watch from a distance, she put the baby into the baby carriage near the front door. Her goal was to push the carriage across the tracks and the road, so she could better see the game.

"We'll go watch your mama play *fútbol*," she said to Maria Christina, though the baby could obviously not understand what was about to happen. Responsibly, the girl told Lilli's mother what she was doing and where she was going.

"Okay," Lilli's mother said. "Just be careful crossing the road, and don't get too close to the game. And stand near some adults who can protect the baby if the ball comes your way."

The girl did everything she was told. She slowly pushed the carriage away from the house and down the dirt path toward the road. When she reached the railroad tracks, she stopped and deliberately looked both ways for oncoming train cars or automobile traffic. She did see a train in the distance approaching on her left, but it was still far away, so far, in fact, that the girl was more concerned about the bus that was about to take off in the opposite direction and the rusted taxi behind it. Intently, she watched the final passenger board the bus, and she waited as the two vehicles prepared to pass her.

When they did so, some of the riders on the bus who had attended the party waved good-bye, and the girl waved back at them. When finally they passed, the girl pushed down on the handle in front of her, so she could gently lift the front wheels of the carriage over the first rail of the track. As she did so, she remembered the train she had noticed earlier and took another glance to her left. Somewhat surprised by how quickly the approaching train had reached her, the girl again took the appropriate action. Rather than try to rush across in front of the train, she calmly decided to wait for the train to pass. With the front wheels already between the two rails of the tracks, she carefully pushed down again on the handle in front of her and pulled the carriage back. Somehow, however, just as those front wheels were about to clear the rail and return to safety, the sagging wheel support got hung up on the lip of the spike that held that particular section of track in place.

If the girl had called for help at that precise moment, any soccer player on the field or any one of the bystanders could have rushed to her side and either pulled the carriage free from the track or at least pulled the smiling baby from the carriage ahead of the approaching train. Unfortunately, this young girl was independent enough and confident enough to think that she could free the carriage from its precarious predicament. "It's okay, Maria Christina," the girl said more to reassure herself than the baby. "I'm going to get this carriage out of here."

Quickly, she pulled back on the carriage, and that pull only caused the carriage to become even more tightly trapped. When that occurred, the girl panicked and finally screamed for help: "*Ayuda me! Ayuda me! Por favor!*"

Had she remained calm, she could have easily picked up the baby and carried her safely away from the train. In her panic, though, she missed the obvious solution and continued to push and pull on the carriage's handle in her attempt to free it. While she struggled and screamed and while those nearby began to realize the seriousness of the situation, the 60-year-old train conductor was innocently watching the soccer game in the semi darkness off to his left.

"Are those guys and girls playing on the same field?" He asked himself as his empty train picked up speed and lumbered away from the town and toward the plantations, a trip he had made thousands of times before. Had he been looking at the tracks in front of him from the outset and observed the carriage, he might have had time to apply the brakes and stop beforehand, but he was not looking forward. Not until he saw an extremely tall American sprint from the soccer field toward the front of his train did this conductor realize that something was amiss.

"*Dios mio!*" He prayed when he finally saw the carriage before him. "Oh my God!" He prayed again as he applied the brakes. "Oh my God!" He prayed a third time, hoping that his God would save the child in the carriage ahead of him and eliminate what looked like a mortal situation.

Diego screamed too as he raced toward the innocent child and as he threw himself, head first and arms stretched out, toward the carriage.

Diego and the train collided, and Diego died instantly, his lungs and heart mortally pierced by the forward point of the train. By the time the train finally came to a full stop, Diego's body had been carried well over 200 yards and thrown onto the nearby grass. When some of the soccer players and bystanders reached him, they all knew immediately he was dead, and a few took off their shirts to cover his wounded body and to absorb the blood. Every single one of them wept uncontrollably in disbelief at what they had witnessed. Two or three of them threw their bodies over him and cried even more.

Chapter 52

Back at the point of impact, everyone else was crying too – even Maria Christina. Somehow before the collision, Diego's outstretched arms had pushed the carriage far enough and hard enough that the baby was thrown completely free, and she skidded along the grass before coming to a stop. Miraculously, she survived the crash with only minor bruises to her body and no facial or head wounds at all.

One of the soccer bystanders had seen her fly from the carriage, and he was the first to find her. He gently picked her up and tried to comfort her until the babysitter and Lilli and Christina and all the others arrived. Lilli grabbed the baby immediately and embraced her, tears cascading over the baby's face. Christina, also weeping, hugged them both, and she glanced at the baby for signs of serious injury.

"*Gracias a Dios*," Lilli managed to say in her distress. "*Gracias a Dios*."

When Lilli eased her grip on the child, Christina spoke softly to Lilli and convinced her to hand the child over. Then, Christina sat in the grass with Maria Christina on her lap, and she closely examined the baby. She marveled that the baby's face was free of cuts or bruises, and the baby's tears and the look in her eyes indicated that she was more frightened than injured. Carefully, Christina felt for broken bones and found none. The only exterior wounds appeared to be the minor cuts on her hands and chest which apparently absorbed most of the landing. "And Diego?" Christina asked finally.

No one in the crowd that had gathered could speak the words. Most simply shook their heads and cried. Lilli and

Christina embraced again, and by that time, Lilli's mother had joined them. Christina handed the child back to Lilli and said, "You stay here with your baby, and I will check on Diego."

Still weeping but trying to appear strong and professional, Christina approached Diego's body. The boys and men who surrounded him stepped back, so Christina could examine him. First, she uncovered his face, and, miraculously, like Maria Christina, his face was unmarked. Surprisingly, too, his eyes were open and appeared to be gazing to the heavens. Christina touched the side of his neck, hoping that he might have some sign of a pulse. He did not. Gently, then, she closed his eyes and kissed his forehead. Her tears escaped finally and baptized him.

As discreetly as she could, Christina next slightly uncovered Diego's chest and peered in at his wounds. She could see that his lungs and his heart had absorbed most of the impact, and she assumed that he died instantly. She quickly covered him again and asked if those around him could form a stretcher of sorts and transport his body to her office.

When Christina stood, she walked back toward Lilli and her mom. Before she reached them and before Diego's body had been moved, though, they all looked toward the road because Padre Roberto's Jeep was flying toward them. When he reached the scene, he repeated Christina's actions, needing to see for himself what he had heard in town only moments earlier. Unable to completely control his own grief, he silently and tearfully motioned for all the others to gather around Diego's body. As they did so, he removed a small vial of holy water from his breast pocket and applied some to his right thumb and rubbed it firmly on Diego's forehead as he prayed.

"I commend you, my dear brother Diego, to Almighty God and entrust you to your Creator. May you return to Him Who formed you from the dust of the earth. May the angels and all the saints come to meet you as you go forth from this life. May Jesus, who was crucified for you, grant you His mercy and His peace. May Christ, who died for you, admit you into His heavenly kingdom. May the blood that He shed be your salvation, and may He forgive you all of your sins and set you among those He has chosen. May you see your Redeemer face to face and enjoy the vision of God forever."

When Padre Roberto finished praying, he stood to embrace Lilli and Christina who had joined the crowd. Everyone watched silently until an older man began softly singing the song "Amazing Grace." Immediately, everyone else joined him, and the crowd sang the entire song before two men arrived with three large, attached boards. Approximately two inches by six inches and eight feet long, these boards would be used as a stretcher to support Diego's body as they carried it to the clinic. While they were preparing the body for transport, Padre Roberto retrieved a large, white cloth from his Jeep and placed it over Diego.

"Should we place the body in the back of your Jeep?" one of the men asked.

"No," Padre Roberto said emphatically, knowing that the Peace Corps officials would want the body transported to San Jose as soon as possible. "Diego's final journey through town should be slow and dignified. Carry him to the clinic, so the people can see the body and say their prayers. If the burden becomes too heavy, simply ask another man to take your place."

So with two men at Diego's head, two men at his waist, and two men at his feet, they set his body on the boards, carefully raised the boards to their shoulders, and began to carry the young ambassador. And though the walk from Lilli's house to the clinic was almost a mile, no one man tired because other men along the way wanted to help transport this Peace Corps Volunteer to his destination. Without stopping, a new man would tap the shoulder of a pall bearer, who would simply step aside once the new man had slid his own shoulder under the load of Diego's body.

Without anyone giving directions to the bystanders at the scene of the accident, they fell in line behind the pall bearers and followed the procession as it moved down the road, and those who were watching from the sides then joined in as well. By the time the procession reached the clinic, hundreds of people followed. And the news of what had happened traveled with them.

"It's the Peace Corps Volunteer," they said. "You know him; it's Diego. He died while saving a baby."

At the clinic, Diego's body was placed on the examining table. Christina had assumed that she would have to officially examine his body and issue the certificate of death, but by the time she and Diego arrived, a doctor from the hospital in the American Zone, the one who also served as the official town coroner, had already assumed control. He met Christina at the clinic entrance, consoled her, and relieved her of any professional responsibilities.

"Go and take care of yourself. We will take care of Diego. We have already contacted the Peace Corps authorities as well."

So Christina, Lilli, Lilli's mom, and Maria Christina along with Padre Roberto exited the clinic, and Padre Roberto, who had driven his Jeep to the clinic, addressed the crowd outside.

"Thank you all for accompanying Diego's body today to this location. We have all lost a good friend," he said, choking up. Then, once he composed himself, he added, "and a good man. Please go now and be with your own loved ones. I don't know when it will happen or where, but I'm sure we will have a formal memorial service for Diego in the near future."

Slowly, the crowd dispersed. A few stayed behind to hug Lilli and Christina and to offer their assistance. When everyone had left, Padre Roberto offered to drive Lilli and her family back to her home, and Christina, rather than stay at her place alone, decided to accompany them.

Though they were all still in shock and totally exhausted by the emotions of the farewell party and the accident, Maria Christina helped them deal with the sadness that enveloped them. Unaware of what had occurred and unfazed by her brush with death, the eight-month-old child smiled and giggled, the only signs of life amid the fading light and the setting sun.

Epilogue

Approximately 20 years after Diego's death, Maria Christina graduated from the University of San Jose with a degree in teaching. She herself did not remember Diego or Christina, but her mom, Lilli, and her grandmother, Rosa, spoke of them often.

With Diego's insurance money, Lilli and her mom decided to move to San Jose where they and the baby would all have better opportunities. Once settled in the capital city, Lilli and her mom both began taking part-time classes at the University while also working part-time and caring for Maria Christina. Together, they raised the child, and they assisted one another.

Within a year of their arrival in San Jose, Rosa opened a small restaurant in San Pedro, the same small suburb where they had settled near the University. To help her run the restaurant, she hired University students, students who, like her, needed part-time work to help them finish their education. Though it took Lilli over six years of part-time schooling, she received her degree in nursing, and two years later, Rosa graduated with a degree in business.

Both Lilli and her mom also found love in the capital city. Rosa met a gentleman in one of her business classes, and while he was a few years younger than she, he, too, had moved to San Jose from the countryside to get an education, and they married the summer after their graduation. The stability of their relationship made life even easier for Lilli and for Maria Christina. With a strong, secure male in their lives, they both thrived. Lilli was thrilled that her mother finally had a male companion to love and appreciate her, and Maria Christina came to view him as her grandfather.

Lilli, meanwhile, remained single until her daughter entered high school. Yes, many men, especially the doctors at the hospital where Lilli worked, had taken an interest in her, but Lilli did not feel strongly attracted to anyone until she met Maria Christina's sophomore English teacher. During an open house at the school, Lilli began talking to him easily and comfortably within minutes. She knew immediately he was the one. They dated for a short time before Lilli introduced him to her mother, and when Lilli and her mom were alone later that evening, Lilli freely admitted, "*Sí, Mama*; he reminds me of Diego."

The Author . . .

Since January of 2000, Jim LaBate has worked as a writing specialist in The Writing Center at Hudson Valley Community College in Troy, New York. There, he received the Chancellor's Award for Excellence in Teaching in 2019.

Originally from Amsterdam, New York, Jim graduated from Saint Mary's Institute and Bishop Scully High School. He earned his bachelor's degree in English from Siena College in Loudonville, New York, and his master's degree, also in English, from The College of Saint Rose in Albany, New York.

Jim has spent his entire career as either a teacher or a writer. He taught physical education as a Peace Corps Volunteer in Golfito, Costa Rica, for two years. He taught high-school English for 10 years (one year at Vincentian Institute in Albany, New York, and nine years at Keveny Memorial Academy in Cohoes, New York). Then, he worked for 10 years as a writer for Newkirk Products in Albany, New York.

Jim lives in Clifton Park, New York, with his wife, Barbara; they have two daughters: Maria and Katrina.

Previous Works

Let's Go, Gaels – a novella by Jim LaBate – tells the story of one week in the life of a 12-year-old boy. The story takes place in a Catholic school in upstate New York in 1964. As the week begins, the narrator is thinking about a speech he has to give in English class on Friday, a big basketball game on Saturday, and a trip to the movies on Saturday night. During the week, however, something happens that changes his life – and his outlook on life – forever. The event moves him further away from his innocent boyhood and closer to his eventual maturity as a man.

Mickey Mantle Day in Amsterdam – another novella by Jim LaBate – is also about growing up. This particular story focuses on baseball and on baseball's biggest name in the 1950's and the 1960's. The story takes place during the summer of 1963 when Mantle is on the disabled list, recovering from a broken foot. When his car breaks down near the "Rug City," the 12-year-old narrator and his dad stop to help, and Mantle's Amsterdam adventure begins. By the time it ends, 24 hours later, both the narrator and the reader have learned a valuable lesson.

Things I Threw in the River: The Story of One Man's Life – In this novel, the first-person narrator lives near the Mohawk River in upstate New York during the 1950s, '60s, '70s, and '80s. He tells a series of related stories about what he threw into the river and why. The first story concerns an incident that occurs when the narrator is four years old, and the final story occurs in 1988 when he is 37. That final story is the most dramatic of all, takes up 50% of the novel, and is based on a real incident.

My Teacher's Password: A Contemporary Novel – Tom Sullivan is a 21-year-old college student, and he's in love with his creative writing professor – as well he should be. Margaret Cavellari is hot! She looks like a cross between Catherine Zeta-Jones and Penelope Cruz. Okay, so no one is really that hot, but Margaret is close. In addition, she's kind. She's funny. She's interesting. And she's a great teacher. So when Tom accidentally discovers her computer password, what will he do? Will he read her e-mail? Will he look at her pictures and her word processing files? Will he go into her gradebook? Naturally, Tom Sullivan is curious. But is he also stupid? Of course he is. Read all about Tom's computer adventures in this contemporary novel.

Writing Is Hard: A Collection of Over 100 Essays – This book serves as an alternative to the traditional writing handbook which typically attempts to explain the entire writing process or to address thoroughly all areas of punctuation, grammar, and usage. Such a text can be overwhelming and intimidating. Instead, LaBate uses each essay to focus on only one small aspect of writing with the hope that the reader will walk away with the key idea, one that can be easily remembered and implemented. Each essay is a self-contained lesson of about 700 words written in an informal, conversational style.

Order Form

Name ____

Address ____

City ________________________ State_____ Zip _________

Let's Go, Gaels	$5.95 x ____	copies =	_________
Mickey Mantle Day in Amsterdam	$7.95 x ____	copies =	_________
Things I Threw in the River	$9.95 x ____	copies =	_________
My Teacher's Password	$9.95 x ____	copies =	_________
Writing Is Hard	$19.95 x ____	copies =	________
Streets of Golfito	$19.95 x ____	copies =	________
Postage and Handling	$3.00 x ____	copies =	_________

Subtotal _________

New York residents add appropriate sales tax _________

Total _________

Please enclose a check for your order and mail to:

Mohawk River Press

P.O. Box 4095
Clifton Park, New York 12065-0850
518-383-2254
www.MohawkRiverPress.com

Made in the USA
Las Vegas, NV
03 February 2021

17059331R00144